PILGRIMAGE

D1558807

Christine Sunderland

CAPSTONE
FICTION

WATERFORD, VIRGINIA

Pilgrimage

Published in the U.S. by:
Capstone Publishing Group LLC
P.O. Box 8
Waterford, VA 20197

Visit Capstone Fiction at
www.capstonefiction.com

Cover design by David LaPlaca/debest design co.
Cover image © 2007 PunchStock
Author photo © 2007 by Brittany Sunderland

ISBN: 978-1-60290-051-6

Acknowledgments

I am deeply indebted to:

The many friends and family members who read my early drafts and encouraged me.

The many clergy and parishioners who have helped me on my own pilgrimage through life, to God, in God.

Editors Margaret Lucke and Alfred J. Garrotto, who helped me with the final drafts.

My dear husband, Harry, who has patiently given me invaluable support and has shown me the amazing worlds of Italy, France, and England.

Life is a pilgrimage to God in God.

Saint Benedict
sixth-century founder of Western monasticism

Preface

In my descriptions of historical persons and places, I have attempted to be accurate. *All other characters are fictional and are not intended to represent any persons living or dead.*

The Church of the Four Crowned Saints in Rome is much as I described, including the organ-playing nun who greets visitors. However, it has long been run by Augustinian nuns, not Franciscans, and there is no orphanage or friary attached to it.

All of the places on the pilgrimage I recommend visiting. They are beautiful and holy, as are many others throughout Europe.

All prayer book references are from *The Book of Common Prayer, according to the use of the Protestant Episcopal Church in the United States of America*, 1928. All scriptural references are from the *King James Bible* except for the Chapter Epigraphs. These epigraphs have been taken from *The Book of Common Prayer* which, when compiled in the sixteenth century, used Psalms from the Miles Coverdale translation, one of the first English translations and a precursor to the King James Bible.

For purposes of orientation in a church, the altar faces east, and other parts of the church are mentioned in reference to the altar, i.e. south aisle, north aisle, etc.

Prologue

The day was balmy, one of those days when nothing could go wrong, when the blue skies and the sun on your skin made you happy and certain. It was Saturday and my clerical job at the bank seemed far away; I was young and my future stretched before me. There would be many days like this, I thought, full of sun, play, and children.

Mollie stacked rubber blocks on a pink blanket in a quiet corner of the back lawn. She could sit up then—she was nearly eight months—and could see her world, but she couldn't yet walk. Her crawl still held the wonder of movement; she wasn't even scooting. So she was content to sit, concentrating on the blocks, full of the promise of life.

Our Vancouver apartment was stuffy that warm afternoon, and we escaped to the crabgrass to try out my son's new wading pool, his third-birthday present from his father and me. With Mollie nearby and Justin hovering close, I pumped air into the white plastic. Justin shifted his weight from foot to foot, raised his hands with impatience, and darted around the lawn in a frenzy of anticipated joy. I had lathered sunscreen on my son's back, arms, legs, and face, and pinned his thrift-shop shorts together at the waist. I pumped, pushing the handle down slowly and pulling back up, watching my son's wiry figure dance across the lawn, return, stare at the emerging plastic sculpture, and pull his pants higher.

I remember how the moment held me in a trance of contentment—the sun, the children, the wading pool taking shape as I pumped. There was also the pleasure of control, the miracle of turning the flat folded plastic into a pool, a cause for my son's glee, a mother's great pleasure.

But where was his father? He said he'd join us, but Charlie remained inside, reading as usual, devoted to writing the Great American Novel when he wasn't sweeping warehouse floors. It had been six years since immigrating to Canada to escape the Vietnam draft of '69; work had been scarce for both of us. We were in dead-end jobs and barely made ends meet, but he wanted more and retreated into his books to find a shortcut to success.

I set down the pump, dragged the green rubber hose to the pool, and let Justin hold it, the water streaming out. *His first pool.* And Mollie was so cute sitting there on her blanket. Where was the Brownie camera I brought from San Francisco? It was in the kitchen next to the phone—I was sure of it.

The water rose an inch, two inches, three. . . . I turned the wall spigot off, moving the iron disc counterclockwise. "That's enough," I said.

Justin dropped the hose, looking disappointed. Nevertheless, he hopped in, and I tossed him his bath toys—the battery-operated tug, the fishing trawler, the police boat.

Mollie crawled toward us over the grass. I lifted her, sat her in the water, and watched her slap her hands on the surface as she screamed with delight. *The camera. I needed the camera.* Where was Charlie?

"Charlie," I screamed, "bring the camera!"

I looked at my beautiful children, so safe; there was barely any water in the pool.

"Watch your sister while I get the camera. I'll just be a sec."

Justin nodded and returned to making noises for his boats as they conducted maneuvers in the mighty sea. Mollie splashed the water and laughed from somewhere in the back of her throat, a gurgle of happiness.

I ran into the kitchen. The camera wasn't next to the phone. I opened drawers and moved stacks of paper littering the dining table. "Charlie, where's the camera?" I gave up, suddenly worried, sick with foreboding, and ran into Justin in the doorway.

"Mama! Mollie fell over."

My heart pounded as I rushed to the pool. I stared, frozen.

Mollie lay facedown in the water, her blond hair fanning like a halo, her yellow gingham jumper puffing out.

"No!"

I pulled her out and laid her on the grass. I put my lips over her tiny ones and breathed slowly in and out, filled with a terrified knowledge. "Charlie! Call an ambulance!"

Dear God, this can't be happening.

Chapter One
Setting Out

I have considered the days of old,
and the years that are past.
Psalm 77:5

Twenty-two years after Mollie drowned, my nightmares returned. Sleeping little, my fatigue weighted me, seeping through my bones, clouding my thoughts. It was time to seek help, to see if Father Rinaldi, my priest and friend, could do anything, anything at all. But I had never told him about Mollie and the thought filled me with dread.

I walked through a cold and damp San Francisco fog past Saint Thomas's Anglican Church, then climbed the stairs to the Victorian rectory's sagging porch. I pushed the bell. The door creaked open, and Father's wife, Martha, smiling through her wrinkles, took my coat. I could smell bread baking, and it was comforting; Martha had been good for him and for all of us, I thought. It was Rome's loss and our gain when Anthony Rinaldi left the Catholic Church to marry.

"He'll just be a minute," Martha said. "He's finishing the Lenten schedule for February. Do you mind waiting here in the hall? Would you like some tea? I've got scones, fresh from the oven."

I smiled weakly. "No thanks. I'll be fine, Martha. Please, don't worry." I sat down in a hall chair as she excused herself and returned to the kitchen.

A slow panic came over me. It wasn't too late to leave with an appropriate excuse, for how could I put such a thing into words? And what could Father do now? It was so long ago; he couldn't bring Mollie back. And if I did confess my part, could I retain my self-esteem? I smoothed my jacket with moist fingers. It was my lecture tweed, one I associated with rapt students and the safe confines of freshman history, with presenting papers at Stanford and chairing scholarly seminars. I had worked hard to restore my life to manageable standards since I came home; this moment might erase it all.

Martha returned. "You can go in now, Madeleine."

I thanked her and, drugged with reluctance, moved toward Father Rinaldi's office, my mind a grim gray.

Usually the books lining the walls, the grandfather clock ticking quietly, and the fire burning in the grate were comforting on a cold February day like this. But today the heat of the fire was suffocating, the clock marking time. I wanted to flee his office and hide myself in the fog.

We chatted about the church's new garden. Then Father leaned forward, his earnest brown eyes searching mine, his parchment skin flushed in patches, his thinning white hair combed carefully over his balding crown.

"You said on the phone you had something you wanted to talk about? Something serious—something troubling you?" His frail shoulders, framed by the red leather chair, were hunched, and the black he wore, broken by the frayed white band too loose for his thin neck, reminded me he had heard worse than my confession.

I breathed deeply and forced the words. There would be no easy way. "My baby girl drowned, and it was my fault."

"Oh, Madeleine." His eyes were intense, questioning. His words held grief tinged with some perplexity that he had not heard of this before. "You never told me."

I could not bear his gaze, the intensity of his love. I looked away, up to the Franciscan crucifix above the mantel, down to the worn carpet, then through the window where children played in a schoolyard, their screams echoing off the pavement. I smoothed a strand of hair behind my ear and fidgeted with my wedding rings; I adjusted my glasses.

It was a mistake to come. He could do nothing about these nightmares and the great fatigue that wrapped me and dragged me into the earth. He had helped me before, with Justin when he was little. He had found an attorney for my divorce from Charlie. He knew many of my secrets, secrets I held close but wanted desperately to share. But what could he do about Mollie?

I walked to the window, seeing only my little girl, floating.

"Tell me about it," Father said softly, his voice far away.

"It was 1975—in Canada." My words came slowly, measured, dragging this unbearable sorrow.

I heard the creak of leather as Father turned. "1975," he repeated quietly. His gaze burned my back.

I turned and our eyes locked as I slowly related the events that never should have happened. He showed no trace of anger or disappointment, only a deep sadness. His hand rested on the chained crucifix around his neck.

"I killed her, Father. I left her alone in a wading pool. I killed her."

"Madeleine, you are right." He sat up straight, his hands gripping the arms of his chair. "You *were* responsible for her death."

I waited, numb, watching him.

"But even this terrible act," he said, "this tragic accident, has been redeemed by Christ."

"I know." I returned to my seat, suddenly bold. "But I wasn't a believer then—and nightmares haunted me. It was hard." In my greener days I had drifted away from the vague faith of my childhood, such as it was. The bearded old man in the sky and the handsome blond Jesus never changed, always pastel and smiling, saccharine. What did they know of hurt? of suffering? or even sin? "Charlie, my first husband, blamed me. I blamed me. Our marriage was already in trouble and this finished it off."

He seemed to be searching his memory. "You told me you had miscarried once."

I nodded. "I wasn't brave enough to confess it, to say it out loud. I lied, Father, and I'm sorry for that." But I did tell my husband Jack, I thought.

"You've been carrying this a long time."

"Yes." The love in his eyes bathed me. Why had I waited?

"Some marriages don't survive the loss of a child." He looked into the fire as though visiting other losses.

"I relived every moment, thinking, if only I hadn't looked for the camera, if only I had carried her inside."

"Grief over the past haunts us all," he said, shaking his head. "Did the nightmares go away when you came home to San Francisco?"

"Not until I married Jack, four years later."

"Love can heal, transform. Martha turned my world upside down, or maybe I should say right side up." He studied his wedding band.

"But, Father, the nightmares have returned."

"Do you know why?"

"They may have been triggered by the parish picnic last September. After you all left . . . there was this terrible accident . . ."

Martha knocked and paused in the doorway. "Anthony dear, the bishop is on the line. Something about last-minute changes before his flight. You can take it in the kitchen if you like."

Father Rinaldi looked at me apologetically. "I'm sorry. Will you excuse me? I'll be right back." He rose wearily and stepped into the hall.

The accident was months ago—why wouldn't the demons leave me alone?

It had been an accident much like mine.

I had watched the little girl toddle far too close to the edge of the sea. She dug her toes in, bent over, and leaned forward to plant her chubby hands in the wet sand, her bottom, wrapped in a swim diaper, raised high. She wore a checked yellow sundress, and her wispy hair caught the light of the setting sun. Losing her balance, she wavered and plopped down on her behind with a gleeful cry, clapping her hands and sending sand flying into the air. *Where was her mother?*

The church picnic had disbanded. Jack and I had lingered on our towels on a stretch of beach near the Cliff House. Jack dozed, his long frame spread out, his hands clasped over his chest. His fair freckled face was beginning to redden and I considered waking him. Instead, I turned back to the child.

She was waddling in the swirling eddies, leaning over, falling, and clapping, in a repeating dance. There had been a brother there, I was sure, and I looked up and down the beach. Perhaps he was with the boys nearby, tossing a Frisbee. I stood and watched the toddler closely, shielding my eyes from the sun dropping to the horizon.

It happened suddenly. She was facedown in the water, her dress floating. I froze, then ran with leaden feet, fighting the sinking sand.

I grabbed her waist and held her up. She blinked, then let out a wail, and I cradled the soaking child in the hollow of my shoulder, looking once again for the brother, then dusting off the sand from her face. The boy was running toward us and with him a worried woman, screaming, "My baby, my baby."

Father Rinaldi lowered himself into the red leather, his face composed, his full attention on me. "Tell me about the dreams."

I breathed deeply and tried to put in words the dark images of my nights, images that left me with a cold dread, a steely loss tinged with evil. "I hold Mollie in my arms, and she shrinks smaller and smaller to a two-inch skeleton, a pipe-cleaner body with soul-searching eyes, Walter Keene eyes. Do you remember the artist from the sixties? I tell myself it will be all right, she's alive, she'll get better and grow. I can see her insides—she's transparent—and I try to put her back together like a surgeon. I wrap her in a blanket. I rock her. Then she disappears."

Pain fleeted across Father's face. "Martha had nightmares like that once, when she miscarried."

"She lost a baby? I didn't know." My words sounded hollow.

"We couldn't have children after that. But God helped her . . . and me . . . through it."

"He did? How?" I studied him. "How did God help her?"

"It was a difficult time—she suffered so." Now *he* stared out the window.

Pausing, I sensed I shouldn't pry. "But you adopted the twins."

He smiled, turning toward me. "Stephanie and Susanna. Yes. They became part of our healing."

"Father," I began again, "something grabs hold of me and I feel pinched, twisted. I envy new mothers. I want to go back in time, have another chance." Here I am, I thought, forty-nine. How could I even dream of such a thing?

"Madeleine, envy will devour you," he whispered, his gaze still on the window.

"It *is* devouring me. It makes me sick. I hate them; I hate myself. It goes on and on. My brother and Kate have four children, *four,* and now she's pregnant again. I hate her, Father; I hate her! I don't want to have anything to do with them, and that's not right, is it?"

His gaze remained on the world outside, his thoughts seeming far away, perhaps with Martha all those years ago. I waited. Was I too extreme?

"Maybe hate is too strong a word," I added.

"You have Justin."

"I love him dearly, but I wanted more children." Jack and I had bought a child-friendly house, a family house with extra bedrooms never filled. When I didn't conceive, we had fought, our first real fights. I wanted to adopt and Jack wanted to try in vitro fertilization, the latest technique. I was horrified; I refused to freeze living embryos. Finally, I let it go. Jack was nearing fifty back then, twelve years my senior, and had his own grown boys as well as Justin.

"And you have Jack. He loves you, Madeleine."

"I do have Jack, don't I?" I rubbed my hands with their brown age spots and fine wrinkles. A phone rang in the outer office. Father had slumped in the chair, his eyes closed, as he often did when he was thinking or praying. Had he fallen asleep? *Dear God,* I thought, *I can't go through this again. I needed to forget, not remember.* I reached for my handbag.

"So," Father said, slowly opening his eyes, "these beasts have returned to haunt you."

I sensed he wanted desperately to take on my suffering, to add it to his load.

"You have confessed with purpose of amendment," he said, opening his palms to heaven. "There is no need for nightmares. You are forgiven." He watched me closely.

Was that it? Could he wave away the pain with open palms and a crucifix?

"But you need something more, I think."

He tapped his fingers together thoughtfully. One minute, two minutes. Why didn't he speak? I wanted him to fix the problem. Three minutes. I reached for my bag and searched for my keys. Most of all, I wanted this to be over.

I glanced at my watch. "Father, I've an appointment." A half-lie, a half-truth.

"Have you ever been on a pilgrimage?" He looked up at me, his eyes hopeful.

A pilgrimage? I saw a busload of strangers traveling to a shrine and sleeping in a church hall. I recalled how difficult my Lenten fast had been and how short-lived.

"No . . ." I wanted to nip the idea before it budded.

"Sometimes, such a journey helps." He half smiled, seeing my dismay. "Madeleine, trust me. Have you forgotten our travels together? I know you like a little luxury."

"Jack does research good restaurants since he retired." Thinking of all the wine-buying trips for Jack's stores lightened my heart, restoring me to the present. I was ready to listen.

"Maddie, we often forget the living victims left behind when a loved one dies. You had a part in the death of your child. Sometimes, when the body is involved, it takes a physical act of penance to erase the guilt, ease the grief from the body's own judgment court, as it were. It's sacramental. Our spirits affect our bodies and vice versa."

I heard his words, but Mollie filled my mind.

He paused. "Are you listening, Maddie?" He touched my knee lightly.

"Yes . . . of course . . ."

"I was saying, our bodies and souls are connected."

"I'm sorry. Sometimes I'm frozen by that pool. I can't move. It's as though time stops."

"I know." He reached for my hands as though his words could travel through them. "You are forgiven, but your spirit won't accept absolution. Your grief brings back your guilt, as though never washed away."

He released my hands and walked to a wall calendar, traced his fingers on the Sundays, then turned.

"Make a pilgrimage through Italy," he said, "to work this evil out of your soul. Include decent restaurants and hotels. You don't have to stay in pilgrim hostels or keep a fast, although the discipline would help, but do visit some holy places, places I loved when I lived there, and pray sincerely for healing. Keep a journal. And let me know about the nightmares, okay? Will you do that, Madeleine? Will you promise?"

I considered his words. Perhaps a trip, even a holy trip, would be possible. Jack loved Italy, especially Florence and Rome. I had taken a year off from teaching at the university, thinking I would work on a book, but hadn't made much of a start. Still, it was a pilgrimage. "I don't know, Father."

"Martha and I have an anniversary coming up, and if God grants me the grace and my doctor permits, we might return to Rome for a few weeks. After all, I'm just a thirty-year-old fellow in an eighty-year-old body. We could show you around, and if my bishop okays the time off, join you for the rest of the journey."

"You might come with us? That would be wonderful. I'll speak to Jack, but I can't promise anything. He does seem at loose ends since he sold the wine stores. He watches his pennies, but he isn't interested in penance. He thinks he's had enough challenges in his life, and now wants pampering." He had worked long and hard, first as an attorney with Gilpin's, then building his own wine import business.

"Then do your best. You could research some of your book in Rome. Wasn't it on the early Church?"

"I'd like to do something on the martyrs. I'm not sure. And the history of popular miracles, maybe weave the two together. Our history chairperson is breathing down my neck. Publish or perish, she says half jokingly. I may perish at this rate. Jack certainly likes having me home, now that *he's* home."

"Do you miss teaching?"

My heart tightened. "I do. It's a bit of a thorn between us, to be honest." The students' questions challenged me. I recalled their faces: thoughtful during lectures, probing in discussions. A few would disagree with my ideas, and the class would leap into a new world of thought. Inevitably, some would be bored, and when a flicker of interest crossed their faces, I was thrilled. Each student's mental maze was slightly different; it was my task to work my way into it, to open new doors of understanding, ways of interpreting the present with the past.

He nodded. "Give him time. He'll come around."

I wasn't so sure.

"How does Jack spend his time? Retirement can be difficult. I'm a great believer in the sanctification of work, myself—I was once involved with Opus Dei."

"We're adjusting to a new schedule, but I think he's enjoying his freedom. He plays golf, jogs, works with the Scouts. I think Jack misses Justin—it's been years since he settled in Colorado."

"I miss him too. He was a challenge as an acolyte but a good lad." Father Rinaldi chuckled. "I often recall the first time you came to Saint Thomas's. He was such a little boy then, around five? He stuttered, didn't he? But he got over that."

Justin didn't speak for months after Mollie drowned. When his speech finally returned, he stuttered, as though his words were waiting for the right moment. The right moment was phantasmal, always dancing ahead of him.

"He hardly ever stutters now, mostly when he's stressed. And it was Justin who pulled me into Saint Thomas's on the way to the park—to hear the organ. I can't believe he's turning twenty-five."

"Is he really? Where has the time gone? Jack said he was drawn in by the music too, but, my dear, he stayed because of you." Father's eyes twinkled.

Dapper Jack Seymour had smiled across the church hall that morning, and I had smiled back. He was curly-haired, wore a gray three-piece suit, fuchsia tie, and matching pocket scarf. I felt my future touch me as I chatted with him, looking up at his closely set blue eyes. Justin, racing around the room, had bumped into him, and he had spilled his

8

coffee.

"It's true about the music—it's wonderful." I sensed I was blushing with the memory.

Father steepled his fingers. "We've been blessed with an outstanding organist."

"Saint Thomas's has been good to us, Father. So have you." He had taught me everything about the Faith, helping me with the first steps of belief. I was raised liberal Protestant, but when I grew up I couldn't see any reason to go to church. Man, they said, was intrinsically good, just misguided by genes and environment. He could be changed with education, taught to be good. God gazed upon us like a benevolent father, and, it seemed to me, I could live my life without church. I was saved, and that was that. Then I met Father Rinaldi and learned it wasn't that simple, or at least, sanctification was an ongoing process.

He smiled. "The family of God is a precious and powerful thing. Now, my dear, are you coming to tomorrow's mass, our Tuesdays in Lent? We missed you on Sunday."

"Jack wanted to spend the weekend in Carmel. He read about a great chef at one of the beach hotels. I'll try to make tomorrow evening—Jack's in San Diego with a Scout meeting."

"Do come. And, Maddie, open your heart. God can't work his miracles if you don't open your heart. Trust me," he added, his eyes full of a confidence I wanted to own, "it will be all right."

He walked me to the front door where he held my head in his hands like a precious jewel, kissing me on each cheek, Italian style.

I left lighter, the heavy weight removed. But the nightmares continued.

"You told Father Rinaldi what?" Jack shouted over the phone. "Sorry, I've got a bad connection."

"I told him about Mollie." I gazed through the kitchen windows to the crashing surf below.

We had found the old Sea Cliff house to the west of the Golden Gate shortly after I proposed to Jack. Over the years we had papered and painted, remodeled and added on, and with each change our roots in the rambling three-story grew deeper, our tendrils winding through the

9

rooms like the ivy pattern on the kitchen walls.

"You said you never would. Hold on, I've got another call."

The line went dead. Should I have waited till he came home? Jack had a temper, and sudden news was not his strong suit. Had I misjudged this one? I picked at a fingernail, cradling the phone with my shoulder.

"Okay," he said, returning, "why the sudden change of heart? What's done is done. Why bring all that up?"

"Jack, the nightmares came back, the ones about Mollie."

"Oh no. Why didn't you tell me?"

"I didn't want to burden you."

"Maybe you should see Lynn Beck. She's helped our store managers from time to time. She's a good therapist."

"Dr. Beck?" I recalled an energetic and friendly face from a gathering in the past. Her eyes searched, evaluated, judged. "Father suggested a trip, Jack."

"My kind of priest! I'm ready and willing. Hey, I've got my Michelin *France* here, an old copy from our buying days. Let's plan something. I was thinking of going back to Burgundy." Jack loved travel and often looked for a reason to justify the expense. His frugal background insisted on a reason, to avoid major guilt.

"A kind of holy trip, Jack."

"A what?"

"Actually, a pilgrimage."

He sighed. "We're not going to a shrine in some remote wilderness, and I refuse to travel with a group. We may not have much, but we can still plan our own route, time our own day."

"He said it could be a comfortable pilgrimage, but he does have a list of churches in Italy. He and Martha might come."

Jack chuckled. "I should've known. Father Rinaldi does enjoy life. We'll make plans when I fly in on Wednesday. Maybe we could go in May before Italy heats up. I know you want to be home for Easter, and Father couldn't be away then anyway."

"That's what I was thinking. How I love you."

"And I love you too, my too-good-for-this-earth Maddie. Now, what did you have for dinner, after this horrendous interview with the venerable Father? And did you remember to feed Miss Kitty?"

"I heated soup, and yes, Miss Kitty is fed."

"Soup? I'd better return and rescue you." Jack was an excellent cook. "I'll call tomorrow night, Maddie."

"Good, but after seven-thirty. I'm going to the Tuesday mass since

10

we missed Sunday."

It was a mass I would never forget.

Tuesday evening I walked through the arched doorway of Saint Thomas's and into the white vaulted chapel, toward the stone altar. A sculpted Madonna stood on a pedestal in the left corner, wrapped in robes of gray and mauve, her eyes pensive, her child on her hip. I lit a blue votive and added three daisies to the vase alongside. Mary steadied me—she was the sacred feminine, the suffering mother. I knelt in the second pew, our usual place, and opened the prayer book to the service for Holy Communion.

Only a few others were there—a young banker who often passed around the collection basket, a elderly editor who kept to himself, and, in the far back, a woman I had not seen before.

Martha sat in front of me, her white head tilted like a sparrow as she waited for her husband to enter from the sacristy. On the altar, six brass candlesticks with tall tapers framed an antique tabernacle holding the Reserved Sacrament. A red candle burned to the side. As Anglicans, we believe that the hosts behind the bronze doors hold the mystical presence of Christ. The red candle signifies that the Sacrament has been reserved there.

The hammered brass of the tabernacle doors rendered a chalice, a sun, and a book. The doors glimmered, as though opening to a purifying love, and I sensed that in that love, answers to questions forever asked could be found. A white tassel hung on the key-handle, a delicate fringe guarding the gates of Paradise.

I wondered about God, my mind cloudy with fatigue. Could he really heal me?

Friends accuse me of living in an unreal world, of being religious and betraying the modern woman. I embarrass them with my walls of crucifixes, icons, and rosaries. But, especially before the tabernacle, I feel God pushing from without or listening from within. Perhaps I have a good imagination, or my world lies parallel to another world and the two merge. Or maybe I'm a genius or a saint, a fool or a lunatic, in touch with a great truth or a great lie.

That Tuesday evening, as my shins pressed against the soft leather

11

kneeler, my arms resting on the oak pew back, I knew Christ would come again in a mysterious way. Soon the bread and wine would be infused with him, a transformation repeated in billions of masses over nearly two thousand years. Even so, to me, each time was new. Each time the seen world collided with the unseen. I said to myself, *the altar, being so strong and heavy, will root this God for me.* It will keep him here, draw him down along with our special words and phrases, our incantations ringing through time. And once he is here, once he becomes part of the bread and the wine, I will have him. I will graft him onto my body; I will consume him. He will ban my ghosts; he will strengthen me.

When I knelt, I prayed like a child. I searched out my heart for sins, sometimes obvious, sometimes wispy and vague and hidden. I repented. Like a child, I waited with breathless excitement, focusing on the chalice and the large round host. That bread was the earthly throne of God— surely a magnificent light would shaft through the skylight and strike the bread and wine. Surely Gabriel would blow his trumpet!

Steven, one of the high school acolytes—and not the Angel Gabriel— entered from the sacristy and lit the candles. Father Rinaldi followed, vested in Lenten purple, his cassock dusting the floor. Slightly stooped, he moved slowly, shyly and purposefully, as though not to be noticed, a pure channel for God. He faced the altar and spoke the words of the liturgy in nearly a monotone, yet with awe and intimate reverence, as though for the first time. Genuflecting, he gathered himself together, one hand gripping the altar. I waited expectantly.

I waited and I watched, carefully repeating the sacred words. Steven rang the Sanctus bells, and as they trilled through the chapel, Father Rinaldi raised the host. I crossed myself, praying *My Lord and My God.*

Then, as he raised the chalice, he wavered. The cup slipped from his hand onto the altar, rolled to the side, and fell to the floor with a hollow clang. Father Rinaldi collapsed slowly, his hand on his heart.

I stared, unable to move.

Martha cried out and ran to him. She knelt on the floor and lifted him up, wrapping him in her arms, like Mary and Jesus in the *Pieta.* She began to weep tiny, raspy sobs of panic, cradling his head, holding her white head next to his silver, their cheeks touching. "No, no, no . . ."

"Martha," he whispered, "it's all right, love, it's all right." He closed his eyes, smiling, and seemed to drift off to sleep, but he was gone from us all.

"I'll call 911," Steven said, running out through a back door.

The banker approached. "Mrs. Rinaldi, let me help." He lifted

Father's small form and carried him to the church hall, Martha at his side.

The editor and I followed. We watched him lay Father Rinaldi on the couch under the portrait of Canon Schuster, one saint gazing upon the other. The woman from the back pew appeared. "I'm a nurse," she said. "Would you like me to look at him?"

"Please," I said, nodding. The room was close. I gripped the arm of the couch and studied the nurse as she moved toward Father's still body. I was acting a part in a strange play, a part with no lines. *Surely I must be dreaming.*

Martha sat with Father's head resting on her lap. She was crying quietly, touching his hair and face. His eyes were closed, and his half smile remained; his wrinkles had disappeared, his skin smooth and pale as a child. I stood behind her, helpless, my hand resting lightly on her shoulder as the nurse took his pulse, her face a trained blank. Steven reappeared, saying the ambulance was on the way.

The nurse looked at me and shook her head. "I'm sorry."

After all had been done that could be done, I returned to the chapel and cleaned up the altar, my heart aching. The chalice lay on the flagstone floor. The consecrated wine, now the mystical Blood of Christ, had spilled onto the corporal, the small linen square that had lain under the chalice, leaving a large magenta stain. The consecrated host remained on the silver plate, waiting to be broken for us few to receive.

I placed the host, now the Reserved Sacrament, in the tabernacle. I washed out the empty chalice in the sacristy sink. The floor appeared clean; all of the wine-blood had spilled on the altar linen. I removed the candlesticks and the service book, folded the corporal, and replaced the sacred vessels. I gazed at the cloth, wondering.

Something prompted me to take the linen with me. In the months that followed, in a journey that changed my life, the cloth was my companion. A little crazy? Maybe, but it has revealed some remarkable places in my soul.

The full Requiem mass would have surprised Father Rinaldi, a simple priest. Wealthy matrons and suited businessmen, toothless rummies and crack-heads, emaciated AIDS victims and homeless wanderers, the old and the young, packed the immense church as the solemn procession followed the gilded crucifix up the broad nave. Jack, serious in his charcoal pinstripe, followed with the other pallbearers, guiding the rolling casket toward the altar.

Justin stood tall beside me at the funeral, his presence reassuring. Leaving his construction business in Colorado, he had returned home with his friend Lisa Jane. He wrapped a heavy arm around my shoulders.

I looked up at him gratefully, then glanced at Lisa Jane on my other side. We had met at Christmas and I had liked her at once—her love of life, her devotion to Justin. Her highlighted chestnut hair flowed down her back; her hoop earrings reflected the candlelight. Fingering a silver cross in the vee of her white blouse, she seemed absorbed by the liturgy in the grand cathedral, the soaring chants, the robed procession. She told me later her Catholic parish at home observed a much simpler rite with guitars and folk songs. She liked this "higher" ritual; it was more artistic, using symbol, metaphor, and poetry. After all, she was an English major with an Art minor, now working on her teaching credential.

I fingered the linen cloth, which the bishop had allowed me to keep, thinking of the stone altar and Father's sturdy faith. I thought of the watching and the waiting and how he wove our prayers into the great miracle each week, as he worked our Lord in among us, like a baker kneading bread or a weaver weaving a fine fabric. I was thankful for his time with us.

I was thankful too for our little church of Saint Thomas. Like the Gregorian plainsong echoing in the cathedral's grand vaults, the chapel's sheer beauty had drawn me in—the rhythmic dance of the liturgy, the poetic Elizabethan language, the seriously festive processions, the sweet swirling incense, the bright flaming candles. But most of all, I liked the objective reality of belief, worshiping Someone real on the altar, Someone who healed, Someone who righted wrongs.

Father had taught me well; I learned that we had fallen away from God in the Garden of Eden and we continued to fall. We were half men, half women, seeking to be whole, living in a gray world, longing for the light. We were created good, but the good had been corrupted, twisted. For once, the human condition made perfect sense.

In the time I had known this priest whose body lay in the wooden coffin before me, I had leapt from despairing doubt to fragile faith to

14

joyous certainty. With his gentle guidance, I came to believe what these Christians preached—in a loving God and in sinful humanity. After all, no one's perfect, a truth I knew all too well. I continued to learn about Anglo-Catholic faith and practice, knowing I had only begun my journey. With each mass, each liturgy, and each sermon, my heart, soul, and mind drew closer to God, and I felt something broken inside me being made whole again. Where would I be today, I wondered with some fear, without having known Father Rinaldi? Without having experienced the mystery and miracle of the mass?

"Mom? You okay? It's nearly over," Justin whispered as he handed me a tissue.

"I'm okay." I nodded. But my lip quivered as I blotted my tears.

We recessed to *Joyful, Joyful We Adore Thee* set to Beethoven's *Ode to Joy*, a hymn Father Rinaldi had loved. The pallbearers stepped alongside the casket, recessing down the aisle, their heads bowed as the pews emptied behind them, one by one. In the last verse, we slipped our hymnals into the pew slots and joined the hundreds of mourners stepping into the March rain.

We headed home to Sea Cliff after the funeral for some lunch, before Justin and Lisa Jane had to catch the evening flight to Denver.

The rain pounded the wooden deck outside the nook, making our society of four safe and warm. The kitchen remodel hadn't given us much more space, but the white counters and glass-paned cupboards lightened things on this dark day, and the green leafy wallpaper was cheery. The old house had been redone many times when we found it fifteen years ago, and we soon added our own memories, good and bad, sweet and sour.

I watched the moment, sitting outside it, as though it held great meaning and transition in our lives. Father Rinaldi was gone from this earth, but not *gone* from us forever. Jack sat next to me, so solid and real, his graying hair and lined face gracing him with even greater solidity. Justin with his Lisa Jane were the future. Where would we go from here, from this moment in time?

I heated leftover soup Jack had made the night before and toasted slices of sourdough, but we picked at the food, our thoughts elsewhere.

Lisa Jane looked as though she didn't want to intrude. She would step carefully as she mapped our family nuances. She sat close to Justin, her dark eyes seeking his.

Justin looked up at me, then glanced at Lisa Jane. "Father R-Rinaldi was like a grandfather to m-me." He had grown a thin beard and cut his blond hair short; construction work had kept his body in shape, and a man's muscles pushed against the white cotton of his shirt sleeves. He was no longer my little boy.

I rose and filled a plate with brownies from Sunday's bake sale. "He loved you like a grandson." My father had died when Justin was five; Justin's other grandfather—Charlie's father—lived several states away. He had never contacted us.

Lisa Jane placed her hand, the olive skin smooth, on Justin's arm, connecting. "I wish I had gotten to know him." She had met Father Rinaldi briefly at Christmas.

Jack leaned back in his chair, folding his hands in his philosopher's manner, raising his brows. "He was a good man. He will live on in all our memories. In that sense he hasn't gone at all." Our tabby, Miss Kitty, jumped on his lap, and he stroked her thick fur as she rhythmically pushed her paws into his leg, purring.

I frowned. I knew Jack believed in many tenets of Christianity, but this implied denial of heaven troubled me. Like all of us, his perceptions were colored by the spirit of the day, the *zeitgeist*, the assumption that this is all there is, ideas worn like a loose mantle. He seemed less concerned with the nuances of faith than I. My father, a liberal pastor, had left his faith and his flock, and I never truly understood why. "We read Tillich and Russell and Rogers," my mother once explained. "They proved Christianity was a myth." Had they never really known Jesus? How could they deny someone they had known?

Justin looked at Jack, then me. "I w-wish I had a chance to say g-good-bye."

"We'll see him again." The words sounded trite and I bit my lip. Expressions of faith were so difficult, so delicate. I often wondered why that was so.

Lisa Jane looked up and nodded. "We will."

"Yeah, Mom, I know, but I w-wanted him to get to know Lisa Jane."

Lisa Jane grinned, and a light flush spread across her cheeks. She ran her fingers through her hair, pulling it up and away from her face, then releasing it to fall in waves over her shoulders.

"He would have loved knowing you better," I said to her.

16

"Thank you, Mrs. Seymour." Her eyes were serious, thoughtful.

Justin smiled for the first time that day, revealing a front tooth slightly gray from a sixth-grade skateboard accident. "He's not much like your Father Ted," he said to Lisa Jane. "He didn't play the guitar, for starters."

"But Father Ted is *young*. He might grow old to be like Father Rinaldi."

Jack laughed. He set Miss Kitty down and rose to make coffee. "Maybe when we visit Denver next time we'll meet this Father Ted. Did you say guitars?"

"When's that?" Justin asked. "I want to show you my new rig. And there's an upscale project near Aspen I'm working on. It's pretty cool, the stonework we've got going."

Jack looked at me as he pulled a tin from the cupboard. "Not sure, really."

"We may be going to Italy in May," I said. "It was Father Rinaldi's idea."

Jack nodded. "That's the plan. I've got the hotels lined up and the airlines, just waiting for a few confirmations."

Justin studied my face. "You look tired, M-Mom."

T makeup hadn't helped. "Not sleeping too well. Father wanted us to visit certain churches—said the trip might help." I searched a kitchen drawer, found the list Father had given me, and handed it to Justin. I wouldn't explain the dreams; I wouldn't make my son relive his sister's death.

Looking at me quizzically, he studied the paper, his blue eyes growing envious.

Santa Maria Maggiore, Roma
Chiesa di Santa Pudenziana, Roma
Chiesa di Santa Prassede, Roma
Chiesa di Sant' Agnese fuori le Mura, Roma
Basilica di San Pietro, Roma
The Duomo Crypt, Milano
Chiesa di San Zaccaria, Venezia
Basilica di San Marco, Venezia
Basilica di San Domenico, Bologna
Sanctuario della Verna, northeast of Firenze
Abbazia di Sant' Antimo, southwest of Siena
Chiesa del Gesu, Roma

"This is sweet."

"We hope to visit twelve churches in three weeks. The Rinaldis were going to come with us, at least for the Rome part."

Justin breathed deeply, working to control his flow of his words. "But you're still going?"

"Jack thinks we should. I'm not so sure." I watched my husband pour water into the coffeemaker and tap the *on* button.

"Maybe Father Rinaldi will watch over you, Mom." My son's eyes mothered me.

"Maybe so," I said, feeling a renewed sadness. "I'm taking his altar linen with me."

"His what?"

"The corporal, the linen that lies under the chalice during mass. When Father died, the wine had been consecrated, turned into Christ's blood. It spilled onto the corporal."

"Wow." Justin looked incredulous.

Lisa Jane leaned forward. "Really? Could we see it?"

I left to find the stained cloth, the size of a large napkin, folded carefully in a bedroom chest. When I returned, Lisa Jane ran her fingers over it. "So you're taking this with you?"

I nodded. "It sounds crazy, but it comforts me."

"And the bishop," Jack added, "is letting your mother keep it. In spite of a persistent outcry from an influential parishioner, a McDougal . . . McDonaugh . . . what was the name, Maddie?"

"McGinty, as I recall. I gather he wants the cloth for the cathedral. He didn't know Father Rinaldi, but considers it a possible relic because of Father's saintliness."

Jack looked at his watch. "We'd better head for the airport."

On Sunday, April 27, we flew over Chicago, the Great Lakes, Nova Scotia, Greenland, and the British Isles. At London Heathrow we boarded a plane for Rome.

Mollie and Father Rinaldi wove through my mind, and I checked my bag often, touching Father's linen cloth. Was Father watching or was he sleeping, waiting for the last trumpet? He had left a gaping hole in my life, and now I mourned both him *and* Mollie. I pulled out my prayer book and turned to the Psalms for the day, reading slowly, singing the words in my head. As I finished, I closed my eyes and let my mind drift.

What, after all, was a pilgrimage? I had looked up *pilgrim* and found it meant a "resident alien, a stranger on earth." I knew that Christians see themselves as aliens in this world, their true home being heaven, and the early monastics sought desert seclusion, an immediate withdrawal from the world. But *pilgrimage*, as a "journey to holy sites," goes back to Saint Helena, Constantine's mother. The empress traveled to Jerusalem in 326 and returned to Rome with pieces of wood from Christ's cross. Pilgrims, traveling to the scenes of their Lord's life, or later to shrines of his saints, sought supernatural help, performed penances, and offered thanksgivings.

"Look, Maddie." Jack had set down his Grisham paperback, a sales receipt marking his place. He peered through the window and focused his camera on emerging lands far below.

I followed his gaze. We flew low along the Italian coast in the late morning light, the hazy waters of the Mediterranean curving in and out. Then, banking east, we began our descent to Fiumicino Airport. I reset my watch. We had been traveling for seventeen hours and had lost a half day in time zones. It was close to noon, Monday, April 28.

Chapter Two
Roma

Why art thou so full of heaviness, O my soul?
and why art thou so disquieted within me?
Psalm 42:6

C hurch bells rang, dissonant tones echoing in the morning air.
I slipped into a terry robe and pulled open damask draperies.
Unlatching tall windows, I pushed open the thick glass, letting in more worldly sounds—horns, shouts, and scooters buzzing.

Seven floors below, traffic jammed the narrow road. Porters slammed doors and blew whistles. Farther along, a broad terrace led to the Spanish Steps, which descended to the Piazza di Spagna, named after the former Spanish consulate. Today pink azaleas covered the Steps, and young people perched among the flowers like lovebirds. Above the Steps stood Trinità dei Monti, Holy Trinity of the Hills, the French church.

Entranced, I gazed over the rooftops and bell towers emerging from the haze, the sun still low. I breathed deeply, inhaling a mixture of exhaust and dew and promised warmth.

Jack, already dressed in khakis, a blue polo, and a green pullover, answered a knock at the door. A smiling waiter wheeled in a linen-covered table set with croissants and brioches, blood-orange juice and sliced melon.

Jack pulled out my chair and kissed me on the forehead. "Welcome to Rome, sleepyhead. It's nearly nine. You had another rough night, didn't you?" His blue eyes crinkled in concern, and I noticed a new freckle on his neck.

I tried to smile. "Let's not talk about it." Talking made the phantoms more real and didn't seem to help, as though they owned my days as well as my nights.

"I worry, though." Taking my hand, he glanced at the folded business section of the morning paper. *"Bless, oh Lord, this food to our use and us to thy service and make us mindful of the needs of others, in Christ's name, Amen."*

I made the Sign of the Cross, thankful but tired, then poured thick black coffee, topping it with hot milk. I reached for a chocolate croissant and looked at the front page.

"Jack, we missed April twenty-first."

"Did we?" Jack's gaze remained on the stock listings.

"Don't you want to know what April twenty-first is, or was?"

"Of course."

"The founding of Rome. Big celebration, according to the paper." The croissant was sweet and buttery and rich.

He looked over his reading glasses with the determined air of a man multitasking. "That must be the Romulus story."

I read on, nodding. "Romulus and Remus. They quarreled over where to found the city, the Palatino or the Aventino, two hills in Rome. Romulus killed Remus, and Rome was founded on the Palatine in 753 BC."

"The Palatino is where the ruins are. Wasn't there some story about a wolf?" Jack turned to the sports page and ran his finger down the scores.

I skimmed the rest. "It says that the brothers were sent down the Tiber for safety to protect them from a wicked uncle and . . . suckled by a wolf and then raised by shepherds."

"I've seen the statue of a wolf with the two children suckling. These Italians *are* full of life." He looked up as he folded the paper neatly.

I smiled, sipping my juice. "Maybe their life will be contagious."

"I hope so." He tossed the paper on the bed. "Now what's today's mission? Is it a three-Rinaldi-star church?" He grinned, giving me his full attention. "Maddie, I do love you, you know, and it will be all right, trust me or trust Father Rinaldi, God rest his soul. We'll ban those nasty nightmares; we'll tame the wild beasts!"

Jack's enthusiasm was heartening, but I worried that my nightmares threatened him; he provided bodily comforts rather than spiritual, or so he thought. If he couldn't heal me or help the healing, I feared he would run away. He wanted to keep the wolves from my door; he saw me as his project, a substitute for his career, now that he was no longer working. At times, his concern crowded me.

"Father wants us to begin with the Basilica di Santa Maria

Maggiore—Mary Major—one of the traditional pilgrimage basilicas. I'm not sure why."

"Pilgrimage basilicas?"

"Originally, pilgrims journeyed to San Pietro—Saint Peter's. But eventually other churches were added: San Paolo fuori le Mura—Saint Paul outside the Walls. San Giovanni in Laterano—Saint John in the Lateran district. Santa Maria Maggiore—Saint Mary Major."

"Pilgrims went to all those churches?"

"That was the short list. Today they visit the catacombs too."

The phone rang and I picked up the old-fashioned black receiver. My brother Michael sounded as if he were in the same room.

"It's a girl, Maddie!" Michael cried. "Kate's so happy."

"Congratulations, Mike." He was younger by three years and I had always mothered him. I should have been happier than I was.

"I . . . just wanted to tell you. I've a few more calls to make. Do you have Mom's number? I lost it."

I recited it. "She's in the rest home now, don't forget. Have you chosen a name?"

"Chelsea Katherine. Seven pounds, three ounces. Better go, Sis . . . *ciao*, as they say."

"Give my love to Kate and kiss Chelsea for me. *Ciao*, Michael."

"Will do." The phone clicked.

The old envy grabbed me, and I swallowed hard, my eyes tearing. I locked myself in the bathroom, stared at my streaky cheeks, and thought how selfish I was not to share their joy.

Why not me? Why couldn't I accept the fact that Justin would be my only child? Why couldn't I be grateful for the life I led? A bitter knot formed in the hollow of my chest. I breathed deeply and returned to the breakfast table.

"Kate had a girl, eight pounds, everyone healthy." I dropped two brown sugar lumps in my empty cup, poured more coffee and hot milk, and stirred hard. Burying my face in the paper, I tried to focus on the book review.

"That's good, right?" Jack asked, his voice uncertain. He began to stack the dishes for room service pick up.

Mary Major stands on a vast square on the Esquilino Hill. Legend says it snowed on the site in August of 352, a rare occurrence. When the Virgin Mary appeared to Pope Liberius, commanding him to build a church within the boundaries of the snowfall, he obeyed. Since then, every August 5 in the Ceremony of the Snow, white petals shower from one of the cupolas onto the congregation.

We crossed a broad parvis and climbed massive stairs. Opening a heavy door, we paused in the narthex. A long straight nave led to a gleaming altar and glittering apse. Forty marble columns ran up the side aisles marking the two hundred feet to the altar.

I stepped into the nave, leaving the dark entrance and turning toward the light apse and its canopied altar. Circular marble tiles covered the floor, and, at the far end, the apsidal mosaic showed Christ crowning his mother. The entire ceiling was coffered in gold—American gold, I recalled, brought back from the New World. Behind me, Jack checked his guidebook as he studied a row of mosaics high on the side walls. Pilgrims and tourists milled about; some sang hymns, some knelt in prayer.

We reached the end of the nave and descended curving stairs to a shrine in the *confessio* beneath the high altar. Whose relics lay here? Mary's body was never claimed; many believe she was taken bodily into heaven, a miraculous event called the Assumption.

"It's the Christmas crib, the manger cradle," Jack said.

Inside a glass ark topped by a cherub rested a small piece of wood. Behind us was an oversized statue of a pope kneeling.

"Now I understand," I said, half to myself, "why this church was first on the list." Here was the beginning of God's great act for man, his momentous intersection in man's time, the birth of his Son, the God-man, in a manger. The child became a man, died and rose from the dead, fulfilling ancient Jewish prophecy. My own loss seemed insignificant in comparison, yet just as real. Maybe I was to take my grief seriously and not to overlook the small, the humble, the seemingly little things of our world. Maybe there *were* no little things.

I heard singing in the distance—it was *Kumbaya*, the lilting chant for peace. We followed the sounds to a golden side chapel where a priest offered mass. He faced the altar, its red candle flaming. High above the altar a Madonna and Child gazed upon the people. We stood in the back, absorbing the mystery of Christ's presence in this basilica of Mary, the simple girl from Nazareth.

Jack pointed to the icon. "That's one of the miraculous Madonnas."

"Really?" I peered, trying to see the faded figures. The icon looked old. Mary's robes were dark and the boy Jesus was draped in red; the figures stood against a golden background, framed in gilt. I was struck by the earthy image in the ornate setting.

Jack whispered, "Gregory the Great processed with this icon through Rome, praying for an end to the plague. In 594."

"And when the plague stopped mysteriously," I added, recalling the story, "the icon was declared miraculous."

"And now she's Protectress of Rome—Our Lady of the Snow."

"It's haunting. I think Saint Luke painted it—that would make it first century." Other Madonnas had claimed Saint Luke's brush as well. How was one to know?

We crossed to the southern transept, where the small body of Sixtus V lay in a large glass coffin. I thought how short life was, our bodies destined to decay, and how, even so, we seek with hope the glorious and the eternal. Here in this grandiose church dedicated to a peasant girl who, in her obedience, became Queen of Heaven, these great opposites—humility and glory—met. They met in the bread and wine on the altar, in the frail body in the glass tomb, in the wood in the silver crèche, in the earthy Madonna and Child. If such things happened, there was hope for me.

We sat in the front row of the nave and watched tourists slip coins into timer slots to turn on lights in the apse, changing the muted tones to vivid blues, greens, and golds. A group sang "Ave Maria," a song for all of us in our earthiness, a hymn to this woman of earth. For Mary had been God's earthly vessel, the vessel of his love.

We stepped outside into dazzling light, and Jack took a picture of the white façade from the far side of the square. He carefully repacked his camera, took my hand, and we walked down the hill through the clear windswept day toward the Via Urbana and the next church on Father Rinaldi's list.

The churches of Santa Pudenziana and Santa Prassede were named after sisters who buried their fellow Christians. In the first century, when believers were eaten by beasts in the Coliseum or—if Roman citizens—beheaded, Pudenziana and Prassede retrieved and cleaned their remains. They anointed their bodies with aromatic oils. They buried them deep in their house wells, believing the bones, having been close to God in life, would be a way to God in death, a road from earth to heaven.

The sisters are thought to be daughters of Senator Pudens, mentioned by Saint Paul in his letter to Timothy. According to tradition, Saint Peter stayed at the Pudens' home, where he celebrated the Holy Supper. Archeologists have found fragments of the Pudens house in the crypt beneath the church of Santa Pudenziana. Nearby Santa Prassede has a similar history.

We descended stairs to Santa Pudenziana, set below street level and surrounded by a Cistercian convent. Entering through humble doors, we sat in a back pew. A nun set cruets of water and wine on the altar in preparation for a mass.

I pointed to the apse and whispered, "Look at that mosaic! See how lifelike the figures are? Christ and the apostles look Roman—not Byzantine."

"They're even wearing togas," Jack said, "and look at the colors of those stones! They weren't exactly poverty-stricken, were they?"

"Not after Constantine made Christianity legal."

"That would make a huge difference, I would think, having the backing of the state."

I nodded. "Wealthy senators and landholders converted."

We walked up the north aisle to the Caetani chapel, covered in frescoes and marble, and I studied a history panel on a wall. "Jack! A Eucharistic miracle occurred here in 1610. Blood spilled from the chalice onto the linen cloth."

"Real blood?"

"Yes." I pulled my linen from my bag and touched the stains. Was this truly Christ's blood? It had to be.

As we walked toward the door, Jack pointed to a large oil painting in the narthex. "Look—the famous sisters."

Two women, bloody pools forming at their feet, concentrated on their work. One placed a skull in a well and the other sponged up blood, her face determined. They were sisterly sisters, I thought, united in their honoring of death, the journey of the soul from earth to heaven. Why couldn't I be united with my sister-in-law in celebrating birth, the creation of earthly life?

We climbed the outer stairs and headed for Santa Prassede. I walked briskly, concentrating on a plastic foldout map, watching for

25

speeding scooters and traffic lights turning to *avante*, burying my envy in movement.

We found Santa Prassede, looked after by Vallombrosian Benedictines. Monastic buildings merged into the ocher walls of the ninth-century basilica, a rebuilding of the fifth-century church. Entering through a side door, we paused in the darkness, realizing we were in the southern transept. As we walked down the aisle toward the foot of the nave, we noticed a glittering bay chapel and paused. Red, blue, and gold mosaics spread across a small apse. Inside, opening to the right, an alcove housed a tall glass reliquary containing a granite column, a rustic contrast to the glittering walls. Tradition claims the column was Christ's whipping post, the beginning of his long Way of the Cross. I shivered, seeing the blood of Jesus and hearing the jeers of the soldiers.

We walked in silence to the narthex doors, where a sculpted figure of a woman squeezed blood from a sponge into an urn. *Blood. Our life and our death. And our salvation, our victory over death.*

Jack scanned the entry in his book. "The slab behind her was her bed and then her tomb; her bones are in the crypt. When this basilica was built, the pope had the remains of twenty-three hundred martyrs moved from the catacombs. Talk about relics."

"Paschal I. He brought many bodies inside the walls to sanctify these altars."

"Probably safer too."

We walked up the nave toward the high altar where a red candle flickered. Above, the apsidal mosaic showed Peter and Paul presenting the sisters to Christ. The figures were Byzantine, iconic, mysterious, a channel for the holy. I knelt in the first pew and tried to pray, but no words came. I sat back and considered the sisters who loved so. I prayed that I could love as they did, that I could love my sister-in-law.

As I prayed for love, I reached for my linen, stained with the blood of sacrifice.

Keys jangled. A monk hurried to the side entrance, waving his hands.

"We'd better get some lunch," Jack whispered.

"They're closing up."

"Pasta time." Jack took a quick picture of the glittering chancel and we headed toward the cleric who pointed to us, bobbing his head. "*Chiuso, chiuso, chiuso. . . .*"

We found a small trattoria near our hotel and lunched on *crostini* with garlic and white beans, *carciofi, fettuccini pommodoro, insalata mista,* and shared a bottle of Chianti.

"What's our next stop?" Jack twirled his pasta into a large spoon with his fork. "This is wonderful. What did they put in the tomato sauce—I think a little balsamic vinegar."

I pulled out the list. "Sant' Agnese fuori le Mura."

"Fuori le Mura?"

" 'Outside the walls.' In ancient Rome it was illegal—for hygienic reasons—to bury the dead within the city walls."

"Makes sense. Want more cheese?"

I took the bowl and spooned the fragrant flakes of parmesan. "In the case of the Christian cemeteries—the catacombs—the martyrs' remains were believed sacred and powerful. So the graves became sites for celebration of the first Holy Suppers. Eventually these *loci* became churches." In my Western Civilization class, my students had been amazed that the early Christians didn't actually live in the catacombs. "A fiction of Hollywood," I explained to them, "one of many."

"So do we see a catacomb?"

I nodded. "One of the smaller ones."

"And who was Agnes?"

Sighing, I sipped my wine, consoled by its bright fruity taste. Like many stories of the early martyrs, Agnes's was a sad one. "She was a third-century martyr, only thirteen, who refused to marry a wealthy pagan."

Jack glanced at me as he speared a cherry tomato. "You married a wealthy pagan."

I laughed, appreciating my husband's lilting humor. "I wouldn't call you wealthy. And certainly not a pagan."

"I suppose not. But I'm more Protestant, and you're more Catholic."

"That's a good way to put it." I generally avoided dwelling on our differences. What good did it do?

Jack reached for the sauce pitcher for his last bit of pasta. "I believe in God and in Christ." He looked up at me, his blue eyes seeking a common understanding. "And I think it's good to worship in church."

I nodded. "It *is* good to worship in church." I dipped a bit of bread in a pool of green olive oil and chewed slowly, enjoying the sharp tang. I knew Jack had difficulty believing in miracles and the efficacy of relics. I understood, for many good Christians didn't believe in such sacramental power, such supernatural interventions. The Protestants of my childhood had warned me against Catholics—I was told they were superstitious, lived in constant fear of God and hell, and weren't allowed to pray. They claimed that Catholics worshiped statues and crucifixes and knelt before tabernacles; they were idolaters and held secret rites. When I returned to the Faith from my collegiate agnosticism, I was amazed to learn how mistaken those depictions had been. Today I found relics and miracles to be real mysteries and fascinating. Some stories were undoubtedly true; some weren't. One used a little reason and did a little research and tried to sort it all out.

"So Agnes was only thirteen?" Jack's words broke my train of thought.

"She was, and after her death, she was beloved in Rome. Several generations later, Constantine's daughter, Constanza, asked to be buried next to Agnes."

"A touching story. And the catacombs sound intriguing. When do they open?"

"Probably not until four—maybe we should take a little nap, do as the Romans do." The time change was hitting me hard this first full day in Italy; two in the afternoon here was five in the morning at home. Then there were my nightmares, waking me again and again.

Jack's lids were drooping and his speech was slowing down. "A nap would do us good. You know . . . I'm beginning to see an order in all of these church visits." He waved for the check.

"It's chronological, I think." The wine had made me drowsy too.

"Maria Maggiore represented Christ's birth."

"And the sister churches reflected the early years of Christianity, the time of the first apostle-bishops."

We asked our waiter which bus to take to Sant' Agnese and bought metro tickets at a nearby newsstand, then headed for our hotel.

Shortly after four, our bus drove through the Porta Pia of the ancient Aurelian Wall and up the Via Nomentata, the old Roman road to the cemeteries. We disembarked near a large complex enclosed by high stone walls. Entering a bricked courtyard, we crossed to the Byzantine facade of seventh-century Sant' Agnese.

We passed through a narrow doorway and paused in a shallow narthex as a funeral was ending, the church three-quarters full. A flower-covered casket rested before the altar under frescoed vaults. The church was bright with pastel stories and glimmering gold. "It's stunning," I whispered.

The mosaic in the apse showed Agnes with a phoenix rising above her; she gazed upon the canopied altar over her underground grave. I recalled that her sister Emerentiana, martyred for praying at Agnes's tomb, was buried with her. Twin staircases curved beneath the altar, but it seemed, with the service going on, we would not be able to visit.

The marble columns lining the nave had been taken from Roman ruins, linking the past with today. Above the columns ran a balustrade, and above the balustrade, light streamed through clerestory windows. Between the windows were mosaics of other virgin martyrs of the early Church: Victoria, Lucy, Agatha, Barbara, Cecilia, Martina, Bibiana, Emerentiana, Rufina, Columba, Julia, Apolonia, Flora, Catherine, Susanna, and Candida.

I shivered. They were so young, these girls, aged twelve to sixteen, to be taking such a stance, refusing to deny their belief in the Galilean fisherman. And they were virgins, making them desirable targets of the state. In the Roman world, virginity—wholeness—was a prized civic possession. The vestal virgins who protected Rome at the time of Agnes represented the city itself when they made offerings to the gods; they had not been penetrated, and Rome would not be breached either. So when Christian virgins were violated—raped or executed—Christianity was seen to be violated. To the Roman world, the attack was both personal and cultural.

Jack motioned me to a side door where others waited.

"We can take the next tour," he whispered, "since the funeral is still going on."

"Tour?"

"Of the catacombs. A guide takes people through every half hour. It's nearly time now."

We joined a small group waiting off the north aisle. A dark young man with long curly hair led us single-file down narrow earthen steps into an underground passageway. Horizontal hollows dating to the second century lined the walls on either side: the empty graves of the first Christians.

The tunnel was about six feet high, and Jack lowered his head. Silently, we followed our guide into the semidarkness, through the smell of damp soil and the chill of moist air, walking through time and suffering. The graves were marked with Christian symbols—the fish, the *Chi-Rho*, the Greek *C* and *H*, the first letters of Christ; carvings also listed names and occupations. A family altar stood in a six-by-eight cavern; the brick walls dated to the fourth-century church. Here the Eucharist had been offered over the martyrs' bones; one day those bones would rise again, perfected.

Long ago the graves had been ransacked by invaders, long ago rifled for relics, and those bones remaining were moved inside the city walls. Finally, layers of mud buried the catacomb of Sant' Agnes until archeologists unearthed it in the nineteenth century.

I descended deeper and deeper into the dark, knowing my new life must come at some cost, some death, feeling my way through the underground labyrinth. But this labyrinth was a Christian one, unlike the old Cretan maze, which led to the monster in its center. This labyrinth led to life, to God, for Christian death opened life's door. These martyrs embraced death willingly. Could I do that? Did I believe I would rise to new life?

I paused before a shallow, short grave and touched the red silt. A child's. It was so small, one of many unwanted babies the Romans left exposed to the elements to die, buried by the Christians. There were many such graves in the catacombs. *So much death.*

At a bend up the way, Jack motioned for me to catch up. I followed him, listening to our guide mingle Italian and English. We had come half-circle and began to ascend, finding ourselves under the high altar of the basilica.

The young man looked at us earnestly. "Here is the grave of Agnes. She lies with her sister Emerentiana. Her head is in Sant' Agnese in Agone on the Piazza Navona, but *we* have her other bones."

I gazed at the silver coffin under the altar. Agnes's tomb both anchored the church and gave it life; it was an underground seed flowering into the basilica and climbing to heaven. Aboveground, the tabernacle held Christ's presence. Above the tabernacle and its canopy, a cross pointed to Agnes's apse mosaic. Higher—outside—the bell tower ascended; the church rose from the depths of the earth to the heights of the heavens.

Jack slipped his arm around my waist, and I clasped his hand, holding onto its warmth. The guide was finishing up the tour, and we followed our group into the south aisle, my thoughts still with the silver tomb and the earthen graves. They were only children, Agnes and Emerentiana, girls on the edge of womanhood. Today they would be considered adolescents, for some a transition time of sexual exploration without responsibility. Did we demand too little from our teens? These virgin martyrs showed a courage and faith beyond that of many adults. Today I reached to understand their experience, to take part in their young adolescent sacrifice. They died and rose; they pointed the way.

Would the death of Mollie and my phantom-filled nights produce such fruits? Must something die in me too?

We paused at the foot of a broad staircase off the south aisle. Jack wiped a red smudge off my cheek like a mother cleaning a baby. "Are you okay?"

"I think so . . . where are we? Where do these stairs lead?"

"Our guide said Santa Constanza, if I heard him right."

"Let's go then. It may close soon."

The stairwell was embedded with slabs and stones of the earlier church.

"How, exactly, did Agnes die?" Jack asked.

"They think she was stabbed in the throat. When she refused to marry the nobleman, the prefect forced her to choose between becoming a vestal virgin who sacrificed to the Roman gods or joining a brothel. She chose the brothel, probably one on the edge of Diocletian's racetrack, today the Piazza Navona. She was stripped naked, caged, and taunted by the mobs. Legend says her blond hair grew long to cover her. When she refused the prefect's advances, she was executed."

We followed a path through the convent garden to Constanza's circular mausoleum where an organist played Mozart's *Requiem*. As the mournful notes filled the rotunda we stepped through a vaulted colonnade of green-and-gold mosaics, birds and vines shimmering in the half light. In the center, an altar rose over Constanza's grave.

Jack scanned a brochure and touched my shoulder. "Costanza had scrofula—what's that?"

"Tuberculosis."

Jack skimmed the slick page, running his finger down the fine print. "So it says that she prayed at Agnes's grave for healing. She fell asleep and dreamt of Agnes. When she awoke, she was cured."

"That's why she wanted to be buried near Agnes. And she became part of Agnes's living legacy."

"Seems more like a dying legacy," Jack said, rubbing his chin. He had forgotten to shave, and a light stubble was forming.

"Dying, and then living. Remember the phoenix?"

"In the mosaic behind the altar? Didn't the phoenix die and rise from ashes?"

The symbols were so very rich, a tapestry of clues and signs. "*Agnes* means 'lamb' in Latin, so she is both a sacrificial lamb *and* a rising phoenix. The Egyptian myth told how the phoenix lived for over five hundred years, dying each night and rising each morning, as an aspect of the sun. It rises from its own ashes." I was suddenly cold, sensing I would have to do the same.

"How does it do that?"

Returning to the entrance, we stepped outside into the cool dusk. The haze over the city reflected the rays of the setting sun.

I watched the sky change as I related the ancient myth, "When it came time for the phoenix to die, it returned to the Temple of the Sun, where it made a nest of cassia and frankincense on the altar. It brought a ball of myrrh, hollowed it out, and buried itself inside. It grew hotter and hotter, finally turning to ashes. Then a new phoenix burst from the 'egg' of myrrh."

"So Agnes was like the phoenix, only rising to heaven."

"Exactly. The burial and heating of the phoenix took three days, which corresponds to the time our Lord was in the tomb before he rose from the dead."

"So Agnes is a Christ-figure too, the lamb of God."

"And the phoenix has flown through the centuries, rebirthing the world as the dove of the Holy Spirit."

Jack checked his watch. "We'd better head back. It's nearly six."

"But do you see the Easter egg connection?" I said as we walked through the gardens to the bus stop. "The egg's a symbol of new life and reflects the three parts of the Trinity."

"Eggs will never be the same." Jack took my hand, and we ran to catch a bus heading toward us.

And Easter would never be the same, I thought. I would think of Agnes, the lamb, and the phoenix rising from the egg.

Chapter Three
San Pietro

My bones are not hid from thee, though I be made secretly,
and fashioned beneath the earth.
Psalm 139:14

Wednesday we toured the Coliseum, the ancient Roman arena. Three tiers of travertine blocks rose above milling pilgrims and sightseers. At the base of the terraces, huge gates remained open, doorways that once released animals, gladiators, or victims, satisfying the people's thirst for blood.

In this stadium Christians were eaten by lions or burned alive. They were shot down by arrows or hacked to death with axes and swords. They were crucified. In the eighteenth century, the pope consecrated the arena to these martyr-saints, creating a *locus* where pilgrims could offer thanksgiving for such sacrificial witness.

Jack focused his camera on the opposite end of the arena. "Look—a giant cross."

"I believe the pope still walks the Stations of the Cross in Lent." I tried to imagine the procession in the candlelit dark through these holy spaces—the prayers and the petitions, as the faithful paused before the fourteen memorials of Christ's path to crucifixion.

We walked on dusty uneven stones as the sun beat down. I shivered.

Jack had opened his guidebook and assumed his lecture mode. It was the Jack who took the Scouts to local historical sights—Fort Point, Mission Dolores, the old Opera House. "This place held seating for forty-five thousand and standing room for another five thousand." He looked at me over his reading glasses.

"Jack, let's leave this place. Let's go to the church we planned to visit today, something living, something hopeful."

He wiped his brow and exchanged his reading glasses for dark ones.

"Another church? You want to skip the Forum, the ruins of antiquity? You want to miss the Mamertine prison?"

"The Mamertine?"

"Tradition has it Saint Peter was chained there."

He had done his homework and I was impressed.

"Let's see something living, please, Jack?" The Coliseum reminded me of my nightmares—an uncontrolled darkness swallowing the light—even in this bright day.

Father Rinaldi had said the nightmares were demons. Did he mean it literally?

Jack shut his book with obvious disappointment and slipped it into his backpack. He took one more wide-angle shot of the arena. "Then to the Basilica di San Clemente, the living cross-section of history, or so you claimed at dinner. You see, I do listen. According to my map we can walk—it's not far." He slipped the cover over his camera.

San Clemente's ongoing excavations have revealed four underground levels. Aboveground stands the twelfth-century basilica; underneath the basilica is the crumbling fourth-century church; under these ruins is the first-century house-church; beneath the house-church lies the rubble of a building destroyed by fire in 68 AD.

We entered San Clemente through a side door and walked to the foot of the nave to view the entire church. Behind the high altar, an apsidal mosaic gleamed gold, green, and red over the *cathedra*, the bishop's chair. The lowest tier of the mosaic showed life-size figures of Christ, Mary, and the apostles. Above, a row of lambs looked up to the haloed Lamb of God. Above the Lamb, four rivers branched into the Tree of Life. The tree's vines covered the rest of the apse with circling birds drinking from shoots, with the central trunk forming a crucifix. Doves—human souls—perched on the crossbeam above the arms of Christ. From the top of the mosaic, the hand of God the Father reached down to an image of Christ Pantokrator, creator of all. Scholars claim that Christ was crucified on the same hill where Adam and Eve ate the forbidden fruit; the tree of Adam's disobedience is replaced by Christ's obedience. The crucifix becomes the Tree of Life, offering eternity through the wine-blood of the vines.

I journeyed through the rich images, the vivid mosaic story, searching for myself, pausing to fly with the birds and drink from the vines. But I sensed I must pause on the cross too.

"There's another phoenix," Jack said, pointing high.

"Where? I just see doves and other birds."

"Way up to the right of the Christ in the blue starry circle."

"I see it! Another resurrection phoenix."

"The book says this mosaic is twelfth-century, but probably copied from the original one, since it seems so fourth-century."

I looked at my husband, his reading glasses sliding off his fine-boned nose, his eyes narrowing in the dim light, so eager to help. "That's amazing, Jack. How do you find all these details?"

He sighed, satisfied. "Just a special talent of mine. Now, are you ready to descend? We came here years ago with Father Rinaldi but I don't remember much of it."

"I don't either."

Jack folded his reading glasses and led me to the door in the south aisle. "I believe the passageway is through here."

We paid an upkeep fee and descended damp stone stairs into the fourth-century church. Passing partial frescoes and dusty sarcophagi, we entered the old nave, whose pillars supported the basilica above, the upper altar aligned with the lower one. The altar was bare, and I imagined the many Eucharists offered in this time of transition from pagan to Christian culture.

We descended more stairs to the house-church, where Christians had met in secret. Water dripped from the walls, and through a grate in the floor I could see a river tumbling, echoing through an underground tunnel.

"How did all this survive?" Jack asked. "These ruins are nearly two thousand years old."

"The early Romans didn't destroy old buildings—they filled them in and built over them. It's only been in the last century that archeologists have dug them out. Pretty recent, really."

Jack pulled out his glasses and a mini-light from his pocket. "Let's see if I can read the entry. 'Executed for following Jewish practices, the owner Clemens gave his name to one of the first gatherings of believers, *Titulus Clementis*.' What were Jewish practices?"

"Probably Christian practices. The first Christians were considered a Jewish sect." Every society has scapegoats, I thought with sadness.

As I stood in the space where these early Christians gathered, I saw

Pudenziana and Prassede and the fiery Paul. I had read that women, no longer considered their husband's property, found a new dignity in Christianity; girls were no longer required to marry at eleven and twelve years of age. There must have been relief too, for the Jewish Christians, men as well, that this revolutionary God had wiped away their sins with his death—the demands of the law had been met. For all other Christians—the Gentiles—the Roman wheel of fate had been destroyed, allowing free will. Most important of all, these newborn Christians encountered a God of love in the God-man Jesus who knew suffering as they did. And they must have been nervous, keeping watch, fearing soldiers breaking down the door, terrified of the tales of torture: burning coals, mutilation, fire, and beasts. They risked so much—God's love must have been powerful indeed.

In this space, Paul consecrated the bread and wine and each believer was filled with Christ's presence. *Lord, fill me too. Let there be room for nothing else. Banish my grief demons as you banished their fear.*

We climbed the stairs, level upon level, the damp and dusty stone holding time in its pores. As I climbed, I thought of my journey, my pilgrimage through this time and this place, through my own span of life and through my spiritual world of healing. Surely, these early Christians, like me, knew grief. They knew what it meant to lose one they loved. They woke to an emptiness they could not fill, a void they lived with, tried to deny. Did they blame themselves for the deaths of their brothers and sisters? Did they feel a guilty grief? A survivor's grief?

I recalled the fourteenth-century mystic, Julian of Norwich, who spoke of turning wounds into honors, allowing Christ to use them. By offering up sufferings, she suggested, wounds were re-created, turned into good. Could Christ use my grief—and my guilt—as well?

As we reached ground level and the basilica, Jack turned to me. "I'm going to get some air. I think you might want some time alone."

"Thanks."

He kissed me lightly and walked down the nave toward an outer courtyard.

Kneeling before the frescoed God and his lambs, I asked Christ to transform my grief, to banish my guilt. I knew he replaced those lambs, that he became the Lamb of God, the perfect sacrifice offered for my sin against Mollie. How could he take my act and turn it into honor? I did not understand for I found no honor in that plastic pool of twenty-two years ago.

Yet Christ looked upon me from his starry heaven in the gilded apse. He knew. He understood. And in spite of everything, he loved me. Perhaps this was a beginning, the first step up the stairs of healing. Just as the Romans filled in their old houses and built over them, God took the material of sin to build upon. Instead of denying the act or excusing it, he mixed it with the gravel of my penitence, cementing a stronger foundation, a new ground floor of my soul.

With a fragile hope, I joined Jack, a patient man dreaming of lunch and a good bottle of wine, in the peaceful cloister. Unthinking, I dabbed my eyes with the linen cloth, mingling my tears with Christ's blood.

"Have you chosen a place?" I peered over his shoulder. The sun shone harshly on the old flagstones, but Jack basked in its warmth, holding his book with one hand and stroking a scrawny white cat with the other.

"There's a place overlooking the Forum. At least we'll see the ruins from a distance."

"Sounds good, but aren't we near that other church Father Rinaldi took us to? Quattro something? It had a lovely cloister. It's only 11:30— we might make it before the noon closing. Then we can call it a day."

Jack frowned. "Okay, one more church. Was that the place where an elderly nun played the organ for us? Let me see here . . . Quattro, Quattro, hmmm . . . Quattro Coronati, here it is."

As he plotted our route, I stood in San Clemente's doorway and gazed at the Christ in the apse. His face held certainty, love, concern. "Children," he said, "believe this and be happy. It is so simple—believe in me." He held up two fingers in blessing, and his halo was divided by the rays of a cross.

I had fond memories of the Chiesa dei Santi Quattro Coronati, the Church of the Four Crowned Saints. "A friend of mine," Father Rinaldi had said, "runs a nunnery here." I recalled a short, graying nun who played the organ and served us lunch, chattering softly in melodic Italian.

We climbed a hill to a fortress-like building with thick walls and a bell tower.

"Do you think," Jack said, reading my thoughts, "that the nuns know about Father's death?"

"We may be the first to tell them—it's only been six weeks."

The medieval church once defended the top of the Coelian Hill, harboring popes fleeing the neighboring Lateran Palace. But the church had even earlier beginnings. Like San Clemente, it was first a house-church, Titulus Aemilianae, rebuilt in the fourth century. Later the side aisles were walled off to create a convent and cloister, producing an extra long nave and an oversized apse.

We passed through two large courtyards, much like a fortified castle. Stepping under a frescoed lintel, we paused, as our eyes adjusted to the dim light. A hand-printed sign announced the nuns sang the daily offices and Sunday mass. A wrought-iron railing divided the nave from a wooden choir and marble altar. Stairs descended to the crypt. The unusual apse was covered with oil paintings telling saints' stories. A red sanctuary lamp burned, suspended near the tabernacle on the altar.

We walked up the aisle and knelt in the front pew. As I prayed for Father Rinaldi, someone played Pachelbel's *Canon in G* to the right of the choir stalls. Could the organist be Sister Agnes?

As we stood, a dark head appeared from behind the organ, and a hand beckoned us to follow. A girl in a wheelchair appeared, a golden retriever padding alongside. She rolled down a makeshift ramp from the choir, through a doorway in the north aisle, and out to the familiar cloister.

A colonnade enclosed a square of grass and palm trees; a fountain bubbled in the center. I breathed deeply, inhaling the aroma of hibiscus and watching the sunlight play on the ocher pillars. Here, for centuries, nuns prayed their daily offices, stepping on the smoothly worn stones, following the path of others before them.

But this girl was not Sister Agnes. Her dark hair was pulled into a thick ponytail, and she didn't wear a habit, but a faded, flowered dress. As she smiled up at us, I thought she looked to be about sixteen, with wide dark eyes. Jack tried out his meager Italian, and she grinned, replying in perfect English.

"Welcome to the Church of the Four Crowned Saints! My name is Elena, and this is Michelangelo." She reached down to stroke the dog's wavy coat.

Jack smiled. I was relieved she spoke our language and with an American accent at that.

"You may wonder," she continued, "who the four crowned saints were, and we do too. One legend says they were soldiers who refused to worship the Roman gods. Another says they were sculptors from

38

Pannonia who refused to carve pagan idols. They died by having a crown driven into their heads. Their remains are in the crypt."

"Thank you," Jack began, "but–"

"Feel free to walk the cloister and ask any questions–the nuns are not available now. If you would like to tour our orphanage, I can show you the way."

"Thank you," I said, echoing Jack, "but we hoped to see Sister Agnes. Is she still here?"

Jack added, "We visited here many years ago with Father Rinaldi."

"We're from San Francisco," I explained, "and Sister Agnes was most gracious. I'm afraid we have sad news for her."

Elena's face dropped. "She knows. When she heard of Father's passing, she retreated to her cell. We bring her a tray at mealtimes, but she eats little."

"I'm sorry," I said, disappointed.

"Won't you stay for tea, and we can talk of these things? I knew Father Rinaldi. Did you know he and Sister Agnes founded this convent?"

Jack and I exchanged glances of surprise.

"He was a good man, a holy man, maybe a *santo*," she continued. "He left the Roman Catholic Church but he never forgot us and has supported our work ever since. Please . . . follow me."

Jack shook his head in disbelief. "I had no idea Father Rinaldi founded this. He sure was a man of surprises."

In their refectory, we sat under a large canvas of *The Last Supper*.

Elena pointed to the painting. "Our *cenacolo*. Most monasteries have one in their dining room, and like most, ours is fifteenth-century and needs restoring. But we have more important work now." Elena spoke to Michelangelo and the dog trotted toward a door. "He will bring a sister to help us."

Soon we were sipping rose-petal tea and nibbling on leftover toasts, listening to Elena's light chatter. She appeared unaware of herself, delighted to share her story with us, to speak of Father Rinaldi's goodness.

"I am one of Father's miracles," Elena said, her eyes shining. "I was a street baby, one of those drugged infants the nomads hold up to car windows when they beg. When the *polizia* raided our camp, I was left behind. One of the officers took me home, then gave me to his aunt, a nun here. Father Rinaldi insisted they keep me."

"So the sisters raised you?" I asked.

She nodded. "And other children followed. When they realized I couldn't walk, one of the American nuns taught me English so that I could guide visitors. They even refitted the organ for me—so here I am!" She opened her palms, grinned, and looked to the heavens with childish delight.

Nervously, I gestured to her legs, covered by a thin quilt. "Can nothing be done?"

She shook her head. "I was born with a spinal defect—my legs are partially paralyzed. They considered putting me in an institution, but Sister Agnes refused. I owe her my life here, and Father Rinaldi too—for he has supported us when times were tough." Her eyes beamed gratitude. "As they often are," she added with a rueful smile.

As I gazed at the young girl I thought of my linen cloth. Should I mention it? I would rather have spoken with Agnes. Could something like this, connected to the life and death of a possible saint, have power to heal? Regardless, it seemed the cloth belonged here, belonged to Father's convent. "I have something for Sister Agnes."

Jack raised his brows in surprise.

"Could you arrange a meeting?" I asked. "Tell her we've come from Saint Thomas's in San Francisco. She could call us at our hotel—I have the number here somewhere." I reached in my handbag for a hotel notepad and tore off the top sheet.

"I shall try," Elena said, slipping the paper into a pocket. "Maybe this will bring her out of seclusion. Until then, may God be with you."

Rolling her chair, she led us back to the church. In the north aisle, she shook our hands and wheeled toward the choir. As I reached the narthex doors, I looked back, taking a mental snapshot of the dark girl and the golden dog lying at her side. She had settled behind the organ, playing 'Gesu, Joy of Man's Desiring,' Michelangelo peering out, one paw on top of the other.

Father hadn't listed Quattro Coronati, but he probably planned on returning with us. He had never mentioned his founding of the convent or his ongoing support. He and Martha lived so simply—how did they manage it? Or was that how they managed, living simply? Would he want me to give up the cloth? *Could* I give it up?

We dined in the rooftop restaurant of our hotel.

Jack set down the wine list and motioned to the waiter. "I still can't believe Father Rinaldi founded that convent and orphanage."

I recalled the crowd at his funeral. "Humility hides many good works, doesn't it?"

Jack pointed to a wine on the list and the waiter shook his head. Jack pointed to another. The waiter shook his head again. Jack finally set the list firmly on the table. "You choose," he said, his voice edged with anger.

Jack watched the waiter's retreating figure. "I hate it when they leave bottles on the list they don't have."

"I know." I saw he needed to breathe deeply, time to calm down. I looked out over the city.

"So what were we talking about?" Jack asked after a moment of silence.

"Father Rinaldi founding the orphanage. His humility."

"He didn't always live humbly. He enjoyed our dinners in Rome, in fact in this restaurant. He liked that Brunello Chianti I just tried to order."

The sun was setting behind the bell tower of Trinità dei Monte off to the right.

I opened my palm toward the skyline. "He loved this too—all the churches."

"He could name every one." Jack rubbed his chin.

I certainly couldn't. There was Saint Peter's in the distance, and maybe—closer to us in the foreground—stood Saint Carlo Boromei's dome, looming large. The domes and crosses of Rome, silhouetted against the pink sky, merged into the dusk. We ordered *farfalle con mozzarella*, *zuppa di piselli*, *aragosta al forno*, and *abbacchio* with garlic and *fagioli*, finishing with giant meringues and fresh strawberries.

We returned to the room and logged onto the Internet to check my e-mail. I plugged my phone cord into the wall and connected with AOL's service provider in Rome.

"There's a note from Justin," I shouted to Jack in the bath.

Subj: Deer Lake Adventures
Date: 97-04-29 18:36:34 EDT
From: Justbury@csd.net (Justin Seymour)
To: MJseymour@aol.com (MOM)

Hi! Thanks for making Lisa Jane feel welcome. She sends her best.

Last night we opened the front door only to find a five-hundred-pound black bear sitting in the bed of my truck helping himself to a bag of garbage! He was only about ten feet away! I grabbed a flashlight and began flashing him and making noise until he casually finished up his meal, climbed out of the truck and meandered into the night. We expect that he will be back considering he scored Alaskan king crab remains and chocolate cake upon his first visit. Business is going well. I am working on coordinating an independent proposal for next spring in which I would design and construct the new Deer Lake Youth and Family Center. Hope all is well with your travels. Take care.

Love, Justin

"Justin and Lisa are living together, Jack. I can tell."

Jack peered through the bathroom door. "How can you tell from an e-mail? Anyway, that's what people do today, Maddie."

"But what about babies? If he really loves her, he should marry her. Commitment is what love is all about."

"Maybe he wants to make sure, so he can really commit."

"Maybe he'll lose her. She's a wonderful girl. I don't want him to lose her. I like Lisa Jane."

"It's his life."

"But they're my grandchildren."

"True. Still, all we can do is to drop a few gentle hints."

"Precisely, and I'm starting now."

Subj: Re: Deer Lake Adventures
Date: 04/29/97
To: Justinbury@csd.net

Dear Justin,

If you love Lisa Jane, propose to her and marry her. That's what love is all about. She's wonderful. Don't let her get away. Love means commitment. Life is short.

Love, Mom

P.S. The Deer Lake project sounds great. Please be careful around bears at night.

As I arrowed *Send Mail* and closed down my laptop, I hoped I hadn't been too direct, but then wasn't that what parents were for? I often wished I had been better prepared for life, with its many demands. My parents gave me such freedom, always approving my choices, wanting to give me self-confidence. Would I have listened to their guidance? Would I have stayed in school and finished my degree before marrying? Maybe not—but nevertheless I often wished they had pushed me more. As it was, married at twenty and divorced at thirty with a young son, I was left with few options. To pay the bills, I typed and filed and counted the minutes in the long dull days in an insurance office the size of a barn.

I reached for my prayer book. Dried palm fronds rested against the page for Evening Prayer and my linen cloth lay on the night table. Tomorrow we would visit Saint Peter's, the great basilica of western Christendom, the loved and hated, cherished and maligned symbol of Christ's church on earth, the people of God.

I looked for the Easter preface, for it was still Eastertide: *Thanks be to God, which giveth us the victory through our Lord Jesus Christ. . . .*

In the morning, Jack and I followed the crowds through a portico circling the piazza of San Pietro where gray plastic chairs, stacked in rows, waited for the next papal audience. We climbed wide stairs and entered the vast space.

Gray, gold, and bronze marble columns lined the six-hundred-foot nave leading to the high altar, where a massive bronze canopy topped by a golden cross rose to Michelangelo's dome. The dark canopy, tarnished by time, contrasted to the light airy space of the church. Below the altar, lamps flamed in a semicircle over Peter's grave. Beyond, in the large apsidal chapel, Peter's episcopal chair hung against the back wall, surrounded by golden rays.

We paused in the narthex, absorbing the scene—the crowds, the swirling marble, the gold, the huge sculpted apostles leaping from the columns. A deep voice, slow and tender, spoke through a loudspeaker system. As Jack angled his camera, I wondered what the fisherman apostle would have thought of this church.

Peter had been a humble man, even if his church was grand. His story—his outspoken devotion and his frightened denials—encouraged me. His story said that mistakes could be rectified, that indeed, the sinner could be saved. The Gospels tell us that Simon Bar-Jona was a fisherman from Bethsaida, a village near the Sea of Tiberias. Jesus renamed him Peter, or 'rock,' promising that on this rock he would build his church. Portrayed as headstrong, open, and graced with holy intuition, Peter was often the first to speak, if sometimes bluntly. Even so, he became the apostles' spokesperson.

The accounts of Peter's impetuous devotion are many. He walked on water to meet Christ and nearly drowned in the rough sea; he sliced the ear off the high priest's servant when the soldiers arrested Jesus in the garden; he raced to the tomb on Easter morning to see if it was truly empty as the women had claimed, and later jumped from his boat to swim to the risen Christ waiting on the shore. Yet three times he denied knowing his Lord, fearful that he too would be arrested in the early hours of that frightening Good Friday.

But Peter grew in faith and courage. In those days of the early Church, he healed and preached, and his authority was soon recognized by the other apostles, those first bishops, an authority reinforced through tradition and written accounts.

When Peter fled the city during Nero's persecution, it is said Christ appeared to him on the Appian Way. Peter asked, "*Quo vadis?*", "Where do you go?" When Christ replied he was going to Rome to be crucified again, Peter returned to the city to face certain death. In 68 AD, he was crucified upside down in an arena where Saint Peter's stands today, within sight of the Egyptian obelisk marking the square.

Jack touched my arm. "This place is huge."

I nodded. "But it began small, as an oratory over Peter's grave, then Constantine's basilica, then this Renaissance church."

Jack looked doubtful. "But how could they be certain that Peter was really buried here?"

"Oral tradition. Constantine dug through sacred Roman burial grounds to build his church—he must have believed that Peter was truly buried here to risk such sacrilege. Recent excavations found the actual grave—a stone says 'Peter is here.' You can visit if you make reservations."

Jack turned his camera toward Michelangelo's *Pieta* in the south aisle. "Lots of famous artists."

I gazed at the sculpted figure of Mary holding her son's body. Jesus' arms and legs dangled, limp and heavy. Her face held grief and amazement, as though she had not yet accepted the horror of her son's death, but even so, understood suffering as part of love.

I turned back to the massive, boisterous nave, the deep echoing voice, the crowds moving slowly over the polished floor.

"The wealth that went into this church," Jack whispered, "could have been used for the poor. It seems such a waste."

"But look at the faces of the people, Jack."

"They *are* enjoying it all."

"They're in love. Somehow, this church is theirs, and they come from every corner of the world."

"And Peter? What would he have said?"

"He was a humble man," I admitted, "but he was also grandiose in his own way. In that sense, the building fits the man. Even so, I understand what you mean. I have trouble with it all too, sometimes."

We headed up the south aisle.

"What's the service that's going on?" Jack asked.

"It's May 1st . . . I don't know—a saint's feast day?"

I thought how the humble apostle personalized this church. His earthy grave beneath the altar and his bishop's chair in the apse made the grand small, pulling heaven to the earth. Other relics—matter made holy—in the basilica would do the same. And indeed, the Reserved Sacrament—Christ's Body and Blood—transformed the massive space of marble and gold. But where was the Sacrament? I looked for the telling red candle or sanctuary lamp.

A red velvet cord barred us from the south transept and we peaked over the heads of the crowd to see who was speaking. Jack could see, but I couldn't.

"It's the pope!" Jack said. "He's right down there in front of the tomb."

I climbed on the lower ledge of a confessional, like Zaccheus in the tree. It was indeed John Paul II. Sitting in front of the flaming ring of lamps over Peter's grave, he leaned toward his flock, his white robes flowing about him, his head nodding to make a point as he read from a text. From war-torn Poland, John Paul had accepted those robes of wealth and power to reveal Christ to the world. In this spring of 1997,

45

the elderly pontiff held on to life by an angelic thread, hoping to save one more soul, heal one more heart, beatify one more man or woman.

His sermon concluded, he climbed onto an electric cart. With hunched shoulders, he waved to his people, a people hungry to believe in spite of all the sinner popes who, like us, make up corrupt humanity. He rolled toward a chancel door, his hand raised in blessing, the great church surrounding him, history surrounding him, this frail descendent of Peter.

Man, in his own way, had passed the Faith through the centuries. He had sculpted and painted matters of belief so that his race would never forget, never return to a world of darkness, never let the lamp go out. Yet each person remained small and mortal, his works and words living on for his children, his own hopes set on another life.

We crossed the transept as the crowd dispersed. I stopped to touch the foot of a bronze Peter, the foot worn smooth by pilgrims' kisses. Forged in the thirteenth century, many years before the towering sculptures of the fifteenth, this Peter was a simple fisherman in a grand palace.

A red lamp burned in the northern transept chapel. Kneeling before the gilded tabernacle, I prayed my thanksgivings for this place so huge and so full of hope. A dusty beam of light fell through the clerestory windows, haloing the common man and woman in the crowd, the dancing particles falling to the marbled earth.

I looked back to the apse holding Peter's chair and the door through which the pope had disappeared. I pulled out my linen cloth. Why had Father Rinaldi sent me here? Maria Maggiore showed me the crèche, the beginnings. The sister churches accused me of self-destroying envy. Sant' Agnese seemed the first step of my pilgrimage, as though the others were a prologue, as I descended to the empty graves of the martyrs. But San Pietro? I touched my cloth, the stain fading more each day into the creamy linen. Peter was the greatest of the martyrs, the leader of the apostle-bishops.

We sat back in the pew and looked about.

"It's like all this stone is singing," Jack said.

"That's it! I'm learning to listen to God, to God singing through his Church, even this marble. Father Rinaldi is saying, *pay attention to material things.*"

"What?" Jack focused his camera on a leaping statue of Saint Matthew.

"Just a crazy thought I had. How about some lunch? But first, let's

46

find a souvenir in one of the shops down the street."

We purchased a six-inch clay figure of Saint Peter. His fishing net hung over his shoulder and he held two large keys, the fisher of men with the keys to the kingdom of God.

Returning to the hotel, we learned Elena had called—Sister Agnes could meet us at three. After sandwiches in the bar, we taxied to Quattro Coronati.

Agnes met us in the cloister, accompanied by a tall, ebony-skinned friar with a close-cropped Afro. The graying nun appeared as I remembered—stooped and frail, with frizzy hair, now white, pulled into a black cap. A few wiry strands escaped, framing a thin face lined like aged porcelain.

She introduced Brother Cristoforo, who nodded seriously, unsmiling. His brown robe was heavily soiled at the hem, his rope belt frayed. He looked to be in his forties, but with his beard, it was difficult to tell.

We sat on a bench, but the friar hovered behind Agnes.

"You may speak . . . in front of Brother Cristoforo." Agnes spoke slowly and carefully, her voice cracking as a slight wheeze escaped her lungs. "He helps with many things now—the orphanage, the vegetable garden. He knew Father Rinaldi well. He was another miracle child. . . . Father found him in Alexandria begging and picking pockets. . . . Father brought him here . . . Cristoforo only seven."

She looked up at the friar fondly. "I remember well. How you say? A rascal. So dirty!" Agnes laughed hoarsely, looking at the friar's hem. "Dirty still!" The monk's lips curved slightly as his thoughtful gaze rested on the elderly woman.

I told her about Father's death and the cloth I saved. With some hesitation, I pulled the linen out of my bag.

Sister Agnes ran her fingers over it, tenderly pausing on the stains, then looked up at me. Her red eyes searched mine.

"You loved him too, I see," Agnes whispered. "I also see . . . you are deeply troubled. You keep the cloth . . . for now . . . for your safe journey . . . but please, maybe upon your return, you leave it here? Father Rinaldi was . . . so much a saint. I will put this corporal on our altar, the altar of his many celebrations, his many masses."

The friar looked at me, his gaze intense. "*Si*, the cloth belongs here."

"We'll see," I said nervously. *Leave it here?* "It means a great deal to me, so I'm not sure."

The friar frowned and folded his arms.

Jack was scrutinizing the dark monk. "Maddie, we can decide that later."

I quickly tucked the cloth in my purse and glanced toward the door.

Sister Agnes reached for Cristoforo's hand and stood. She embraced me, her head coming to my chest. Fragile though she was, *she* strengthened *me*.

Jack bowed to Agnes and held her hand between his own. "Thank you for taking the time to see us, Sister."

"*Prego*. I must go. *Per favore*—I have many prayers to offer. . . ." She shuffled away, nodding her head.

Elena appeared with Michelangelo and followed Agnes into the church. What had she seen and heard? Did the cloth seem a new hope to her? *Was* it a new hope?

"You like to see the orphanage?" the friar asked. "We have many children now." He raised his heavy brows; his grave expression gave no hint of his thoughts. He was all browns—russet robe, chocolate skin, and chestnut eyes. His short curly hair formed a black halo about his face. He glanced at my handbag.

"We'd love to," Jack replied as though hoping to make peace.

I had mixed feelings about seeing the orphanage, but I knew Jack would enjoy visiting. Since Justin had moved out, the house was too quiet. My brother had settled in Maine with his family, but Jack's three sons had produced six grandchildren, and they filled the rooms at Christmas. He shopped for their gifts, waiting in line at toy stores, arranging colorful packages under the tree. During the year, he drove the children to church and had them baptized and confirmed; on our wine buying trips, he bought them puppets in Tuscany and dolls in Provence.

I told myself it would be good for me to see the children; after all I often helped with the children at church. When the grandchildren visited, we baked cookies together. Sometimes we colored and cut and pasted, making artistic masterpieces. On sunny days I piled them into Justin's old red wagon and pulled them along the sidewalk. Yes, it would be good for both of us to see the orphanage that Father Rinaldi had founded.

Brother Cristoforo led us through the cloister, past a well-tended vegetable garden. "This is my *giardino*." He waved a hand over the neat green rows. "It is good work—planting, growing, feeding—is it not? The artichokes are not good this year. And they are my favorite. *Allora*."

I smiled, more at ease. "My father had a garden." I saw in my mind his tomato plants with their wild leaves and pungent aroma. "We like artichokes too," I added.

We walked down a path to a long stone building. "Here the sisters sleep, how do you say, the dormitory. . . . Now, here the children sleep. Kitchen here, nurse here, school here. . . . Children learn reading, learn jobs. Sometimes, they sing in mass."

"How many do you have?" asked Jack.

"*Quarantadue*—forty-two—babies to sixteen years. Then they find work outside to help the convent."

He regarded us in silence, glancing at my bag, and I realized suddenly that Father Rinaldi's death could have a financial impact on the orphanage. Had Father left them anything in his will?

We peeked into a workshop where a young nun helped students take apart a car engine. Farther along, students sat at a table, writing in notebooks, as an older sister pointed to algebraic equations on a blackboard. She smiled at us, revealing a missing tooth, and exchanged nods with the friar.

Our last stop was the nursery. "Only two babies now," Brother Cristoforo said, "and it is more quiet."

A young woman, soon to give birth, bottle-fed an infant. A toddler played on the floor with a wooden spoon and a pan. Flies buzzed. The girl looked up and grinned, her teeth white against her olive skin. In spite of the ceiling fan, the humid air pressed down. I breathed deeply to calm my nerves, but the air was thick.

"We find homes," the friar was saying, "for their babies. Adoption is very good, no? Carlina stays with us now. She helps."

I felt Jack's gaze, and he slipped his arm around my waist. I could not take my eyes off the rounded stomach of the lovely girl, her long, wavy black hair falling to her waist, her attention focused on the baby in her arms.

How desperately I wanted to turn the clock back, return to the moment before that summer day in Canada, before I ran into the house; I wanted to reconstruct the time as if those events never happened—leapfrog back over those years. I wanted a second chance. The what-ifs danced a mournful dirge in my mind, winding about my thoughts, tying them tighter and tighter as a panic rose from someplace deep.

Carlina wore a silver crucifix. It glowed against her moist skin and caught the light from the window as she swayed. She hummed something familiar—*Fairest Lord Jesus, ruler of all nature.* . . . The crucified Christ on the chain was the same frescoed Christ of San Clemente.

Have mercy, Lord. Transform my bleeding heart. I reached for my linen, my knees shaking as the evening chants echoed, the women's voices high and lilting.

Jack mumbled some quick thanks and farewells, and we headed back to the hotel.

It rained that night, and my nightmare took new shapes. The skeleton baby with its bulging eyes was gone and I floated down a dark hallway, reaching for a child that disappeared at the next turn. . . . I ran to catch her, to tell her not to go on, to warn her, to save her. . . . The passageway descended and she ran around a corner into what I knew was certain death. . . . My eyes kept closing and I couldn't see where I was going. . . . Something grabbed my shoulder. . . . I awoke with a start.

"Maddie, Maddie, wake up, honey." It was Jack, touching me gently.

I surfaced. "Sorry. . . ."

The digital clock read 3:07. The rain fell steadily. Somewhere a gutter dripped.

"Go back to sleep, honey." He rolled over. "It's just a dream."

I snuggled into his broad back, his weedy smell filling me with home, and clung to him, my heart drumming in my ears. He turned, and as he wrapped his body about me, I laced my fingers into his and felt his early morning beard on my cheek. Our bodies would banish loneliness— and nightmares—and fill one other with the wonder of the opposite, making us complete—one, not two. We buried the dream far down in my soul's crypt, and Jack's love shoveled more earth upon its grave.

In the morning the streets were slick from the rain, reflecting sudden sun. The rental agency had given us a luxury car since they were out of midsize, and we looked forward to the drive to Milano. But we hadn't planned on the additional passenger and the additional stop along the way.

50

Chapter Four
Milano

He brought me also out of the horrible pit, out of the mire and clay,
and set my feet upon the rock, and ordered my goings.
Psalm 40:2

B rother Cristoforo waited in the lobby, his long face somber, his coarse robes wet from the rain and smelling of damp peat moss. I had not noticed how tall he was, taller than Jack's six-three.

"You need a driver, Signori," the friar said.

"*Grazie*," Jack said, "but no thank you."

"Sister Agnes said you need a driver." He sounded confused.

"Sister Agnes?" I asked.

Jack looked at me, I looked at Cristoforo, and the friar gazed longingly at the car through the revolving glass doors.

Cristoforo raised his arms wide, then clapped his hands. "I remember now! She wishes to give you a gift. In memory of Father Rinaldi. And I like to drive—I drove Father and Mrs. Rinaldi many times."

Martha. Her image reassured me.

"But where will you stay, Brother?" Jack asked.

"No problem. I have many friends in Italy. Where do you go first?"

Intrigued with the offer, I pulled out the list of churches.

The friar held the paper in his thick hands and squinted at the writing. "*Si*, I know these churches."

I pulled Jack aside. "It's not a bad idea. We might like being chauffeured. It's a nice gesture on Agnes's part. He speaks the language. And you've never driven in Europe."

Jack looked doubtful. "True, we've always had someone drive us, haven't we? A local broker took us around on our buying trips." He turned to Cristoforo and shook his hand. "*Grazie*, Brother, we accept your kind offer."

The friar pulled out a cell phone. "I call Sister Agnes. We go to Milano first, *sì*?"

A cell phone? Did friars have cell phones these days? But then Cristoforo was the only friar I knew; maybe I was out of touch. *My* cell phone remained in the glove compartment of my car for emergencies—I still couldn't get used to using it.

"*Sì*, Milano." Jack smiled and shook his head at the high-tech monk.

"Maybe by way of Orvieto," I said, "and Bolsena."

"Orvieto? Bolsena?" Jack stared at me. "When did we decide on Orvieto? Or Bolsena?"

"Maybe just Orvieto, if we can't do Bolsena." I knew I should have mentioned it earlier, for I saw the old impatience in Jack's eyes, a look from his working days, his days under pressure. I had wanted to see the little church in Bolsena, but I would compromise with Orvieto. "We can have lunch in Orvieto and see the cathedral. We need lunch somewhere, and it's on the way."

Cristoforo clapped his phone shut. "*Sì*, the *duomo*. It has a miracle cloth. I carry your bags?" He carried a stained knapsack over one shoulder.

"They're in the car," Jack said as he led us out the door.

"This your car?" The friar's eyes grew wide.

"We got upgraded by the rental agency," Jack said with some satisfaction.

I let Jack have the front passenger seat for his long legs and I sat in back, sinking into the soft leather.

Cristoforo settled himself behind the wheel and played with the controls and mirrors, making adjustments. He turned the key in the ignition with care, and the engine caught, purring quietly. He maneuvered the car through the wet city streets, one hand on the steering wheel, one hand on the horn, and we were soon outside the walls. We sped north on the autostrada, passing cars and dodging suicidal drivers. Jack gripped the dashboard and I tightened my seat belt as fields flew by.

It was nearly noon when I saw Orvieto in the distance. The medieval city rose high on a rocky outcrop, its cathedral parting the gray sky. We exited the highway and wound through vineyards up to the medieval town.

Orvieto had been a center of pottery manufacture for the Etruscans and Romans, and during the Middle Ages its strategic location made it the object of many wars. But it wasn't pottery or war that intrigued me. I had read about Orvieto when I researched miracles in Italy, and when I checked our route from Rome to Milan I recalled the story. The cathedral owned a mysterious cloth, rather like the altar linen in Santa Pudenziana, rather like mine.

As the noon bells rang, we parked outside the walls. Brother Cristoforo gave us directions to the cathedral and we agreed to meet at the car in two hours.

"I have friends to see." He nodded and loped down a side street, pulling out his cell, punching numbers and holding the phone against his ear.

We walked toward the town center, the streets curiously quiet, the narrow lanes dappled with splashes of sun and shade.

Jack turned to me. "You should have mentioned the stop earlier, Maddie."

"I only just thought of it. Do you really mind?"

"I was looking forward to going straight to Milan and settling in. We only have two days in Milan."

"It won't take long."

"So what's the story here? What's so important?"

"I read about Orvieto in my research. The cathedral has a miraculous cloth. Peter of Prague–"

"Your research? I thought you were easing out of all that. Next you'll want to go back to teaching."

"My research for the book. And I do miss the students. What if I taught part-time next year? Maybe just European history. I took this year off since you retired, but–"

"I'd rather you were home, Maddie."

"Why? You have golf and you have the Scouts."

"Take up tennis again."

"It's not the same."

"So," he said, making a peace of sorts, "tell me about this Peter of Prague."

We passed closed shops and open trattorias; silverware clinked in upstairs windows. "Peter of Prague didn't believe in the Real Presence of Christ in the bread and the wine. So in 1263 he made a pilgrimage to Rome for greater faith. On the way home, he celebrated mass in the church of Santa Cristina in Bolsena, a little south of here. As he consecrated the bread and wine, blood dripped from the host, soaking the corporal underneath. Peter came home a believer."

"Real blood dripped from the host? That's like the other church we saw—near Maria Maggiore."

I nodded. "Real blood, according to witnesses. The pope brought the cloth to Orvieto and decreed the Feast of Corpus Christi, the festival of the Body and Blood of Christ. They built a cathedral to enshrine the cloth. In June the townspeople dress up in medieval costumes and process through the streets with the linen in a glass reliquary."

"I see why you're interested. It sounds remarkable even to this old materialist."

Jack's skepticism had been slightly breached, and I grinned with the small victory. Like many, he sometimes gave in to the temptation to be a "buffet Christian," grazing on Christianity, picking the parts he liked. He loved to sing so he liked the hymns and the organ music. He appreciated thoughtful sermons that organized his mind and stirred his heart. He liked the sense of doing right on a Sunday, observing the day properly, a Victorian sense of duty. And I valued his respect for duty, for someone once said duty is the discipline of love. It pushes us to act charitably even when we don't feel like it; duty had saved our culture from the chaos of moral relativity. Duty had saved our society from self-destructing, at least for now.

We turned a corner and suddenly the cathedral facade rose before us, its two-tiered gables of ocher, blue, and gold shining in the sun. Jack pulled open one of the massive front doors. Stepping inside, we paused, and soon could see the colors and shapes of the nave: green-and-white striped pillars ran to the high altar and pink-and-blue frescoes covered the apse.

In this cavernous space, I carried my linen square like a pilgrim's shell, a relic-charm, a vestige of hope. Halfway down the central aisle Jack checked his guidebook. He turned left at the transept and entered a glittering side chapel.

Jack pointed above the altar. "It's here."

Housed behind intricate gold-work was the miracle cloth of Bolsena.

"It's covered," I said, disappointed. "At least I can't see it."

"Beautifully covered." Jack skimmed the guidebook. "It seems the reliquary is only opened on Easter and the Feast of Corpus Christi."

We sat in a pew and studied the golden chest; enameled tiles on its face told the story of Peter of Prague. *Blessed are those who believe but do not see*, Christ said. But many of us need to see to believe, need to have material proofs. Here, in Orvieto, seven hundred years ago, God gave us one of those proofs.

54

I opened my handbag and felt for my cloth. Was this square of linen a relic too? Would this journey of faith work a miracle in my soul? Would Father's last Eucharist and the spilled wine-blood help me? I didn't know, but I understood the doubts of that priest from Prague.

Incarnation, sacramental. Father Rinaldi had repeated those words over the years. He said to look around and see the sacramental in all creation. I remembered the theme, woven through sermons and conversations. See the Spirit incarnate, he said, in the flesh of each of us. What is language itself, if not a sensory vehicle for something we cannot see? He claimed we use words to house our thoughts, to give them form and substance, things our ears can grasp, our senses can know.

I knelt before the hidden cloth from Bolsena and prayed for faith, just as Peter of Prague prayed in Rome. Maybe God could work the miracle of no more nightmares. Maybe I could allow the invisible to heal what was all too visible for me each night.

I touched my linen, rough against my fingers, as a bell tolled one.

When I looked up, Jack was gone. I glimpsed him wandering toward the south transept, his book swinging in his hand. I folded my cloth, packed it in my bag, and rose to join him.

"Time for lunch." I wrapped my arm around his waist.

He kissed me lightly on the head. "And I'm starving."

"And after lunch, Milan."

Brother Cristoforo unloaded our bags at the door of our hotel on Via Gesu in Milan.

"I return on Monday as you say," he said, his deep voice smooth as velvet. "If you need me, here I be."

He handed me a card with a local phone number, nodded, and strode down the street.

As Jack checked in, I picked up a hotel brochure and explored the white lobby frescoed with pastel images. The brochure told how a devout woman converted her house to a convent in 1328, which, like so many in Italy, eventually became a hotel. As I returned to the reception counter, Jack's voice was rising.

"How could you lose our reservation? Your name, Signore?"

My husband's expectations were high, and he took failure seriously, having worked so hard himself. But soon we were ushered into a quiet room overlooking a grassy cloister and a bubbling fountain. A bell tolled four as champagne, fruit, and flowers arrived with an apology from the manager.

Jack sighed as he unfastened the luggage straps. "Milan is such an elegant city, don't you think, Maddie? Maybe we should do a little window-shopping tomorrow. We might find you something nice, a pretty reward for all these church visits."

Since the Via Gesu neighborhood was near the cathedral, it was once the home of monasteries and convents. Today it boasted designer shops: Ungaro, Fendi, Frette, Ferragamo, Valentino.

"Sure," I said reluctantly, "but what about the cathedral? It's the *duomo* that we're supposed to visit—actually, the crypt."

"All in due time, Maddie. We'll go there for Sunday mass—that should be special. So we'll have Saturday to explore the town."

The morning looked dry, but rain was forecast. Sipping a cappuccino and nibbling a muffin, I reviewed my notes on Milan's famous figures, Ambrose and Augustine. Both were Church fathers, men who guided the early centuries of Christianity; they formulated the canons and creeds, sorting fact from fiction.

Jack had finished the *Herald Tribune* and was now searching his travel documents.

"Listen to this, Jack."

"Not now, Maddie, I'm trying to find something." He frowned and swore.

I returned to my notes.

When Ambrose, the Roman governor of the province, visited Milan in 374 AD, he climbed into the pulpit of the cathedral to quell a rowdy crowd gathered to elect a new bishop. As they vehemently argued their choices, Ambrose urged peaceful deliberations. Then a voice shouted from the crowd, "Ambrose, Bishop!" and they elected him unanimously. They persuaded him to accept; he was baptized and consecrated eight days later.

56

Jack would have loved this story, but he was racing about the room, checking pockets and drawers.

"What are you missing?"

"My packet of hotel reservations, all the confirmations and certificates. It's got to be here somewhere."

"It'll turn up."

Jack sat down, troubled but resigned, and reached for a slice of toast. "I'll ask at the desk on the way out. Maybe I left it on the counter when we checked in."

I filled him in on Ambrose's unusual election.

"Amazing verve, these people." Jack strained to be interested.

"So Ambrose gave away his possessions and studied Scripture and doctrine. Since he was a governor, he was an effective leader. He fought Arianism, a major heresy at the time."

"Arianism?" Jack asked automatically as he sipped his coffee.

"The Arians believed Christ was not actually God, but rather a created being exalted above other created beings, a kind of first Adam, who reappears in Bethlehem. It was a big-time reason for wars and alliances—opinions were heated."

"We'd better get going, before it starts raining." Jack dialed for the waiter to pick up the dishes.

"And Ambrose converted and baptized Augustine of Hippo." I packed my handbag—dark glasses, notes, umbrella.

Jack was checking the side pockets in his carry-on. "Wasn't Augustine the one who did all those nasty things and wrote about them in a book of confessions? See, I'm not as dumb as you think. Darn, where are those papers?"

"He sought the truth."

Jack turned to me, smiling paternally, "Kind of like you, the way you're always asking questions. Not everyone is cursed like that, you know, Madeleine." He wrapped a yellow tie around the collar of his denim shirt, his Saturday casual look.

"I like to think *blessed*. Anyway, Augustine sought a personal God, unlike the classical gods."

"I know the rest. He met Ambrose and Ambrose preached to him until he gave in." Jack chuckled. "Does that sound familiar?"

I sighed and found the map. Sometimes I did overdo it. "Sort of."

As we approached the concierge's counter, a short, balding man with wire-rimmed glasses departed, and a clerk shoved an envelope into our mail slot. The clerk turned and asked if he could help. Jack gave him our room number, and he pulled out the envelope.

Jack sighed with relief. "Whew, I thought I had lost these. The young man said someone just turned them in."

"I wonder what happened to them."

We stepped outside.

"So where to now?" Jack asked, looking up the street. "You said something about a circle?"

"We'll head for Basilica di San Ambrogio, one of Ambrose's basilicas. There are actually five, I believe, along the Roman wall."

With a map and some guesswork, we followed the ring road that replaced the fourth-century wall. Cemeteries in Milan, as in Rome, lay outside the walls, where the graves of the martyrs became holy *loci*, places venerated by gatherings of the living. When Constantine legalized Christianity, Ambrose built basilicas over these *martyria*, spacing them along the circumference. I wanted to find those layered churches, to touch those early days. Feeling a pilgrim's thanksgiving for those first witnesses, I would lay my flowers of prayer over their graves.

As we walked, I tried to visualize these fourth-century Milanese, called the followers of the *Christus*, or the Messianists. With Christianity legalized, they proceeded to define creeds, fight heresies, and form liturgies.

Their world was changing rapidly. As the old pagan order disintegrated, Christian basilicas replaced pagan temples. The Goths approached the gates of Rome and the military took greater power. And, as turmoil cried for structure, Christians laid the foundations of Western civilization. In the coming centuries, bishops would protect that civilization through the dark years of invasion and illiteracy.

Sixth-century Gregory the Great would send Augustine of Canterbury to England. British Patrick would Christianize Ireland, the scene of his boyhood slavery. Irish Columbanus would convert Gaul, today France. All of these religious, monks and nuns under Benedictine obedience, would create libraries of thought and parchment, ensuring the survival of literacy and law, the legacy of the classical world. And through the Eucharist, they would ensure the survival of Christianity, that explosion of the infinite into the finite, God reaching into our world, God touching us.

We continued along cracked sidewalks of unfashionable neighborhoods, carefully crossing busy intersections, alert to scooters buzzing around corners. We studied our map to find the Roman wall, today replaced by streetcar lines, delis, and hotels.

The wind picked up, and the sky grew dark and threatening. Finally, we turned a corner and two ocher bell towers appeared, the city crowding in upon the Basilica of Saint Ambrose.

Stepping through an arched portal, we crossed a broad square, and entered a colonnaded court. Catechumens studying to be baptized had gathered in this courtyard, waiting for the rite that would prepare them for the Eucharist. Here too, Christians had sought sanctuary. Today, it was a place of reflection before entering the basilica. I touched the Roman slabs embedded in the walls and turned toward the church doors.

We entered the dusky light and paused. At the far end, a canopy of crimson and blue porphyry stood over the high altar. Three naves, lined by pillars and high galleries, ran under a vaulted russet ceiling to a dome far above. Behind the altar, a wooden choir curved along a golden apse. The colors of the church settled upon my senses, rich earthy colors of another time.

I touched an ancient Roman column, cool against my palm.

"What's below?" Jack peered into the *confessio* beneath the high altar.

We descended stairs to a porphyry sarcophagus with a glass panel, containing the bodies of Ambrose and two other saints. Ambrose's body was clothed in bishop's crimson. I stared at the skulls, both grisly and holy, for there were no death masks.

"Who are the others?" Jack asked.

"Gervasius and Protasius, second-century martyrs. Ambrose discovered their bodies nearby and brought them here to sanctify the church."

"Martyrs' relics were a valuable find in those days, I'll bet."

"They were. In fact, Ambrose processed through Milan with their bones. Christians believed such relics gave the church—and the city itself—authenticity. Gervasius and Protasius are Milan's patron saints."

"Ambrose was a true politician."

"And knew the power of martyrdom, the power of absolute devotion."

"The ultimate sacrifice."

"They must have been filled with the courage of God. Miraculous healings at their graves were soon reported."

We ascended to the nave and I knelt in the first pew, praying for wisdom to sort fact from fiction, truth from heresy, in my own short span of life. For surely, one day my body would be like these corpses in the beautiful tomb, merely dry bones.

Yet the words and deeds of Ambrose lived on in Augustine of Hippo and successive bishops over the next sixteen centuries. When Milan was threatened by the Goths, the Church held firm and in time influenced them through education and law. In a way, these immigrants, however "uncivilized," were baptized by the Christian world. Like Augustine, they entered the pool of Christ and emerged new creatures, forming a new culture: Western civilization.

I wanted this too. I wanted this transformation, and perhaps I, like the Goths, would have to allow it to occur in God's time, not mine. It took them several centuries, and I prayed my renewal would be sooner. *Give me patience, Lord.*

As I knelt, I sensed someone watching us. Uneasy, I remembered the card that Cristoforo handed Jack, something about *Ambrogio.* I looked about, and a door closed silently to my left, probably leading to the cloister.

We checked the gardens and they were empty; a moist wind blew the lemon trees, scattering leaves on the flagstones. From far away I heard someone whistling. Was it "Holy, Holy, Holy, Lord God Almighty"? One of Father Rinaldi's favorite hymns.

After lunch, at the fashionable hour of three, the iron grates of the local shops clattered, rolling up and open, revealing their wares behind glass.

We walked up Via Gesu to Via Monte Napoleone, a long narrow street of elegant townhouses, now boutiques selling shoes, clothing, and fine linens. We passed suited women swaying with a runway step, intent upon their business, their stiletto heels tapping beneath short, tight skirts, their designer bags dangling from be-ringed fingers, nails a glossy red. Men in silk suits carried supple leather cases. They processed up and down the sidewalk, avoiding touch, strangers rushing to an undefined location.

Cars jammed the medieval road, horns honking. Exhaust fumes, mingled with eau de cologne, smarted the eyes.

But the vias leapt through time—San Spirito, Gesu, San Andrea. Other worshipers once walked here, solemn and serious too, in their cowls, their starched collars, their wimples. They wore humbler clothing, rough sacking of earthy hues, and for many, delight came from within. Steeple bells marked their hours as they fed the hungry and nursed the sick.

Today the bells continue to toll as shoppers clip along the sidewalk; the avenues still bear holy names. Small reminders linger, washing the present with the past.

A light rain fell as we peered through windows, trying to see the last of the spring collection, and we ran, dripping, into Valentino.

There, on a back sale rack, Jack found a little black dress, nipped in at the waist, with soft silk falling in folds and a sweetheart neck perfect for pearls. "For my *bella signora*," he said. "Happy Birthday."

"Thank you, sweetie," I said, kissing him. "A size six—do you really think I might squeeze into it?" But I tried it on and it fit—barely.

We dined in the Art Deco restaurant in the hotel basement, the former crypt of the convent chapel. They served us *minestrone alla Milanese, costoletta di vitello, verdura alla griglia*, and ravioli with Gorgonzola. I swirled my wine in the balloon glass and watched the legs form along the sides. "Isn't it ironic that the fashion houses are located where all the convents used to be?"

Jack munched thoughtfully. "Not that ironic. Our bodies and souls are related, right? At least my doctor says if I don't worry so much, my blood pressure will go down, and my ulcers will recede. Of course, that's easy for him to say. He probably doesn't have all his savings in stocks and bonds."

"But what drives us to want new clothes? We want to be beautiful, I'd say . . . to be loved . . . especially if we're turning fifty. That's hardly materialistic."

"What about power? When we're loved, we control the relationship. We broker acceptance or rejection." Jack gazed at me with his blue eyes. "I'm certainly in your power, my Madeleine . . . especially with that dress you're wearing . . . and here comes your birthday dessert."

And what a day to visit decomposed bodies, I thought, even if they *were* saints; then again, perhaps a fitting reminder.

The materialistic Tiramisu arrived—cake and coffee cream and liqueur.

Jack raised his glass. "To another fifty years . . ."

I raised mine. "With you."

Sunday morning the skies cleared, swept clean by wind and rain.

Jack grabbed his blue blazer. "Hurry up, Maddie. We're late. I hate to be late. Is my tie crooked?"

"The cathedral's not far." I centered the burgundy tie on his crisp white shirt, then slipped on my sweater, one that matched the cornflower blue in my skirt.

Pushed by the wind, we walked the six blocks to the towering Gothic *duomo*. Standing in the massive square, we scanned the white stone facade and lacy spires, then rushed up the broad stairs and entered the packed church. We stepped down the central aisle between giant columns and finally found seats halfway up. Light and color streamed through stained glass, transformed by the sun into rainbow prisms.

The organ boomed and I looked back to the foot of the nave. White-robed clergy processed up the aisle, journeying the long path from narthex to altar, from beginnings to ends to beginnings again, from birth to death to life. The censor led, throwing incense before him, preparing the way for the crucifer. The others followed slowly, their hands folded, their eyes veiled, holding their solemnity close, as though offering themselves to God. The bishop came last, the shepherd of his flock, wearing the golden miter that signaled his authority and carrying the staff that commanded him to gather, feed, and protect.

The mass began, the Italian mingling with Latin. *Signore, pietà! Cristo, pietà! Signore, pietà!* Lord have mercy! Christ have mercy! Lord have mercy!

I gazed at the gilded tabernacle housing Christ's Presence. *Open my heart to healing, O Lord. Show me the way to forgetfulness.* . . . . My nightmares continued. Mollie ran through the dark underground passage, far too far ahead as waters rushed in my ears, her matchstick form merging into the stone walls.

But here all was light, dancing in the air and glancing off polished marble. Tiles circled immense columns rising to the brilliant glass panels, and I thought how Christ was like those columns, linking earth to heaven, for he too ascended, from this world to his Father. Indeed, he claimed he was the *only* way to heaven.

And today, on this altar, he would return in the bread and wine.

The priests, I knew, were human like me. They too had sinned, some more seriously than I, some less. But they also had been forgiven. It was good that the action of the mass did not depend on their purity.

As the priests held their hands over the bread and wine, saying the sacred words of consecration, I recognized Christ's command at the Last Supper. *For in the night in which he was betrayed, he took Bread; and when he had given thanks, he brake it, and gave it to his disciples, saying, Take, eat, this is my Body, which is given for you.*

The bells, high in the towers, rang deliriously, announcing the mysterious transformation to all Milan.

The priests glided down the chancel steps and offered the white hosts, the tangible love of God, free for the taking, like Christ feeding the hungry nearly two thousand years ago. Robed in God's majesty, these outward and visible signs of God's love linked the apostolic centuries. And in the space of the present, they united their people to eternity, to the promise of resurrection.

The faithful came forward, their faces penitent and hopeful, open and unguarded. They consumed their Lord, returning to their seats transformed by an infinite yet corporeal love, imminent yet eminent. Local Milanese and dusty tourists, young and old, rich and poor, received Jesus into their bodies and souls. The organ thundered, and the clergy recessed down the aisle in solemn victory, in a transfigured moment of golden glory.

"Let's find the entrance to the crypt," I whispered as the nave cleared.

We found a ticket booth in the narthex, pushed our way through a turnstile, and descended into the crypt, once the fourth-century Church of Saint Tecla. Stepping carefully on raised boardwalks, I inhaled the damp air. A stone wall circled a large earthen basin bordered by brick slabs, about twelve feet in diameter.

In this pool, Ambrose baptized Augustine. I pictured other white-robed catechumens, descending into the waters as sinners and ascending saved, donning the power of the Holy Spirit. Through the dark nights of Lent they studied and prayed, and on Easter Eve were baptized and confirmed in a fanfare of procession and song.

As I stared at the pool, Mollie flashed before me, Mollie in her watery grave, facedown, still. How I longed to change that pool of death into one of life. How I ached to undo the years.

As I walked through the dusty aisles, I prayed this trip would rebaptize me, cleanse and heal me in my own pool of time. I understood why Father sent me here. I needed to desire this, to want this, to be willing to give up my ghosts, just as these catechumens gave up their past, to be reborn. I had to accept God's grace, his transforming power. Was I willing? Did I hold on to my sorrow in the same way I clasped my linen cloth?

"How about lunch?" Jack whispered. "I read of a great place just opposite the piazza. They have stuffed zucchini flowers—you'll love it."

Jack's trattoria was busy. Waiters bustled between crowded tables and families chatted across generations in the weekly ritual of Sunday brunch. I circled the buffet: platters of anchovies in olive oil; yellow, red, and green grilled vegetables alongside poached salmon; jellied terrines sliced and arranged in gardens of basil; marinated tomatoes with tiny green beans, cold sliced potatoes, tuna, olives, and lemons.

Hoping to walk off lunch, we headed for the city *parco*. It was quiet this Sunday afternoon in Milan; stores were closed, and Milanese strolled arm in arm, walking their dogs. Some residents had left town for the weekend, emptying the streets for we *pedoni*.

Jack and I followed gravel paths through the park under giant shade trees; the gardens had seen better days, but even so retained the bygone elegance of a wealthy great aunt. Vendors sold pink swirls of cotton candy and children's toys, and a carousel clanged.

My mind pulsed with marble and stone, martyrs and relics, and time fleeing. I was becoming the great aunt, without the bygone elegance—only bygone terror—and my demons were gaining ground. I wanted to ride the carousel, but I was too old. I was fifty and longed to be reborn, to enter that underground crypt and emerge new, cleansed, washed of midnight ghosts.

Something rustled in the trees behind us, and I thought I saw our friar, but the tall figure disappeared down another path.

Chapter Five
Lago di Como

Thou shalt show me the path of life:
in thy presence is the fulness of joy,
and at thy right hand there is pleasure for evermore.
Psalm 16:12

On Monday, May 5th, nearly one week into my pilgrimage, Jack surprised me with a side trip to Lake Como, one of five finger lakes spreading south from the Alps into Italy. Years ago, we had visited the Hotel Villa d'Este, an hour north of Milan, as guests of a Lombard wine broker. They had an excellent wine list and a renowned cooking school. Jack could bring home new ways to roast lamb, sauté fish, and season pasta with fresh herbs.

With our friar at the wheel, we were soon climbing the Alpine foothills, winding through tunnels, and descending to Como's emerald waters. We skirted the western shore, passed through the village of Cernobbio, and arrived at the gates of Villa d'Este. Brother Cristoforo dropped us off at the front door and left to find lodgings nearby, promising to return in two days to drive us to Venice.

Once a sixteenth-century cardinal's palace, Villa d'Este had become a world-class resort with a floating swimming pool, formal gardens, neoclassic statuary, sporting club, and spa. I had forgotten how beautiful it was.

We entered our third-floor room overlooking the lake. Red velvet chairs on a sea-green carpet faced a walled-in fireplace, and white cotton draperies billowed about French doors. We unpacked and I joined Jack on our narrow balcony.

Below, the glassy water undulated hypnotically. A mystical mist settled over the water like an ancient veil—did royalty once live on the opposite hillside? Red-roofed villas dotted the forested shore and church bells echoed over the water. There was little evidence of the robed clerics who once walked the gardens below—only jacketed waiters and well-dressed guests. The old world where princes were bishops, where the aristocracy found—or bought—their vocations in the Church, had crumbled. But clearly an aristocracy remained, perhaps of a different sort.

I heard the crunch of gravel and peered over the railing.

"There's Cristoforo," I said, pointing.

Our friar stood under a shady plane tree. He looked up as he fingered beads looping from his pocket. Raising a hand in greeting, he slipped quietly away.

I turned my face to the thin sun piercing the mist, half dreaming of Coleridge's ancient mariner. Did I too carry an albatross? With a jarring roar, a seaplane broke the silence as it lifted off from the glassy surface. An occasional bird chirped, and a motorboat droned in the distance, muted by the fog.

"So what are you wearing to the dinner dance tonight?" Jack's low voice broke my trance.

"Dinner dance?"

"It's their spring celebration and we have reservations—a show, a band, the works."

We gathered for cocktails with others on the lakeside terrace, holding our *coupes de champagne* and watching skiers skim the water, their flags high. I scanned the crowd, thinking our friar might appear without warning, but there were no familiar faces. My cloth lay neatly in my evening bag.

Linen-covered tables dotted the lawn; a stage had been erected. We sat in gold-painted chairs, nibbling chicken breasts with eggplant and pumpkin ravioli with mushrooms. I could see Jack was taking note of the herbs and cheeses; he tilted and swirled his wine, studied the color, and inhaled the bouquet. "Ah," he sighed appreciatively.

The show began, the performers leaping and careening through spotlights; soon the stage was cleared for the diners to dance. I wasn't much of a dancer, but I made up for my lack of skill with enthusiasm. I set my bag carefully under my wrap and we joined the others, swinging to a fifties jitterbug, and for the time the happy beat carried me back to high school and DJs and top singles. I laughed as I swung past Jack, our hands sliding, and I was thankful for my husband, his love of life, his embrace of the moment. The next dance was slow, and he held me close, cheek to cheek, my fingers laced with his, lying against his chest. Mollie seemed far away.

When we returned to the table, I reached for my bag. "It's gone!" I cried. My shawl was there, but no handbag.

"What's gone?"

"My purse . . ."

"It's probably in the grass."

We searched and finally called a waiter, who assured us he would find it, and to check the front desk in the morning.

"Jack, my cloth was in that bag."

"Was there anything else? Wallet? Credit cards?"

"My wallet's in the room safe."

"That's a relief—you can always get another bag."

"But the cloth!"

"They'll find it; I'm sure of it."

I felt sick, but made an effort not to spoil the evening. Surely, it would turn up in the morning.

It was nearly daylight when Cernobbio bells echoed over the water, waking us. The lake lapped the wooden dock below our windows and a cool breeze ruffled the cotton curtains, throwing shadows on the opposite wall.

"So, birthday girl, what would you like to do today?" Jack whispered in my ear.

Find my bag. Find Father's linen cloth. The reality of the loss came to me suddenly. "Let's find the church that woke us up. I want to offer thanks for another year, and for you." He smelled of spice and sweet syrup.

"*Si, si, mia bella,*" Jack said softly. "We'll thank God, and then let's take the ferry to Bellagio for lunch."

We stopped in the hotel office on the way to breakfast.

"A boy turned it in," the clerk said as he handed me the black leather clutch.

Just as I packed it—compact, lipstick, comb, and linen cloth. Perhaps it was, after all, just lost and found. I kissed the cloth without thinking and the clerk raised his eyebrows. "A memento, *signore* . . . a precious memento."

Chiesa del Redentore—Church of the Redeemer—was half a block from the village square. We entered the baroque church and I gazed at the light-filled nave. Yellow, green, and peach frescoes covered the vaults. Marble aisles opened onto gilded chapels. Above the altar, Christ hung on a golden cross, offering his body, his suffering sacrifice.

I knelt in the first pew and gazed at the red candle burning on the altar. I made the Sign of the Cross and prayed an *Our Father*. Then, in fitful phrases, I thanked God for another year of life on this earth; I thanked him for Jack; I asked for peace. I waited in the silence and soon he eased my tired heart, my dusty body, my pilgrim's soul. In the quiet of this weekday morning, I listened for his voice, welcomed his presence. *Take not thy Holy Spirit from me.*

I prayed for redemption, that my sin of neglect be transformed into love. Then I took the cloth from my bag and spread it on the pew back. As I stared at the tabernacle, waiting and watching, a gust of wind blew through the entry doors, and the red candle flickered. *I must send my sister flowers.* The thought came to me like a burst of light.

A door squeaked and I turned to spot Jack in the back pew, dozing. A tall black-robed man stood behind him in the shadows. He peered from under a cowl. He wore wire-rimmed glasses. This was not Cristoforo.

The cleric had left by the time I reached Jack and gently tapped his shoulder. "Let's catch the next ferry to Bellagio. It's almost lunchtime."

Were we being followed? Someone back home wanted my cloth—a Mr. McGinty. Maybe our friar wanted it too. He was constantly staring at my bag and suddenly appearing. Could the corporal linen be that valuable?

The ferry to Bellagio motored smoothly up the undulating lake, through dark deeps and shiny shallows. Churches stood on rocky cliffs or nestled in green banks, their Lombard towers straight and stalwart, like the Alps behind them.

We stopped at Moltrasio, Argegno, and Isola Comacina, each name barreling through a loudspeaker. Hotels crowded the lakefronts; window boxes spilled red geraniums. Tourists, chatting in many languages, boarded, stepping carefully on steel ramps thrown out with a loud clatter by the boatman.

We disembarked at Bellagio, a pretty village on a peninsula in the center of the lake. We followed cobblestone lanes past shops selling leather goods, Como silk, and carved figurines, and soon arrived at the Grand Hotel Serbollini, an elegant old resort with gardens that cascaded to the shore. A few guests took pictures from an upper terrace. Jacketed waiters served lunch on flowered linen to discreet couples as silverware and plates clinked lightly. A few remaining diners lingered quietly over a coffee, a glass of wine, a bowl of cherries.

We took a table near the edge of the terrace and ordered from simple menus, then stared across the lake to the forests rising from the water.

I glanced around the terrace. "Don't look now," I said as I took a bite of pasta, "but I think I've seen that man in the corner before—he was standing behind you in church this morning." How could I be sure? This man wore sunglasses and a Panama hat with a feather. He was clean-shaven and pale. "Only he wore a black robe with a hood—like a monk."

"What man in church?"

"He was in the back, right behind you, and he was staring at me."

"That shouldn't be so unusual. Monks often inhabit churches." He chuckled, clearly pleased with himself.

"Well, he seemed a little sinister. . . . Maybe he's following us."

"And this fellow here is like that monk?" Jack turned, glancing quickly. He frowned and set down his wineglass. "You're blowing this way out of proportion. Why would anyone want to follow us?"

"Lots of reasons."

"Name one."

"The linen cloth might be a relic . . ."

"Sure it's a relic. And I'm Saint Peter. You're tired—your mind is playing tricks on you."

I *was* tired. *So tired.* Was I losing my mind? "Maybe you're right." I tried the wine. *Fruity. Nice.* But the straw-hat man looked *so* familiar.

"Listen," Jack said, "I've an idea."

"An idea?"

"Lynn Beck. You remember the doctor I told you about?"

"From your business connections?"

He nodded. "Her daughter in Zurich is a specialist in your kind of problem."

"My kind of problem?"

"You know—religious visions, that sort of thing, para . . . para something. . . ."

"You want me see a shrink."

"She's a therapist. I could give her a call while we're here. Zurich isn't that far away."

"No, Jack." I tried to stem the panic.

"Simply testing the waters. No need to get huffy. Anyway, Lynn said she didn't entirely approve of her daughter's style . . . or was it her way with patients . . . can't recall exactly. So maybe it's just as well. Now—tell me about this place. All you know."

His diversion worked, and I gratefully took the bait.

"Stendhal and Twain wrote here and Liszt composed." I held on to facts, and my panic began to subside. If Jack didn't understand, who would? "Percy and Mary Shelley stayed at our hotel." I glanced through a local pamphlet, slick with color photos, trying not to look at the pale man. "Donizetti, Listz, Rossini, and Bellini all came here."

"Wasn't there something about Churchill?"

"Here it is. . . . He came to the lake to convalesce after the war. He painted."

"Maybe you should try painting?"

"Me paint? Much too difficult. Listen to this." I could play his game—I could watch Big Hat and read at the same time. "Here are some famous names for you. Elizabeth Taylor and Nicky Hilton, Rita Hayworth and Orson Welles, Clark Gable and Carol Lombard, William Randolph Hearst and Marion Davies, Ava Gardner and Frank Sinatra, Aristotle Onassis and Maria Callas. They all came to Lake Como."

"Now, those names I can relate to." Coming from a working-class family in east Oakland, Jack grew up idolizing the famous, reading about them in newspapers, hearing the latest gossip on his crystal set radio, and seeing them on TV. They fed his ambition as he worked through law school and climbed the corporate ladder.

Jack pulled out his reading glasses to study the check, and I returned to my history lesson. The pale-faced suspect waved to the waiter.

"It says here," I continued, "that in Dongo, up the lake, Mussolini and his mistress were captured and shot. Their bodies were hung upside down in a square in Milan, the square where the Nazis committed their worst crimes."

Jack handed the waiter his credit card. "That seems fitting, but I think I can pass on Dongo. What else, Professor?"

I skimmed ahead. "The lake was first settled by five thousand colonists sent by Julius Caesar. The Plinys—Roman writers—were born in this area. In fact, the younger Pliny had a villa right here in Bellagio. Virgil visited too. And Queen Caroline of England lived at our hotel after George IV tried to divorce her."

Jack signed the credit slip and put away his card. "It's amazing. I've been here twice before and never knew the juicy details." He smiled his pretend-amazement look, eyebrows raised. "Was he the King George of the American Revolution?"

"That was his father. *This* George was *Georgie Porgie, puddin' and pie, kissed the girls and made them cry.* . . . He was a bit of a roué, to say the least."

"Really? Come on, let's walk off this lunch."

"Where do you get your energy?" But a stroll through the medieval streets of Bellagio sounded pleasant enough.

I glanced in my bag for my cloth. It was still neatly folded. And Pale Face was gone.

"Many years, my dear, of go-go-go, I guess," he said as we left the restaurant. "Did I ever tell you the story of my passing the bar exam?"

"Tell it again," I urged, as we climbed a cobblestone path lined with shops.

"I was so poor," he sighed, holding his youth in the timber of his voice. "I worked in a warehouse forty hours a week, but I was too thin for the lifting, so I strengthened my wrists with tape."

"How did you find time to study?"

"Late at night. I had a wife and two children, a lot at stake. So I was determined."

"Didn't you come into an inheritance the last few months?" I was touched again by his quiet strength and focus.

"Uncle Harry died and left me enough to quit work and study full-time my last semester. I've been going ever since, with a motor that won't turn off, I suppose." He smiled. "Maybe now with age and retirement, I'll shift into a lower gear, and my ulcers will too."

We wandered the old lanes—I bought a silver teaspoon with *Bellagio* on its handle—and boarded the 3:20 ferry back to Cernobbio. We sat in plastic chairs in the stern. There was no sign of the stranger. Lulled by the deep drone of the engine, we glided over the sparkling blue-green waters. The present nearly washed away the past as the sun burned my skin, mellowing my almost-forgotten pain. I dozed, my head dropping, then rising with a jerk.

In the morning, as Jack reviewed our bill as though it were his last will and testament, I stepped outside to say good-bye to Lake Como. I sprawled on a white lawn chair under the plane tree and looked up at the enormous branches full with spring leaves. The tree presided over the gardens, the lake, and the villa itself, watching our passing, unnoticed by us, providing both shade and beauty.

Perhaps God was like the plane tree—with us, yet not always dominant. His love sheltered us, and yet for those who did not seek him, he was merely a background to life, a beautiful perfection gone unnoticed.

Wearing that thought like a soft shawl, I approached the car as our friar loaded our luggage onto the trunk. The porters stared at his rough cassock, his swinging rope belt, and his dangling rosary. We fastened our seat belts and headed for Venice at high speed, as I prayed to Saint Christopher, patron saint of travelers.

I wondered about the hooded monk in the back of Il Redentore and the fellow at lunch in Bellagio. I wondered about Mr. McGinty and Cristoforo too, our mysterious driver. I checked on my cloth, secure in my bag. In Venice, I would speak seriously to Jack about dismissing this friar. Cristoforo could take the next train to Rome. We would manage somehow.

Chapter Six
Venezia

Let the floods clap their hands,
and let the hills be joyful together before the Lord.
Psalm 98:9

As Cristoforo pumped gas at a highway rest stop, I spoke with Jack about dismissing the friar. Jack wanted to keep him on—he liked having a chauffeur who helped with the luggage and language.

So we arrived in Venice, my nightmares, fears, and suspicions still close companions. Mollie visited in the day now as well as the night, in strange places, a phantom of love reaching out—her first smile, her first rolling over, her first sitting up. I saw the tilt of her head and the concentration in her eyes when she watched my lips move, absorbing my speech. I felt the warm weight of her, her soft flesh in my arms, and saw her trembling lip before she cried. In the night, her dying figure terrified me.

Cristoforo parked the car in a lot outside of town and loaded our bags into the hotel launch. He helped us board, his dark face inscrutable as we stepped over the luggage and made our way through the low-ceilinged cabin to the open stern.

The sky was partly cloudy, and a salty sea breeze slapped my cheeks. High gray-green waters washed the sleek polished sides of the boat and splashed the docks lining the canal. The friar sat up front with the driver, and the two soon appeared deep in conversation.

We motored down narrow waterways through the ancient city of villas, sailing under stone bridges, past frescoed lintels and red doors. We turned into the Canal Grande where aged hotels tilted into the waters, their striped awnings shading wooden decks, and red-and-white poles marked berths. The canal opened into a wide bay and we crossed to Isola della Giudecca and the Cipriani Hotel.

The launch idled alongside the dock, its motor humming, the shellac burning in a sudden shaft of sun. I balanced myself against the rock of the boat and stepped up, grabbing the porter's thick hand for support. The man's weathered face broke into a grin, white teeth flashing against a dark tan. "*Buona sera, Signora*, and welcome to the Cipriani!"

We followed a path under a long canopy, through a garden of red and yellow pansies, and into the lobby. Soon a swarthy clerk led us down an outer pathway and up narrow stairs. Through a dormer window of our attic room we looked across the canal to Piazza San Marco on the opposite shore. The *vaporettos*, Venice's waterbuses, blew their horns below our window.

Jack stood behind me and wrapped his arms about my waist. "We have a good view."

I looked at the churning sea. "Isn't the water rather high?"

"They say it's been raining the last three days, and with the tides and full moon, they expect some flooding."

"I hope we can get around." I recalled pictures of Venetian floods—the waters could rise suddenly.

While Jack showered, I lay on the bed, exhausted, fatigue wrapping me like a shroud.

Mollie, Mollie, is it you I see? Do you haunt me? Do you hate me? Don't run away, Mollie; stay, please, stay. Come back to me, my little girl; breathe, Mollie, breathe. . . . Last night I screamed in my sleep, and Jack shook me gently, once again pulling me out of a dark fear.

We dined in the hotel restaurant looking out on the channel. A perfect mushroom soup was followed by stuffed artichokes and fresh sea bass with basil and tomato. We sipped a local red wine and ended the meal with poached pears and vanilla ice cream.

I savored the last of the ice cream. "So we see San Marco tomorrow. Do you know the story of Mark's body?"

Jack smiled. "I'm afraid I don't."

"They say the Venetians stole it from Alexandria in the early ninth century."

"How in the world did they steal it?" Jack was interested; he enjoyed thrillers and mysteries.

"They hid his relics in a shipment of pork, hoping the Muslims wouldn't search it."

"Clever. But stealing a body—isn't that rather un-Christian? I mean stealing is bad enough—but a body? Grave robbers?"

"Christians, like everyone else, don't always practice what they preach."

"You sound like Father Rinaldi—religion and philosophy should be judged by the tenets, not the practitioners."

"Exactly." I reached for a miniature cream puff.

"What else is on Father's list? We have only one day in Venice, so we'd better make the most of it."

"I have the list here somewhere." I pulled it out of my bag and handed it to him.

He took out a pen and checked off the churches we had visited.

Santa Maria Maggiore, RomaX
Chiesa di Santa Pudenziana, RomaX
Chiesa di Santa Prassede, RomaX
Chiesa di Sant' Agnese fuori le Mura, RomaX
Basilica di San Pietro, RomaX
The Duomo Crypt, MilanoX
Chiesa di San Zaccaria, Venezia
Basilica di San Marco, Venezia
Basilica di San Domenico, Bologna
Sanctuario della Verna, northeast of Firenze
Abbazia di Sant' Antimo, southwest Siena
Chiesa del Gesu, Roma

"Six down and six to go. But San Zaccaria?" he asked. "I've never heard of that one. San Marco should be fun. San Marco is an experience, not a church."

If only I could bottle my husband's present enthusiasm. I knew he was growing impatient with this world of churches and history. In fact, Jack's gaze was presently focused on a young woman whose neckline showed off a well-endowed bust. Her skin was creamy and her eyes dark, her blond hair long and straight. She flashed a wide white smile to an attentive waiter.

I shrank, sensing my lesser figure, freckled skin, myopic eyes, and mousy hair. She dined alone.

"Someone you know?" I hoped to sound more teasing than accusing.

"No, but she sure looks familiar."

It rained all night and into the morning, a steady spring rain with no wind. Armed with coats and umbrellas, we boarded the hotel launch and sailed to Saint Mark's Square, the heart of Venice. I stared through the cabin windows, rubbing the glass with a tissue to clear the condensation, trying to see the Piazza San Marco, shrouded in silvery fog. Chiesa di San Giorgio Maggiore, a Benedictine monastery with a giant bell tower, loomed on an island to the right. On the left, Santa Maria della Salute, a huge, domed circular church built in the sixteenth century as a thanksgiving for the end of the plague, guarded the Grand Canal.

We disembarked near Piazza San Marco and followed a path of flagstones still above water level, working our way through the crowds. Guides with raised umbrellas shouted in several languages and schoolchildren jumped in puddles, squealing with delight. We climbed onto a two-foot high boardwalk that bridged deeper water, and I looked back to the sea sloshing over the quay. Reaching the opposite side of the square, we peered through the rain to the frescoed facade of San Marco. The golden pediments and domes touched the stormy heavens as four bronze horses stood fierce and free on the balustrade.

Jack frowned. "Look at the lines, in spite of this weather. I'm not standing in any lines, Madeleine, especially in the rain. It's a waste of time."

"Say—it's Ascension Day—there should be masses all day at San Marco. And we can get in through the side door if we go to a mass."

"Good idea. And afterwards we can lunch at the Hotel Danieli around the corner."

A posted schedule announced that the next mass was at eleven o'clock.

"So where to now?" Jack asked. "We've got an hour to kill—let's get away from these crowds."

"How about walking and seeing where we end up? This is a good walking town." The quiet streets with no cars turned Venice into a city from another time, magical.

76

The rain continued to pour, and we paused under the awning of a shopwindow to check the guidebook. Jack skimmed a page, running his finger down the fine print. "You're right about Ascension Day. It's a big deal here. They have a regatta of gondolas that sail out to the Lido."

"Really?"

"They have a ceremony called the Marriage of the Sea, where the mayor throws a wedding ring into the waters."

I grinned. "That's wonderful." *Only in Venice.*

He slipped the book into my bag. Taking my hand, he led me away from San Marco.

The rain had eased into a mist as we followed a cobbled lane to one of Venice's four hundred *ponti*. Beneath the bridge, red gondolas, their cushions and chairs protected by tarps, bobbed in the canal. We padded down a narrow *calle* between high palazzo walls that opened onto a square with the words *Piazza di Santa Maria Formosa* carved into a house façade. A church, covered in scaffolding, stood at one end. We crossed the piazza, and as Jack paused to stroke a thin cat, a little girl approached me. She wore what looked like a school uniform—a navy jumper and yellow galoshes. Her curly blond hair formed ringlets about her head.

She handed me a card and smiled.

Jack looked up as the cat darted away. "You'd better give her something, Maddie."

As I rummaged in my bag, she ran off to a group of children dressed similarly. They followed a teacher with a raised umbrella.

I read the card: *Santa Maria dei Miracoli.*

"She's gone," I said, disappointed. I would have liked to ask her about the church.

Jack looked about. "Do we know where we are? At least the rain stopped."

"Sure, sort of, but let's just wander a bit, and see what comes up. Venice isn't that big, really."

We passed a shop of masks and costumes, a reminder of the Mardi Gras *Carnivale* in February. Mardi Gras, "fat Tuesday," originally celebrated the cooking of the last meat products—usually suet—before Ash Wednesday, the first day of the Lenten fast, but had evolved into more of a masquerade ball than a religious observance. Venice gloried in the masquerade with masks of all kinds: clowns, devils, countesses, and cats peered through the glass, offering the chance to be someone else.

The faces behind the windows tempted me to escape, to leave my past behind, to reinvent myself. Did I want to run? Or give in to the temptation? Was it even possible to escape oneself? I pulled myself away and followed Jack up the lane.

We continued past storefronts filled with glass and lace, then followed a *fondamenta* along a canal. The waters were rising, seeping onto the walks, the next bridge inaccessible.

"Let me see the map," Jack said. He slipped on his reading glasses and unfolded the plan, squinting and tracing lines with his finger. "I think we can get to the Rialto Bridge by taking this route. That would be interesting—all the food stalls are in that area."

I recalled tiers of sliced fresh coconut watered by a fountain, and neat rows of nectarines and tomatoes. It began to rain lightly, and I opened my umbrella as I followed Jack down another alley.

We wound about, turning again and again, finding silent dead ends. Suddenly, as though out of nowhere, a church appeared, as though birthed by the canals on either side. Its Renaissance façade stood solitary with tiers of white marble and coral crosses. A half-circle porch led to a small bronze door with a Madonna and Child over the lintel.

"What a pretty church," I said. "I wonder what it's called."

Jack pulled out the guidebook and searched, shaking his head. I studied the map, but between the winding streets and canals, I was lost in a serpentine maze with microscopic script.

"The door's open and it's starting to rain," he said. "Let's go in."

We entered and paused in the narthex. Polychrome marble covered the walls of the single nave in geometrical patterns of greens, gray-blues, corals, and ambers. Red-carpeted steps led to the chancel; from there, green steps led to a simple stone altar. A silver tabernacle stood on the altar with its flaming candle; above the tabernacle was an icon of a fully figured Madonna and Child. Above the icon a large cross was suspended in a green marble apse. Opaque windows filtered light onto the tabernacle.

As we looked about, Vivaldi's "Four Seasons" played from the loft, then abruptly stopped. A young black-robed priest descended and handed me a prayer card. He nodded, smiled a welcome, and returned to the organ loft. The lilting notes resumed, and we knelt in a pew.

"He's playing Vivaldi," Jack whispered, then sat back. "Remember? Vivaldi was born here. This is nice," he added as he looked about, his hand patting the polished pew back.

"That must be one of the miraculous Madonnas," I said. I took out my corporal and clasped it between my palms. The beauty of the space was close and intense. The aroma of roses mingled with the Baroque melody and held me as though I belonged there at that moment; somehow that time and place were mine. Was it an accident that we happened upon this church?

I prayed an *Our Father* and a *Hail Mary*. Falling silent, I allowed my words, my thoughts, my fears, my longings to be suspended. I kept my eyes on the colorful icon of Mary and Jesus, then shifted my gaze to the tabernacle holding Christ's Presence.

Once again, the music stopped suddenly. I looked around for Jack and spotted him in the loft, talking to the organist.

I glanced at the prayer card. A reproduction of the vivid icon was on one side, a prayer in Italian on the other. Under the prayer was the name *Santa Maria dei Miracoli*, the same as on the card from the little girl.

"The priest is from Chicago," Jack said, as we stepped outside into a glaring shaft of sun. The skies had partially cleared, and the rays burned through the moist air. "How about that? And that's not just an organ loft. It was the nuns' choir, connected to their convent by way of a closed passage over the alley."

"The nuns' choir?" Cloistered nuns often observed the liturgy from hidden galleries.

"The very same." He smiled with satisfaction and slipped on his dark glasses.

"Now we know where we are," I said, looking at the map. "At least, I think we do."

"Good, it's getting late. You can't miss a mass, Maddie."

As we headed back to San Marco, one winding lane at a time, I wondered about the little girl, thankful for the mysterious miracle church.

We entered Saint Mark's through the north door. The service was beginning, and we found seats toward the front, then looked about, having fallen into a world of golden vaults.

They say Venice was founded on March 25, 491 AD, the Feast of the Annunciation, when the Goths drove the Venets offshore. By the eighth century, the settlement of marshy islands was taking shape, and Venice, protected by the sea, grew into a flourishing port, surviving attacks from both east and west. A crossroads of the Crusades, Venice collected treasure from eastern capitals: San Marco's bronze horses came from Byzantium as well as icons, sculptures, and relics. In the thirteenth century the Venetian merchant Marco Polo, returning from China, opened trade routes of goods and ideas that placed Venice in the center of a new era of discovery. The city gloried in its wealth, stunning the world with art and music.

Venice's original patron saint, the eastern martyr Theodorus, was replaced by the Western evangelist Saint Mark, who traveled with Paul and assisted Peter in Rome; his Gospel is thought to be based on Peter's sermons. After Peter's death, he became Bishop of Alexandria, where he was martyred.

When Venice "rescued" Mark's relics from Alexandria and entombed them in the doge's chapel, the city adopted the saint's lion symbol, the winged lion. The lion was derived from Mark's identification as the first of "the four living creatures" in the Book of Revelation, Saint John's vision of the Apocalypse. As John relates in this last book of the New Testament, an Angel of the Lord appeared to him on the island of Patmos off the coast of Turkey and showed him a lion, a calf, a man, and an eagle, images thought to represent the four Evangelists.

The doge's chapel evolved into the Basilica di San Marco, its walls covered with precious stones from the East. I looked from vault to vault until my neck ached. San Marco fused the East with the West, the Byzantine with the Romanesque. Three naves formed the three arms of the Greek-cross plan, and the chancel and high altar, partially hidden by an iconostasis, became the fourth arm. Five domes vaulted the three naves, the chancel, and the transept midpoint, all glittering with golden mosaics. A painted crucifix hung in the center, slightly dwarfed by the brilliant vaults.

The mosaics covering the domes told the ancient stories of salvation, and here, in these glittering tiles, suffering was made beautiful. Poverty and hunger, trial, torture, and brutal death—physical defeats redeemed by God—were transfigured into grace and victory. Across one dome, Christ, in vivid robes, rode a white donkey; the saints glowed in jeweled tones.

Soon every seat in the nave was taken, and guards protected the congregation from tourists who crowded the side aisles.

The organ boomed as a procession came down the central aisle. Mitered bishops and somber priests in robes of white and gold glided through billowing incense, following the crucifer and torchbearers. Soon they approached the high altar as a choir sang from the chancel galleries.

The mass began, and chants ascended through the sweet clouds as the ancient rite of love and sacrifice called a longing people to their God. A suited woman read lessons from a lectern, her soft Italian weaving through the congregation. Then an elderly priest, carrying a certainty borne of time, shuffled forward to preach, his voice soft and intense, his head tilted in appeal, his right hand cupped, carving small portions of the air. He carefully cupped and offered his words in a measured effort, as though laying before us his own tale of redemption.

We sat on canvas chairs over sinking paving stones, riding the Venetian waters in an ancient ark protecting centuries of the faithful, the Communion of Saints. We sang *Alleluia* and I prayed that I too could ascend into God's glory, that I with my silly sufferings, my earthy darkness, my mysterious demons, I could emerge from the watery world of earth and sea and fly with the angels, that I could be forgiven my sins, trapped as I was in my prison of self. For I *had* sinned. I had, in the words of my prayer book, *left undone those things which I ought to have done, and done those things which I ought not to have done.* I should have stood watch by Mollie's pool; I should not have left her alone. But God forgave me, forgave it all. My linen cloth was damp between my palms, the air close with the crowd and the humidity pressing in from outside.

A younger priest, robed in green, consecrated the bread and wine before Saint Mark's grave, and the people lined up to receive Christ. The clergy recessed down the aisle, and the golden vaults fell into shadow as the lights switched off. Time had encapsulated into a giant jeweled moment, holding me, and now it moved on, ticking once again.

We paid a fee in the right transept and followed a queue into the ambulatory, winding behind the altar, past the apostle's tomb that lay under a wall of emeralds and rubies, the *pal d'oro*.

Jack studied the gold work, the patterns of precious stones. "Amazing."

"Matter honoring spirit," I said quietly. "They seem like opposites, but in this place they're united." I didn't find fault with these exquisite expressions of pride and ownership, these grandiose gestures glorifying the humble saints of a simpler time. How, after all, did one glorify humility? Had this gold not been hammered into such splendor, would we honor these men and women of God? Would we even remember them? I knew the motives were often twisted, but in the end, I was glad San Marco was here. It testified to sacrificial love, to the gilded and gloried God the Father and the offering of his Son. Once again, God had taken man's impure motives and used them in his plan.

Could he do that with me?

We moved slowly toward the side doors to confront the crowds outside, the rain pouring steadily.

The Hotel Danieli on the flooded quay boasted a terrace restaurant, but today we lunched inside, gazing through the windows at the rain spattering the white enamel tables.

"San Marco," I said, "was like standing still in time. Normally I sense time rushing ahead of me."

"Because of all the history or all the gold?"

"The history." I searched for words that would not come.

"What are you having?" Jack peered into the menu.

I tried again. "Usually I feel like life is a giant ride. . . ." I scanned the list of dishes. "Could you order for me?" Indeed, time skidded over our present and slid into our past, carrying us with it. We reached for today as it disappeared into yesterday, gone. We desperately tried to catch glimpses of our lives, of our world, to make sense of it all, to understand where we had been, and to see where we were going. But in the golden basilica, time stood still.

Jack ordered *tagliatelli* and ravioli and two green salads, to be followed by sea bass in olive oil. He chose a local white wine.

"It's my turning fifty, I suppose. It's as if I'm counting the days I have left, as though such a thing was possible. We really just have so much time, don't we?"

"Our days are numbered. Isn't that from the Bible?"

"The Psalms, I think." What would I do with the days I had left?

"Many would call this a midlife crisis, my dear, taking stock and finding things missing. I suppose I should have had one years ago, but couldn't find the time."

"Maybe you're right." I noticed a short man sit at a table nearby. He wore wire-rimmed glasses and a Forty-Niners cap. His face was pale and smooth. He had a black mustache, but no sign of black hair—he could even be bald under that cap. He wore a green plaid shirt and khakis, and spoke rapid Italian to the waiter. Our eyes locked, and he quickly looked away. The cowled figure in Il Redentore and the straw-hat man in

Bellagio came to mind.

"Jack, do we know that man over there? The one alone, against the wall?"

Jack put his guidebook down and peered over his reading glasses. "I don't believe so. Why?"

"No reason."

"Maybe a little souvenir shopping would be fun this afternoon, take your mind off things—a small chandelier from Murano, a nice handbag from the leather district, a tapestry to keep away those San Francisco chills. . . ."

"I don't think we can sail to Murano Island in this rain, and we don't really need a chandelier. I like the handbag idea, but first we need to see San Zaccaria."

"I'd forgotten about Zaccaria."

"The church claims the saint's relics."

"The father of John the Baptist?" Jack looked up from his plate, doubt mapping his face. Sunday school had taught him well.

"They claim to. Do you recall the story? Zaccaria and Elizabeth were childless. He prayed for a child, and an angel appeared to him, answering his prayer."

"Wasn't Zaccaria the one who couldn't speak?"

I nodded. "An angel told Zaccaria that his elderly wife would have a son, and they were to name him John. But Zaccaria made a mistake—he doubted the angel."

"I remember—the angel struck him dumb because he doubted. Better not doubt, Maddie!"

I laughed and tasted my wine. It was cold and fruity with a crisp finish. "So for nine months he was speechless. When they took the baby to the temple to be circumcised and named, Zaccaria wrote on a tablet *His name is John* and his speech returned."

"He sounds like a very patient man, like someone I know intimately."

I raised my glass. "You certainly are patient, and you must be looking forward to Harry's Bar tonight."

Jack touched his glass to mine. "It's supposed to be the best dinner in Venice."

The pale fellow against the wall sipped his espresso, reading a rumpled copy of the *Herald Tribune*; he must speak English. But who was he? And what did he want?

I cut into a spinach ravioli and concentrated on the father of John the Baptist.

A side street opened into a quiet square, empty except for strutting pigeons and wandering tourists as we approached the vast five-tiered façade of San Zaccaria.

We paused in the back, our eyes adjusting to the light. Handel's *Messiah* played through a sound system. Soon I could see oil paintings hanging from dark walls. Sun shafted through clerestory windows, lighting particles of dancing dust, landing in the monks' choir. Fading frescoes ran along the apse.

Moving up and down the aisles, we searched for Zaccaria's tomb.

Finally, on the south wall, we found a sarcophagus with the dim letters *ZACCARIA*. Through a glass panel, we saw a body, or at least a death mask, of an old man. So here rested the father of John the Baptist, silent once again.

But there was another body resting below his. His letters read *ATHANASIUS*.

"That's one of the Church fathers—he wrote our creed." I studied the Latin description, and indeed, it said something about *Father of the Church*. "The man of certainty and the man of doubt, Athanasius and Zaccaria. How appropriate."

I knelt in a nearby pew. As I gazed upon the tombs, I prayed for healing, for understanding, for faith that I could be healed. "Only believe, and . . . be made well," Christ said. Because Zaccaria did not believe, he was stricken. If I could banish my doubts, I could banish the nightmares. Was that the answer?

Jack touched my arm and whispered he would wait outside. I nodded.

I considered the history of this shadowy church. In the ninth century, this community of monks served a town besieged by wars. The monks offered sanctuary and guidance. They gave men and women purpose and meaning, making sense of their lives.

And Zaccaria was an example of both faith and doubt. Like these monks, he lived through a somber time, waiting for that child foretold by the angel, wondering if his speech would return. Who was this son, John? "And the light shines in the darkness. . . . He was not the light, but came that he might bear witness of the light." John the Evangelist wrote of John the Baptist. The latter would claim, "I am the voice of one crying in the wilderness, 'Make straight the way of the Lord.' "

Touching my linen cloth, I prayed that I could see beyond the dark and into the light, that I could believe and be made well.

The rain had stopped. Outside, Jack was speaking to a slim girl with long blond hair, who turned quickly and walked toward San Marco. Her black leather skirt molded to her body. Her four-inch red heels clicked on the paving stones and she swung a large handbag.

Jack was too quick to explain.

"She gave me directions to the leather district, near the Rialto. She was the girl we saw at dinner at the hotel, remember? She's from New York and studying art. She said her dinner date last night was a no-show. How about that?" His face was flushed.

"How about that?" I felt a strange twinge. I slipped my arm through his, and he smiled at me.

"Are you jealous? She's young enough to be my daughter."

"Maybe just a little. She's awfully attractive."

But he *had* mapped out our route. We crossed Piazza San Marco and made our way along the narrow *calli*, finally coming to a dock where *treghetti* ferried passengers across the Grand Canal. But the service was closed due to flooding, so we rerouted, climbing onto boardwalks, finally reaching the Rialto Bridge.

The Rialto district, home to the first Venetian settlements along the Rio Alto, the upper river, was a major banking center in the Middle Ages. Over time, areas were cleared for produce markets; today craft and souvenir stalls thrive as well.

The rain stopped as we reached the other side of the canal and worked our way through the crowded bazaars selling tees, fans, glass, jewelry, lace, and leather goods. Melons, nectarines, tomatoes, and strawberries were displayed in neat rows in canvas stalls, and, just as I recalled, carts with miniature fountains offered fresh coconut.

We followed lanes opening onto pretty squares and bridges arching canals, past windows with masks, costumes, wigs, and satin capes. We roamed through the leather district, admiring handbags and jackets, rich brocaded fabrics and tasseled pillows, carved maple cupids and crèches. The paths were passable here, so close to the Grand Canal, but as we moved farther away, the waters deepened.

Suddenly, in the silence of the empty street, I heard light footsteps. I turned and caught sight of a brown robe disappearing around a corner.

"There's Cristoforo," I said, pointing. The height and gait were familiar. I was sure it was the friar with his distinctive Afro and the lumbering pace of a large man covering the ground easily.

"There must be hundreds of friars in Venice, Maddie, not to worry. Here, let's buy you a carved angel. They're Alpine maple."

The three-inch cupid played a violin. Jack was diverting me, I knew, but the angel was lovely and somehow comforting, far better than a handbag.

That evening we sipped sparkling wine in the hotel bar and gazed at the rising, churning sea. Bells rang six across the water, saluting the end of the day.

Venice was a charming puzzle; the city of Mardi Gras *festivale* continued its masquerade throughout the year. The streets meandered in a maze of silver and crystal, sculpture and paintings, jesters' cone hats and ladies' black lace fans. The churches were at once dark and light, holding centuries of art and prayer. Layer upon layer intertwined, weaving a tapestry of time and space.

Images of the mysterious and colorful city crowded in my mind. A cat curled in a corner, sickly and looking for a handout, too weak to cry. Through small doorways we glimpsed cloistered gardens, and beyond, workmen sanded floors.

We followed the signs—*San Marco per Ferraria–Accademia–Traghetto*— and found ourselves in silent dead ends, a bank clerk peering from a window above. Venice hid behind her many façades and blind corners, reflecting light like cut glass, and, like that Murano crystal, giving off a new color, a changing style, with every turn.

San Marco seemed far away and the little miracle church even farther. San Zaccaria rested in a corner of my mind, to be examined another day. But the pale face at lunch, the retreating brown robe, and the swinging hips of the blond had unnerved me.

Did my fears reflect my tortured mind, as facets of my soul spun into the dark through serpentine mazes, the floodwaters rising . . . or did I simply need a good night's sleep?

We found Harry's Bar on the Grand Canal near the Piazza San Marco. Pushing our way through the crowded bar, we climbed narrow stairs to the second floor restaurant and squeezed into a table near a window.

Jack lowered his large frame into the wooden chair. "If anyone sits next to us, they'll have to crawl over me." He unfolded his napkin in front of his face, arms tight against his chest, nearly knocking over a single pink rose in its glass vase. Other diners began to arrive, and soon chatter filled the room, drowning our conversation.

"What did you say?" I leaned forward.

"Don't look now, but our friar likes Harry's too. I thought I should warn you."

I glanced over Jack's shoulder. It was indeed Cristoforo. He looked away, motioning to the waiter.

"Can't you see he's following us?"

"Never mind, my princess," Jack teased. "I'm here to protect you. Anyway, he just left."

"Jack, let's send him back . . . to Rome . . . please. We can manage without him."

"Here comes our first course."

The service was efficient, and the flavors simple—fresh asparagus, sole in a flaky crust, sea bass with tomatoes and olives, creamy lemon tarts, and a cold bottle of Vigna Alpoggio, a Tuscan Chardonnay.

"To Venice." Jack raised his glass.

The wine soothed my nerves, and Cristoforo didn't seem so menacing. "To San Marco and San Zaccaria!"

"I've been thinking," Jack said, peering into his glass and inhaling the pungent bouquet, "about that Zaccaria. It was such a beginning to his fatherhood, losing his speech and all. And he had such a son—he *makes straight the way of the Lord.* You can never tell what the future may hold. Sometimes I wish I had spent more time with my boys, although I have to say I'm proud of how they turned out, in spite of the divorce."

I looked into his blue eyes—"bluer than a dachshund's belly

crawling in a blueberry patch," as both Jack and Jack Benny would say. I touched his curly, silver-streaked hair, and tried to imagine his younger days as father to three boys on visiting Saturdays. When I met Jack, the boys were nearly grown and living with their mother; it was a part his past I didn't share.

"You did the best you could," I said, "which is saying a lot for Jack Seymour. You know you did a great job with Justin."

"We had our moments."

"Remember the time Justin took out the car and ran into a cement wall, before he had his license?"

"I do recall that."

"And the time the principal warned us Justin was close to going on probation?"

"We were on a buying trip when that call came."

"And we worried about drugs, alcohol, and driving, not to mention casual sex and AIDS. But you were there, you were a father, and he knew you cared."

"I did care and I do care. You know he means the world to me."

"All of our sons have been a source of satisfaction."

"But poor Zaccaria—his son died so young."

"But he gave Elizabeth and Zaccaria *joy*. Maybe our boys will visit us when we're old and gray, in our rest home."

"They'll drive us to our doctors' appointments."

"Pick up our prescriptions."

"And buy our bran flakes."

As I crawled between the cool crisp sheets that night, church bells clanged, crying to the world not to forget—*recall, recall, recall* they rang. A light in the darkness . . . and I drifted to sleep halfway through my evening prayers . . . *Lighten our darkness, we beseech thee, O Lord. . . .*

Early Friday morning our bags were packed and stacked in the lobby. As

Jack worked on the hotel bill, I walked out to the quay and gazed at the mysterious city across the waters.

A hesitant morning sun parted black clouds rolling high above the ocher rooftops. Construction cranes intersected the sky, angling over steeples and domes. The canal water was high, swelling and crashing onto concrete stairs disappearing into the sea. Across the channel I could see Saint Mark's Square, where a stalwart bell tower stood opposite the lacy stone of the Doges Palace and the frescoed façade of San Marco.

How peaceful it all appeared, belying the hoards swarming the boardwalks and pushing through the dry places, elbowing and shouting, hungry for Venice's treasures—even belying the rising sea. Thunder rolled in the distance, and as the sun shot between the clouds, bells rang nine.

Venice had showed me a ray of light in the darkness. I would not forget silent Zaccaria.

But what would I find in Bologna?

Chapter Seven
Bologna

O send out thy light and thy truth,
that they may lead me, and bring me unto thy holy hill, and to thy dwelling.
Psalm 43:3

B rother Cristoforo met us on the hotel dock, his brown robes sprayed with salt water. He loaded our luggage onto the launch as though he knew no other life than the sea, humming the hymn, "God the Omnipotent! King who ordainest . . . ."

We motored through the maze of canals and wheeled our luggage to our car in the parking lot. Heading south on the A13, we crossed the broad agricultural valley of the River Po and turned west toward medieval Bologna, the city of Saint Dominic. Our friar driver whispered his morning office as he sped down the autostrada, his large hands wrapped tenderly around the steering wheel.

In the sixth century BC, Etruscans named the settlement Felsina. Conquering Romans renamed it Bononia, a name thought to come from *bona*, a word used for new Roman towns. Bononia changed hands over the years as Goths, Greeks, Lombards, Franks, and popes all conquered and in turn were conquered. In the twelfth century, the town became an independent city-state with thick fortified walls and home to one of the first universities in Europe.

We checked into a hotel that had known better days; sooty portraits covered the walls and voices echoed in the cavernous lobby.

"How long here?" Brother Cristoforo set down our bags.

"Two nights," Jack replied. "The rate's good and I can see why, but at least it's centrally located, right on the main square."

"I return on Sunday? I must report to the monastery here."

"Fine," Jack said and headed to the front desk to register.

Cristoforo turned to me. "You be careful?"

I nodded, puzzled, but before I had a chance to ask the friar what he meant, he handed the car keys to a porter and stepped out through the revolving doors.

As Cristoforo left, a woman entered. Her hair was tucked under a baseball cap; she wore horn-rimmed glasses and carried a briefcase. She looked familiar.

Jack joined me at the elevator as she approached the counter.

"Jack—who's that woman?" I glanced at his face for some hint of recognition.

"What woman?"

I turned and she was gone.

We followed a young man down long creaking corridors to our room.

Saturday morning *fortissimo* bells clanged outside our window.

I dragged myself out of the deep feather bed, draped with a graying velvet canopy of an unknown color, and dropped my feet to the warped flooring. Jack groaned and slipped into his robe. Sneezing and cursing the dust, he creaked his way along warped floorboards to the bath down the hall.

I pulled open faded maroon panels hanging on large rings and unlatched the tall window to let in fresh air. Leaning on the peeling sill, I stared at the piazza. Bright sun burned on russet stone as the cathedral bells continued to clang from the opposite side of the square. *Bologna.*

The night had been filled with Mollie. I chased her through the dark, through blinding rain. I followed her down strange alleys, trying to see through my tightly closed lids. I waded through rising waters as masked faces rose between us, cat-eyes knowing and not telling, laughing at me, laughing at the joke of living.

Flippancy, I thought, as I stared at the square, remembering my night. How painful that slick façade was, smooth outside and eating away inside, pretty surfaces covering up inner rot. Was that what I learned in Venice? The silence of Zaccaria in the city of masquerade—the oiled surfaces of form and color—the glittering vaults of heavenly fantasy? Was any of it real?

Today, real sun baked the real square, burning my dreams, and I looked forward to a good walk. It was, after all, our first time in Bologna.

The Basilica di San Domenico was on Father Rinaldi's list, and we mapped our route carefully. The Dominicans had played a major role in Western thought—was this why Father Rinaldi chose San Domenico?

We walked through porticoes of tawny stone, past open stalls of fruit and vegetables shaded by awnings, to the thirteenth-century basilica. The ocher façade and rose window faced a neat cobblestone square. Stepping inside, we found Dominic's marble chapel off the south aisle, his head resting in an ornate glass reliquary under a suspended Michelangelo angel. Four cherubim in the ceiling dangled altar lamps from long cords.

Dominic Guzman was born in Spain around 1170. Before his birth, his mother dreamed "she bore a dog in her womb and that it broke away from her with a burning torch in its mouth wherewith it set the world aflame." The dog became the symbol of the Dominican Order and the source of its name, *Domini canes*, "the watchdogs of the Lord."

A brilliant and effective priest, Dominic was troubled by the laxity of many religious orders and the growth of the Albigensian heresy in southern France. He founded the Order of Preachers, disciplined monks who traveled, preaching, converting, and establishing teaching communities throughout Italy, France, and Spain. It is said his preaching converted one hundred thousand people in Lombardy alone. He developed the rosary, prayer beads that kept track of meditations on the life of Christ and requests to Mary for intercession. The first meeting of the Dominicans was in Bologna, and it was in Bologna where Dominic died.

We sat in a pew in the massive nave, near Dominic's relics off the southern aisle. Monks chanted the rosary nearby, some wandering about, some kneeling. Scaffolding encased the dome behind a side altar, and the singing of the monks merged with the hammering in the back, a curious counterpoint of two restorations, one of spirit and one of matter.

I prayed my own *Hail Mary, full of grace, blessed art thou among women and blessed is the fruit of thy womb, Jesus.* Once again, I asked for healing, for rest, for peace.

They say Dominic prayed unceasingly, as Saint Paul tells us to do. Perhaps he had one foot in each world, one in heaven and one on earth.

Maybe the worlds were the same; maybe prayer opened a door to heaven here and now, inviting God to enter our world, our bodies. *Teach me to pray, Lord. Open my eyes.*

What was the significance of Dominic in my quest? Prayer? Heresy? Rosaries?

We purchased a rosary in the gift shop—white glass beads strung between silver roses and a silver crucifix—and headed back.

As we turned up a narrow side street to our hotel entrance, we saw a crowd queuing to enter a church on the opposite side of the road. Tour buses blocked traffic. I stared at the commotion, then looked at Jack, who was examining the map. "What's happening here?" I asked.

"It must be Saint Peter's Cathedral," Jack said. "We didn't plan a visit, but shall we check it out?" The broad façade, newly painted, was nearly flush with the sidewalk and blended in with the buildings on either side. We hadn't noticed it when we had set out earlier.

We squeezed through the crowd, picked up a leaflet from a table by the door, and stared at the massive, brightly lit nave.

Jack looked over the packed congregation. "A sign outside said something about a weeklong 'congress'."

"What feast day is it? Ascension was two days ago." I recalled that Bologna, like Venice, was famous for its celebration of the Ascension, which continued for eight days. "It must be the Ascension Festival of Mary. See the icon? I think they brought it from a shrine somewhere outside of town."

More than a thousand pilgrims sang hymns and chanted prayers, honoring an icon of the Virgin and Child on the high altar.

"It's said to be a miraculous image." I scanned the leaflet. "Every Ascension Day since the early fifteenth century, the Bolognese carry the icon through a two-mile colonnade down the hill to this church."

The singing soared through the vaults.

Jack shook his head in amazement. "Such a crowd! I wouldn't have believed it. Not today, not in 1997—even in Italy."

"Many believe Saint Luke painted it."

"That *would* be old. How did it get here?"

"A pilgrim brought it from Constantinople, and the Bolognese built a hermitage to enshrine it."

"Let's find a seat," Jack said, "but where? There seems to be standing room only."

"Jack, look. . . ."

Wheelchairs rolled up the center aisle toward the altar, carrying the sick and the crippled, pushed by nuns in white robes and caps. We followed and found seats far to the side, but close to the icon.

I knelt and gazed at this gentle and compassionate rendering of the mother of Jesus. She had a long, delicate nose and the dark hair and skin of an Eastern Mediterranean people. The icon was plated with silver; only her mysterious face and her child could be seen. Her large almond eyes enclosed me, absorbing my anguish. She knew suffering—she knew me.

Hail Mary, full of grace, the Lord is with thee. . . . Her femaleness, her motherhood comforted me.

Images of my journey appeared in my mind: the Madonna in Rome's Maria Maggiore and her crèche resting beneath the high altar, a homely and comforting beginning; Prassede and Pudenziana, the sisters who loved so, their hands bloody with the bodies of their fellow Christians; Agnes, the young martyr buried in the catacombs made holy by her blood. I saw Augustine, water dripping from his white baptismal robe, stepping from the pool in the candlelight of Easter Eve, and Zaccaria's silent tomb, challenging my doubt. I thought of Father Rinaldi and the wine-blood spilled on the altar of his own death, a double sacrifice offered.

And here was the mother of the Christ, the mother of the crucified one, the sacrificed one. She knew the agony of losing a child. Today her grief was mine and mine hers, for Christ's suffering enclosed mine. Was she nearby when my child died?

Holy Mary, Mother of God, pray for us sinners now and at the hour of our death. . . .

I clutched my rosary, entangled in my relic-cloth, and appreciated Dominic. Mary, my new mother-sister, wove through my soul, her love purging my self-pity. She was the sacred feminine, the new Eve, the mother of us all. I would not forget her.

Jack wrapped an arm around my shaking shoulders and I wiped my eyes, relief surging through me. We made our way through side doors where buses waited and nuns helped the sick into the church.

Jack pointed to a bus. "There's our friar."

Brother Cristoforo stood behind a wheelchair as he waited for the bus doors to open. He looked around, saw us, and nodded as we approached. "I often help the hospice here. Many sick, many need help."

The doors folded open, and in one graceful motion, Cristoforo lifted a slumped boy out of his chair and carried him up the steps. What hymn was the friar humming? "Sing of Mary, pure and lowly. . . ."

We squeezed into a corner table at a local trattoria and ordered turbot with potatoes, grilled vegetables, and porcini mushrooms. The waiter poured a fruity Chianti.

I passed Jack toasts topped with garlicky tapenade. "So what do you think about Dominic and his purging the faith of heresy?"

"Preaching isn't exactly purging."

"The Dominicans enforced the Spanish Inquisition, but that was after Dominic's time."

"That sounds like purging, all right. Maybe Dominic wouldn't have gone that far."

I nodded. "Institutions don't always remain true to the founder's purpose."

Our dinner arrived. Green, yellow, and red sweet peppers fanned on a plate with darker slices of eggplant. White filets of fish nestled in beds of mushrooms.

I tasted the eggplant, glistening in olive oil. "Wow."

Jack tried the turbot. "Excellent."

"This *is* good. What's the herb in the vegetables?"

"Savory, I think. Or something like it. And the porcinis are interesting with the fish." He paused, tasting the different flavors, and sipped his wine. "So did Dominic go too far? Man can't seem to get it right."

"You can say that again. The Dominicans believed they taught the truth. They saved souls by fighting heresy. But some used force, denying free will."

"And here's to free will. . . ." Jack raised his glass of Brunello. "May I always be free to choose my reds and my whites."

Our glasses touched. "But you agree," I said, "that each of us must decide, in the end."

"Decide?"

"Decide what is true and what is false. Some say there are no truths, no blacks, no whites—only grays—or that the truth changes with one's own perspective, one's journey."

"That's rubbish." Jack spoke as though analyzing a contract. "An apple is an apple, and an orange is an orange. You know that. Even these gray-area people know that. We descend the stairs or ride the elevator—

instead of jumping—because we know, and I mean *know*, the truth of gravity. There are many truths that everyone accepts as true in the absolute sense, even if they don't understand them. How else could they function from day to day?"

"So what about belief in God, or the Christian creeds? Are they objectively true?"

"Again, either God exists or he doesn't. I don't see where my own belief or unbelief will make any difference as to his existence, or lack thereof. The problem lies in my recognizing and accepting the truth. And that is where, sometimes, an educated guess must be made, as we do every day in other areas of our lives."

"You're talking about taking a leap of faith?"

"You could call it that." He swirled his wine, watching the legs form on the insides of the glass.

"So each of us, using our education and experience, seek the truth."

"My mother would have included the guidance of the Holy Spirit."

"I would agree with her." I knew Gertrude for only a year before she died. She was tiny and bent, but she had a fierce spirit. She was what they called a "do-gooder." A devout Methodist, she ran the local PTA, collected clothing for the poorer children, organized food drives, and was awarded Mother of the Year. Jack had taken me to Oakland's Rose Garden and proudly pointed out her name on a plaque. "She was an amazing woman."

Jack was studying the dessert menu.

"My mother?" He looked up. "She was that all right. I think she taught me that work could be satisfying. Now Maddie, did you notice what they have for dessert?"

I glanced at the list. "Profiteroles. Oh my." I leaned toward my husband, swirling my wine. "Your mother believed in the absolute nature of truth."

"She did and tried to explain it to me many times. She would say truth exists apart from us. It's our understanding of the truth that changes. I never fully grasped the concept until I studied law."

"The redefining of experience?"

He sighed. "Witnesses who color the truth. What can you do if you can't prove perjury?"

"Like historians who reinvent the past, angling it to suit their purposes. They are, to my mind, also guilty of perjury."

"So, with regards to heresy and free will . . ."

He wanted to tie the problem in a neat package, as though

presenting a summary to clients.

The waiter hovered, and I glanced again at the menu. The lemon tart looked good too, but I knew I should settle for a decaf coffee. My slacks seemed to be shrinking.

"If I understand it right," Jack continued, pouring the last of the wine, "your fourth-century fellows—what were their names—Ambrose and Augustine? They thought they could define the *true* Christian doctrine. Dominic too. They all saw their view of the truth seriously threatened by heresy and thus . . . their Church threatened. So they preached their truth to all, at times forcing belief. Hence religious wars."

"Today Christians must feel equally threatened."

"I'm sure. They've been marginalized considerably by secular culture. Then there's the rise of fundamentalism in the Near East."

"So what are you having?" I hoped he would choose. "We could share."

"Profiteroles."

"Me too . . . and decaf. Can we divide an order?"

Jack shook his head. "Not this time—the truth is, I'd like my own."

That night I checked my e-mail. Justin! I arrowed the *Read* button, and up flashed my son's letter, written hours before, an electronic feat that continued to delight me.

Hi Mom,

My youth center project came through! We begin design this fall, construction next spring. A real feather in my cap! I know how you feel about Lisa Jane and me living together, but we feel that it is better to find out now if we are compatible. Better now than later, right? Don't worry, Mom, it will be okay.

Love, Justin

The wine from dinner inspired and empowered me to solve the world's problems, especially Justin's. Of course, his problem was that he didn't know he had one.

Dear Justin,

Congratulations! That's quite a coup (the youth center).

Don't treat your relationship with Lisa Jane lightly. Sex is a serious business, not a tryout for compatibility. Nor a sport. Sex is the fruit of commitment. Commitment is the fruit of love.

Love, Mom

P.S. How about a Rocky Mountain wedding? Buy her a ring.

I read it through and clicked *Send Mail* before I lost my nerve.

I placed my rosary alongside my prayer book on the nightstand, rested the dried palms between the onionskin pages, and stood my San Pietro figurine nearby. We had bought a small icon of the Madonna di San Luca, and I leaned it against the wall next to Peter, the silver edges gleaming in the lamplight, the dark almond eyes reassuring.

Jack came out of the bath and crawled into bed. I said a quick bedtime prayer and folded into his arms, sinking into the deep feather bed, the day's sun warm beneath my skin.

Tomorrow, Florence. I wondered what Saint Francis would tell me, the author of the *Canticle of the Sun*, the lover of all creation. But I knew he was a man of fasting and penitence, as well as joy. Florence was the door to Francis country, and we would be staying in a monastery.

We would arrive on Ascension Sunday, nearly two weeks into my pilgrimage.

Chapter Eight
Firenze

In his hand are all the corners of the earth;
and the strength of the hills is his also.
Psalm 95:4

Cristoforo took the A1 south to Florence, through forests and tunnels, and into the green hills of Tuscany.

"Firenze!" The friar sighed wistfully as he turned onto another highway. "We are near."

We followed an outer ring road to the Firenze Sud exit, crossed the Arno, and ascended into the hills, passing Renaissance villas hidden behind stone walls and glimpsing lush gardens through iron gates. Beyond the village of San Domenico, we turned up a narrow drive surrounded by manicured gardens—hedged squares of grass, statuary, and fountains—and pulled up to the creamy stone façade of Villa San Michele, high above Florence.

A sixteenth-century Franciscan monastery, Villa San Michele had seen successive owners. An arched portico shaded the entrance, flanked by giant pots of sunflowers.

Cristoforo braked and the tires screeched. He opened our doors and flung out his arms. "*Bene, bene, signori.* We are here, in Firenze, Florence—the city of greatness, the city of *santi*, the city of my brothers." He looked up the hill. "I have friends in Fiesole, the village up the hill."

"Good." Jack helped me out of the car.

"You be okay?" the friar asked as he rubbed his large hands together. "I see you tomorrow? You be careful?"

"Of course, Cristoforo." Jack looked worried. He glanced at me, then back at the friar.

The friar shouldered his pack. "At five o'clock I go to prayers in Fiesole cathedral, if you need me." He disappeared up a rocky path into the trees.

I too wondered what worried him. Did he share my fears? Maybe someone really *was* following us, and I wasn't imagining things.

"Now you can sleep in a monk's cell." Jack looked up at the Michelangelo façade with its simple panel insets. "I believe this building's protected by the government."

"It looks like the original Renaissance façade."

"As I recall, historic landmarks can't be modified—they can only restore what's here. We stayed in Florence on our buying trip and taxied up here for cocktails, remember?"

"Barely." We had drinks with a swarthy wine broker who spoke little English and seemed more interested in me than in Jack's deal. I was both flustered and flattered.

Bells rang noon as we stepped into the lobby, once the chapel. A stone altar with an empty tabernacle filled the small apse, and a wooden confessional and marble sarcophagus stood in side bays. The reception counter lined the right side of the nave.

I was startled and a bit unnerved to see a once-holy place turned into a lobby, and I recalled Christ throwing the moneychangers out of the temple. Then I remembered why churches were deconsecrated. Church buildings were, in the end, merely matter, consecrated by God through his Church. Even so, I was uncomfortable with the business of the clerks, the computer screens, and the phones. Centuries of prayers and countless Eucharists had been offered in this space.

A young porter jangled his keys and motioned to us to follow.

"I show you around," he said, "before you go to the room?"

"*Si*," Jack said, "*bene*."

We followed him through a TV lounge, once the sacristy, crossed a glassed-in dining room, once the cloister, and entered the bar, once the refectory, where a restored *Last Supper* covered the end wall. Other frescoes had survived time and war—washed-out figures of ocher and blue, partial saints and sinners, their stories half hidden. The porter continued outside to a sun-drenched loggia running the length of the villa, and through the loggia's gentle arches we gazed down to Florence's steeples and towers. Linen-covered tables had been set for lunch; a shiny baby grand stood next to a sideboard stocked with liquors, lemons, oranges, olives, and pistachio nuts.

Like Villa d'Este, Villa San Michele was a startling contrast to its past—here friars once prayed their offices, walking the loggia in the silence of the mountain. But the peace had remained.

100

We followed a gravel path through a garden of lemon trees and white umbrellas, sling chairs, and wrought-iron tables tilting in the grass, through Roman ruins—crumbling walls, fountains, and pillars—and under an arbor of climbing jasmine. Above the gardens, a swimming pool had been terraced out of the mountainside.

"It's so beautiful," I said, turning to gaze at the city far below. Florence's red roofs burned in a warm haze. "I think I can see the *duomo*."

"And now I take you to your room." The porter smiled with satisfaction as he led us back to the villa.

We climbed narrow stone stairs, and the porter opened a heavy door with a massive iron key. The room, about eight-by-ten, faced south, with tall windows opening to the broad sky and the valley below. Our luggage was stacked in the corner.

"*Bene?*" The porter smiled.

"*Bene, bene . . . molto bene.*" Jack said, staring. "This sure beats staying in town."

"It's like being on the edge of the world," I said, "or flying with the birds."

We unpacked, then lunched on the loggia—melon and prosciutto, green salads with tuna carpaccio—and took the path up the hill to the village.

As we climbed, I recalled Fiesole's story. Commanding the hilltop above the swampy Arno valley as early as the sixth century BC, the town was a strategic crossroads for the Etruscans. Around 80 BC the Romans settled military veterans here and called it Faesulae; later some of the Faesulae residents moved to the valley where they founded Florence. Florence grew as Fiesole declined.

We reached the summit and descended through Fiesole's back streets and neat villas to the town square, the Piazza Mino, once the Roman forum. Bells rang five o'clock as we entered the cathedral on the opposite side of the piazza.

This Ascension Sunday a small congregation had gathered for afternoon prayers in the medieval basilica, the air thick with roses and incense. Roman columns led to a raised chancel where the domed apse glimmered with gold and red frescoes; above the high altar a gilded Madonna and Child was flanked by Saint Peter and Saint Romolus, Fiesole's bishop and patron saint. Romolus's relics lay in the crypt.

Two priests and three acolytes entered from the north aisle, took their places at a modern altar at the head of the nave, and led the antiphonal chanting of the Psalms.

As we listened to the prayers weave through the vaults, I prayed my thanksgivings for this holy day, this day of Christ's return to heaven. I prayed that I might ascend too, that through his community of believers, his body the Church, I might be reborn. At that moment, in this quiet cathedral, with this small group of faithful, I was confident I could. I held my altar cloth, giving thanks once again for Father Rinaldi. I sensed I was close to something important, here in the land of Francis, close to what my old priest wanted for me. I would open my heart—I would not let fear steal my focus.

Cristoforo knelt in a side pew, his head bowed, his rosary hanging from his thick hands. As the service concluded, he joined us.

"Welcome, *Signori*," he said. "You like to see my *convento*?"

I looked at Jack. We nodded.

The friar led us up a steep drive to the Convento di San Francesco, where a few humble buildings lined a square of weedy grass. A plaque, printed in English capitals and flanked by two flags, one American and one Italian, was embedded in a wall:

CHURCH AND CONVENT OF SAN FRANCISCO

HERE STOOD THE CITY'S ANCIENT FORTRESS, WHICH
WAS DESTROYED BY FLORENTINES IN 1010. LATER AN
ORATORY ROSE ON THIS SITE. IT WAS FOLLOWED BY
A CONVENT OF NUNS, WHICH IN 1407 WAS TAKEN
OVER BY FRANCISCAN MONKS, WHO ENLARGED AND
ENRICHED THE CHURCH.
THE LAST RESTORATION WAS IN 1905.

We entered the church through a low doorway. Twelve friars knelt in a small choir, singing the last of vespers. Soon they made the Sign of the Cross and processed out. Tourists entered, wandered about, pointing to paintings in vivid blues, reds, and golds, and exited through the north aisle to a museum. A lone tourist stood near a group, his head down, reading a guidebook. He was balding and pale with wire-rimmed glasses.

I looked for Jack, who was following the friar out the door.

Cristoforo led us outside to a broad promontory overlooking Florence where an iron cross stood silhouetted against the sky.

Jack whistled through his teeth. "What a piece of real estate."

Cristoforo nodded. "We keep the best for God."

"I guess so."

"Jack . . . ," I whispered, "one of the tourists in the chapel . . . looks like the man I saw in Cernobbio and maybe Bellagio."

"What?" the friar asked, overhearing me.

"I didn't tell you, Cristoforo. Jack thinks I'm imagining things."

Jack sighed and turned to the friar. "Maddie's been a little on edge lately. Don't worry about it."

Cristoforo glanced at me, then at Jack, as though he wondered whom to believe.

Jack took my hand. "Let's go back to the hotel. It's after six and I'd like a swim before dinner."

"I see you later, *Signori*," Cristoforo said, bowing.

I looked back and waved, but I could not read his face.

We took the gravel path up to the sun-warmed pool and settled in lounge chairs under white umbrellas, a waterfall cascading behind us. I stepped into the cool water and swam slowly, glancing up through the lacy leaves of an overhanging olive tree to bits of blue sky. I slipped in and out of shade, from shallows to depths and back again, raising my face to the sun and absorbing its last rays. I would ignore the pale man in the chapel. Allowing my muscle memory to guide me through the water, I glided into a world of cloisters and country churches, cobbled lanes and ocher towns in green valleys.

I toweled off and lay on the lounge chair. Jack dozed, his hands clasped on his chest, his book having fallen in the grass. Breathing in the fresh evening air, I gazed over Florence. Terra cotta roofs clustered around the cathedral and golden domes caught the last of the sun. Puffy clouds drifted across the sky.

I stretched, feeling the warm ache of exercise. Far below, a soccer stadium's giant lamps, bright against the approaching dusk, overpowered the *duomo*. With all of our advances, we were closer to the

Roman world of games than the Renaissance world of art and spirit.

I understood how the body could eclipse the soul. Maybe the monastics were right.

We dined on the loggia as the sun set and lights appeared in the valley. A tuxedoed pianist played Broadway tunes, his bushy head bent low over the ivory keys, his fingers dancing. A waiter poured champagne and we toasted Florence.

What would this artistic city in the land of Saint Francis grant us these two days? I saw no Cristoforo on the loggia, no suspicious pale face with glasses, no ingénue with long hair. With my cloth in my bag, secure on my lap, what could touch me? And Saint Francis! He was such a happy fool, a saintly beggar, calling himself the *jongleur*—a troubadour/juggler—of God. He would set fire to my demons, burning them to ash with the love of Christ.

We feasted on Tuscan vegetable soup, thick and fragrant, made from pureed tomatoes and bread, then artichokes carefully quartered and sautéed in pungent olive oil, and finally *bistecca Fiorentina* with sweetly intense rosemary.

"Jack," I said, "do you think Cristoforo is guarding us?" While at first I suspected the dark friar of wanting the cloth for himself, his clear concern for us had changed my mind. His worry was genuine, and I wondered why.

"I thought that might be the case, but I didn't want to mention it, to add to your fears. He could be, but from what or whom?"

"Maybe he's protecting the cloth. Should I lock it up?"

"Why would he want to protect the cloth? Come on, Maddie, it's only a piece of linen."

I didn't lock up the linen, deciding my fears were unfounded. The serious friar was simply being attentive to two hapless Americans who had known his beloved Father Rinaldi. Maybe he saw the trip as a way of giving something back to the priest who saved him from the streets of Alexandria. And Sister Agnes *had* told him to take care of us.

Early Monday morning, the breakfast buffet was laid out in the cloister: melon, mozzarella balls bobbing in water, Tuscan smoked meats, bowls of strawberries, kiwi, and pineapple, yogurt cups, pitchers of blood-orange, apple, and pineapple juice, crusty bread, croissants, and pastries. I read the labels of twelve kinds of honey, lost in indecision; we loaded our plates and found a table on the loggia. The May sun teased through the crisp morning air, promising a warm spring day.

I gazed down to Florence's red roofs peeking through the morning mist. A long green band, the River Arno, snaked through the valley, heading west to the Mediterranean. Such a location on such a river had produced the great mercantile banking houses of this Renaissance crossroads.

The Romans called the settlement *Florentia*—flourishing—and laid out their forums, temples, baths, arenas, and straight streets, including the Via Flamina to Rome. Merchants from Rome and the East introduced exotic spices and dyes. They also introduced Christianity, so when Ambrose of Milan visited in 393, he found a sizable Christian community.

But by the Middle Ages, family feuds and inter-city wars had bloodied Florence. Searching for civil order through a renaissance of cultural ideals, Florentines looked to ancient Rome. They did not doubt their own beliefs, but sought a rebirth of the Christian way, an enlightenment, a new Jerusalem.

Giotto painted with classical realism, breaking away from the medieval icon style, using pigments from eastern dies in his wall frescoes. The devout Michelangelo sculpted muscular figures, celebrating God's creation.

Today, we would visit Florence, and tomorrow, Cortona, Assisi, and La Verna. Would I too experience a renaissance?

The hotel shuttle dropped us off in the center of town, and we headed for the Franciscan Basilica di Santa Croce.

We followed the map as we walked toward the river. Crossing the broad Piazza della Signoria, we passed the Uffizi galleries, and continued to another huge square bordered by houses and leather factories. Pigeons fluttered about tourists who scattered crumbs and posed for pictures. On the far side of the square, we climbed the broad steps to the white façade of Santa Croce and paused before the giant bronze doors. I looked back over the piazza as Jack focused his camera.

"Do you remember," I said as he clicked, "poor young Lucy in Forester's novel *Room with a View?* She saw that terrible knife fight in the piazza?"

"I recall the movie. She was so innocent, so sweet."

"She desperately wanted to know the world, the real world she thought was out there. She fainted when she saw the duel."

"The real world can be ugly."

We entered the thirteenth-century Santa Croce. In 1221 Franciscans took over a local oratory in order to serve the textile community. As Florence grew in wealth, families financed the present basilica by purchasing patron chapels for their family burials.

Giant columns led to an apse of carved wood and jeweled stained glass.

"It doesn't seem very Franciscan," Jack said. "Even the gravestones covering the floor are polished." He scanned his guide. "There once were frescoes and a monks' choir. Some of the frescoes have been restored in the transept chapels."

I pointed to etchings in a stone plaque. "Rossini, Michelangelo, Galileo. What would simple Francis have said?"

"He would have liked the preaching space. You said it was built to hold the crowds, and it sure is."

Jack dropped coins in a metal box, lighting the pinks, blues, and golds of the chapel walls. Guides led groups from tomb to fresco, lecturing on Renaissance technique. We followed tourists out to a sacristy museum, where Francis's robe of faded brown sacking and his rope belt were displayed behind glass. Beyond the sacristy, a leather factory produced handbags and wallets—cutting, stitching, and imprinting. I noticed a tall, dark monk whispering to another at the end of a worktable. I couldn't hear, but they seemed to be arguing.

"There's Cristoforo," I whispered.

"He's a Franciscan, Maddie, and this is a Franciscan community."

"True, but I wish he wasn't following us."

Jack frowned. "Do you want to see the famous Fra Angelicos before we find a lunch place?"

"Sure." I knew he was diverting me, but Fra Angelico and his

106

followers were artists I had always admired. There were both rustic innocence and holy glory in their work, pulling one into a world that bridged heaven and earth.

"And after, let's go to the Excelsior for lunch—on the river."

We crossed town to the San Marco Convent, now museum, and toured the cells, the pastel frescoes of Christ's life filling our senses.

"They were painted by the brothers themselves," I said.

"You can sort of see God shining through the paint." Jack stood back and scratched his chin. "Maybe we should do a few walls like this at home—what do you think?"

"I think you are trying to make me feel better—and it's working."

We wandered from cell to cell, down frescoed corridors, and I pictured those days, the life of those monks. I found it difficult to imagine a time so foreign to our own world—the searing belief, the turmoil and intrigue, each Florentine taking a deadly side. But perhaps we were close to such a time, when believers must take a stand.

I turned to Jack. "Savonarola was prior here."

"Wasn't he the one who burned books?" He pulled out his guidebook.

"What does it say about him? He's been a pretty controversial figure lately."

Jack adjusted his reading glasses. "In the fifteenth century, San Marco's prior, Girolamo Savonarola, lit a 'bonfire of vanities,' burning books, art, and costumes, in the Piazza di Signoria. He considered them heretical."

"I wonder if they were." Recent scholarship claimed that the objects burned were mostly pornographic.

"The truth question again." Jack gazed through a window to the cloister below.

I nodded. "I believe Savonarola saw the future, some kind of doom, perhaps the Apocalypse, the Second Coming, the Last Judgment, and he worried for his people."

We left San Marco and headed toward the river for lunch.

Jack had latched on to the problem of the Renaissance prior. "It seems to me that Savonarola should have worried more about their souls than their bodies—his area of responsibility, as it were."

I smiled. "But the lusts of the flesh corrupt the life of the spirit, an idea Christianity inherited from Jewish and Roman thought." I supposed the opposite was true as well; a damaged soul could hurt one's body. Was that the cause of my nightmares?

Maneuvering through the crowds, we crossed the cathedral square. Jack checked street names against the map. "Control of the body is necessary; I can see that." He pointed ahead. "I think this road takes us to the river and our lunch place."

"I'm glad—I'm famished."

He slipped the map into his pocket. "It's an interesting problem, really. Not all passion is desirable. We sometimes overstep boundaries. We can't seem to help it, and hence the law."

"Manners are a kind of law too."

"Like keeping your elbows off the table?"

"Which gives others space to dine." Did families even dine together anymore?

"Or chewing with an open mouth, revealing a whole lot more than I want to see."

"I'll say. Or hog the conversation. Or hog anything." I recalled the many business dinners we had attended over the years; the many occasions that taught one how to behave at table—speaking quietly to one's neighbor, passing dishes to the left, which fork to use. The rules made the evening more enjoyable for everyone.

"Here we are," Jack said as he opened the hotel door for me. "I recall they make a good club sandwich. We can practice our manners."

The Excelsior bar was decorated in what Jack called modern Victorian, dark but comfortable with large potted palms, Oriental rugs, and leather swivel chairs, a reminder of the English in Florence. The waiter brought us club sandwiches, sparkling water, and cappuccinos. As we ate, our napkins unfolded properly on our laps, a young girl approached me and handed me a rose.

"Why thank you," I said.

"You go to San Miniato?" she asked. Dark curls framed an oval face, black eyes, and long lashes. She wore a blue jumper with a white frilly blouse.

"San Miniato?" I looked about the room for her mother.

"*Si*, it is very beautiful. We visited today."

"Where is this San Miniato?"

"Across the river," she said, nodding.

I turned to Jack and smiled, then slipped the flower into the bouquet on the table.

When I looked for her, she was gone. She reminded me of the child in Venice who suggested the miracle church. Where had these children come from?

"She disappeared," I said to Jack.

"Sorry, I was reading the wine list."

"Let's look up San Miniato. Maybe we can walk there."

With some reluctance, he turned to the index of his guidebook. "We were planning a little wine browsing this afternoon."

"Can't we do both?"

He looked at his watch. "I'm thinking of sending a few cases home if I can find something good. But the shops won't be open for another hour anyway." He ran his finger down the list and flipped to the page. "I think we can walk. It's a good mile from here, but the church might be worth it. It's eleventh-century, built over the grave of third-century Saint Minus. There seems to be a pattern—medieval churches built over martyrs' graves, earlier oratories."

"Minus?" I had never heard of a Saint Minus. "Do they say who he was?"

"Let's see—he was martyred by Emperor Decius. He survived the lions in the arena, then beheaded. He carried his head to this hilltop. How's that for miracles?"

"Thank you," I said, kissing him. "Maybe we'll find some great wine buys afterwards."

The waiter smiled as he approached and handed Jack the check.

We crossed the Ponte Vecchio. The original Roman bridge had been replaced by tanners, the tanners' bridge replaced by butchers, then replaced by jewelers. Halfway across, we paused to take pictures. Below us, in the misty Florentine light, the Arno rolled under more bridges of arching stone.

Reaching the shore, we turned left and followed the river past the Ponte alle Grazie to the Piazza Poggi. From there a winding path led us to the broad Piazzale Michelangiolo. We continued up wide stairs to a second viewing terrace. In the distance amber domes rose over terra cotta roofs; the Ponte Vecchio with its jumble of old houses bridged the silty river.

Behind us presided the Basilica di San Miniato, with its Romanesque façade of green-and-white marble. We climbed to the open doors and entered the half-light as distant voices chanted through the damp air; the singing seemed to come from the far end of the massive frescoed nave.

The high altar was curiously enclosed with a wrought-iron railing.

"Like a church within a church," I said.

Jack had already looked it up. "It's called the Chapel of the Crucifix. It once housed a miraculous crucifix that's been removed to San Trinità."

"San Trinità?" I made a mental note.

Staircases ascended on each side of the altar-chapel to a raised chancel, reminding me of Fiesole's cathedral. A second set of stairs curved down to the crypt.

We followed the somber chanting to the crypt, where seven white-robed monks knelt before an altar. They sang the last of the afternoon Psalms, and we joined them in the concluding *Amen*.

I peered into the dim light. San Miniato's relics rested under the crypt altar, sanctifying the high altar above. A red candle burned next to the tabernacle. All but one of the monks processed out; the lone one remained kneeling, his head in his hands. I pulled out my linen and let the prayers of the centuries settle upon me.

I prayed for peace, the peace of the heart, *the peace that passeth all understanding*, for indeed, it was un-understandable, incomprehensible, this peace of God. A war waged within me, one side punishing the other for a deed I could not undo, a loss I could not regain. I wanted to end the war, to banish the combatants, to be left only with Christ's peace. We kill each other on the battlefield, defending or invading. We kill each other at home with neglect or abuse. We kill our own selves with warring wills doing battle in our hearts. *Lord, banish my will and grow your peace in my heart—for Mollie.*

A bell rang, seeming far away, muted by the stone. I rose to find Jack waiting outside on the terrace in the translucent light, aiming and focusing. Then silently, in the still air of the late afternoon, we descended the hill a different route, down wide straight stairs bordered with cypresses and the Stations of the Cross.

We continued to the river, and browsed wine shops on the way to the *duomo* piazza. There we waited in the shade of the bell tower for our hotel shuttle, weary.

Sipping welcome martinis, dry, straight up with a twist, we sat on the loggia and gazed upon Florence. We dined on cannelloni, curried shrimp, and broiled fish as the moon emerged from behind a cloud.

I mopped a pool of olive oil with a last bit of bread.

"We never went into an art museum, and we were in Florence," Jack said.

"An art-filled city." I smiled. It did seem strange.

"But there was plenty of art in the churches, I would say." Jack swirled his wine, a translucent ruby red.

I paused, pondering the question of art. "Art is religious in a way, as an expression of man's spirit. It's fitting that such expressions should be used by the Church and would be an artist's highest calling."

"I read Michelangelo was a devout Christian."

I nodded and gazed down to the Florentine lights. "And he reflected the Christian view of creation—the beauty and sanctity of the human body, the promise of salvation and eternal life."

"Today's sculptures aren't always so beautiful."

I recalled an outdoor exhibit of fat naked women in obscene postures with men with enlarged genitals. The style reminded me of primitive tribal works, where fertility and orgiastic pleasure were central themes. "Art does indeed reflect the times. Our world is cynical and despairing, often bestial."

We sat in the quiet of the evening, each roaming through our own thoughts.

Jack broke the silence. "But churches are more than art—they go beyond."

"They do. They participate in reality—they're not only reflections or expressions. In the mass, sacrifice is realized. Redemption is active. Things happen that change people in real time."

"And you've often said that you sensed the history of the particular church as well."

"All those prayers over the years. It's encouraging really, as though I am invited to share my belief with Christians throughout time . . . and space, too."

111

Jack looked pensive. "It seems today God is farther away than he was in the past."

"That's sad if true. But God meets us where we are, if we search for him. We must open the door first, I guess, to enter his world and allow him into ours. And sometimes great art helps us do that."

Jack speared a small square of white fish. "I don't have much artistic knowledge, I'm afraid. But I know what I like."

"And what do you like?" I smiled. Jack had purchased a few paintings over the years and his choice generally reflected our travels—a garden path in Tuscany, a chateau in Provence, wildflowers in a field.

"Beauty. Something that pulls me into itself, out of myself. Those frescoes in San Marco's convent were incredible."

"The Renaissance reflected a time of great faith and the artists expressed that vision. To be surrounded by heaven on canvas is captivating—one loses a sense of time."

"Inspiring, really."

The waiter handed us dessert menus, and we peered inside. What would the temptation be? "These desserts are works of art."

"The chef is indeed inspired. But let's do the cheese course tonight." Jack leaned back and looked out to the moonlit sky.

We ordered the cheese course—a pungent triangle of fresh chèvre, a slice of dry Pecorino, a crumble of moldy Gorgonzola. The silence wrapped around us. Only a few diners remained, whispering at a far table.

"We do the Francis tour tomorrow," Jack said as though handing me a gift to encourage me.

I grinned. "Yes—the gentle saint, who cared not a fig for art of any kind, or cities for that matter. He wouldn't have believed motor scooters possible. First Cortona, then Assisi, then La Verna. It'll be a long day, but a perfect loop on the map."

"*Bene.* I'm glad to see your smile again."

In our room, I skimmed a short biography of Francis I had brought with me. With access to many primary sources, historians have a great deal of material. A short summary of his life was nearly impossible.

Born in Assisi in 1181, the son of a prosperous cloth

merchant, Francis Bernadone grew up hearing the tales of wandering troubadours. While fighting Perugia as a young soldier, he was captured. In prison, he had a vision of God; when released, he returned home a changed man.

"I am about to take a wife of surpassing fairness," Francis announced, referring to "Lady Poverty." He journeyed to Rome and gave his money to Saint Peter's Basilica; he exchanged his clothes with a beggar. Returning to Assisi, he prayed in the church of San Damiano, where God spoke from the altar crucifix: "Repair my house, which is falling into ruin!" Taking the message literally, Francis sold his father's cloth and tried to give the proceeds to the priest who refused them. Furious, Francis's father beat his son and locked him in the basement of their family home. Francis escaped and returned to San Damiano for sanctuary.

Brought before the bishop, Francis stripped off his clothes. "Hitherto I have called you my father on earth," he said to his father, "but henceforth I desire to say only 'Our Father who art in heaven.'"

He wandered the countryside, singing to God, calling himself a *jongleur* for God, a troubadour-juggler-fool. Highwaymen robbed him and threw him in the snow. In Gubbio, friends gave him a cloak, a rope, and a staff, the clothes of a begging pilgrim. In Assisi, he rebuilt San Damiano and restored two other chapels. He nursed lepers, searching for God's will in his life.

In 1208, in the church of Santa Maria degli Angeli in the valley below Assisi, the Gospel reading commanded Christ's disciples to give up all they owned, and preach repentance and the coming of the Kingdom of God. Francis renounced his few possessions and donned rough peasant sacking. Soon others followed, embracing poverty and preaching God's love.

The Penitents of Assisi traveled to Rome for approval of their order. At first the pope refused their request, but after a dream where Francis propped up the collapsing Basilica of Saint John Lateran—the pope's cathedral and symbol of the Church—he agreed to the new order.

Now called the Friars Minor, Francis and his followers

lived in small huts in the valley below Assisi; in 1211, they were given a chapel called the Porziuncola. They traveled the countryside, preaching and living humbly. The order grew.

Stories of Saint Francis spread throughout Italy. He healed lepers; he nursed the dying; he tamed a dangerous wolf; birds obeyed him. He created a live nativity scene in Greccio—an early crèche. He crusaded to Egypt to convert the Sultan. In 1224, on Monte Verna, east of Florence, he received the stigmata, the five wounds of Christ, from a seraphim angel: his hands and feet were pierced, his side was slashed, and he began a slow hemorrhage.

Two years later, at the age of forty-five, he lay dying. He asked to be buried with the criminals; but after his death his body was placed in the crypt of the Assisi basilica built by his followers.

Jack yawned as he slipped between the sheets. "I can't believe we've been gone two weeks. Do you realize we only have one week left? And you still have nightmares."

I looked into his blue eyes. "But they *are* changing."

"That's good?"

"Something is happening inside me—I feel like God is rearranging my mind; I'm trying to trust him with it, and not get impatient."

"Good plan—maybe the psyche is like a fine wine—it needs proper care, to be allowed to ferment in the right conditions."

"I like the image."

"But, Maddie, if all this doesn't work . . ."

"Yes?"

"Will you agree to some therapy when we get home? It can't hurt."

I breathed deeply. "Okay, if the pilgrimage doesn't work. That makes sense." But I *would* believe that it *would* work. That's what I learned in San Zaccaria.

"And Maddie—about Cristoforo. I'll ask him what's going on when the time is right."

"When will that be?"

"Soon."

"Then I'll trust you too—to pick the right time." Jack's political acumen, his "street smarts" as he called them, give him an enviable sense of timing, and of people.

"What are you reading?"

"One of my bio summaries for the students. They're useful in Western Civ."

"Let me take a look." He reached for his reading glasses.

I turned to my Evening Prayer office, running my hand over the dried palms lying in the fold. It was now Ascensiontide, so the preface was different: *Christ is not entered into the holy places made with hands, which are the figures of the true; but into heaven itself, now to appear in the presence of God for us.*

Jack handed me the page. "Pretty cool guy, as Justin would say. He's certainly a famous one."

"Our world likes Francis. Ecology. Animals. They see him as a medieval hippie." I set my book down, turned out the light, and snuggled in close.

He rubbed my back, his hands massaging my spine, lingering on the shoulders, moving down. "Will there be a quiz? I love your quizzes," he whispered.

"Might be. It all depends on how good you are."

"I'll be very, very, good."

We fit together, Jack and I, and our movements, our rhythms, our explorations of one another, were at once familiar and new. Always, he took me far away, to another country, uniting my body and soul, giving me a foretaste of heaven.

Chapter Nine
Assisi

Let the floods clap their hands,
and let the hills be joyful together before the Lord.
Psalm 98:9

Early Tuesday morning we drove south to Cortona, a walled medieval village built into a mountainside. We circled the outer wall and climbed into a forested canyon, where Le Celle, one of Francis's hermitages, hung from the cliff. We parked at a gatehouse and descended a wide path into a gorge; stone buildings with tiny windows appeared on the opposite side. The monastery hovered over the broad valley like an ancient angel praying for Tuscany.

The morning sun streamed between dark clouds into the canyon, lighting on a black-robed Capuchin stooping over his garden. His white beard moved up and down rhythmically, following the motion of his hoe, and he worked slowly in his clogs, his bare heels exposed to the cold wind. He didn't look up as we passed in the crisp morning silence.

A river tumbled through the gorge. We looked past the Capuchin, to the west, to the Val de Chiani, a green plain splashed with sun. Crossing a stone bridge, we entered through a low doorway. Off the dark entry, we found Francis's low-ceilinged cell, where he had retreated after preaching in the valley. Through an iron grate, I could see his bed carved from the rock. A painting of Mary hung over a stone altar.

Francis first came to Cortona in 1211, traveling north from Rome, preaching in the towns. The villagers gave him this abandoned mill, and soon other friars joined him. Thirteen years later, his feet and hands hemorrhaging from the stigmata, he returned here to rest. After his death, and with the energetic building of Franciscan basilicas, the humbler Le Celle declined. But eventually the order grew lax, and in 1517, members seeking to follow the original rule established the reformed Capuchins, named for their hooded cowls, or caps. Some settled at Le Celle. Today they offer retreats; they pray for the world.

In the silence of the forest we followed trails to other chapels, cells, sanctuaries, and Stations of the Cross. Pausing on a rocky promontory, Cristoforo, his thick eyebrows rising and falling, pointed down the hill to Francis's cell.

"You see how simple it is for Francis," he whispered. "He comes to Le Celle for peace, away from towns, away from crowds. Not clean and comfortable. Our cells are more simple." He moved away, into forest, fingering his rosary beads.

Jack was reading my notes. "Here's a quote from Francis—'Wherever we are, wherever we go, we bring our cell with us. Our brother body is our cell and our soul is the hermit living in that cell in order to pray to God and meditate.' "

"He *was* kind of like the hippies in the sixties." How proud we were of our poverty, I thought, thumbing our noses at the establishment—and our parents—with all their material addictions.

Jack shook his head. "The hippies seemed a bit strange to me. I grew up in the forties with the hardships of war—blackouts, food lines—and memories of the Depression. Being poor was not desirable, not something you would choose. But weren't you sort of a hippie, Maddie?"

I looked at my husband. At times our twelve-year age difference seemed a great divide. "I was definitely influenced by the 'natural' idea—living off the land, few possessions; I was even a vegetarian for a time. I think some of us saw simplicity as a way to God, as if fewer goods meant fewer distractions, so that we might hear his voice, might draw nearer. By stripping away the hustle of acquiring, we felt we could embrace something true, something real."

Jack put his arm around me as he looked out to the plain dappled with moving shadows. "You were 'waiting on God.' Who said that?"

"Father Rinaldi, but I'm sure he wasn't the first. Some would say a vow of poverty releases the soul from diversions, allowing peace in God."

"For the hippies it was peace in drugs, I'm afraid."

"I think many of us confused God with drugs, or drugs with God. Remember the 'flower children' of San Francisco? Their name was a half-appropriate connection to the city's saint. Like Francis, they rejected their parents' materialism, thinking it killed love. So they became poor, though their idea of 'love,' being so 'free,' may have been closer to lust. But the analogy ends there. I recall a fellow in college brewing hard drugs in his room. That would have been September '65."

"Remember the psychedelic vans and painted school buses? That was a clear contrast to the cells of Francis."

"I sure do." I gazed down to the riverbed where Cristoforo was speaking to the Capuchin. "I had some friends who made their way across the country and ended up in a Vermont commune. One day they questioned their choices and returned to school to become investment bankers."

"The hippies became yuppies."

I nodded. "They were some of the lucky ones—they didn't fry their brains on LSD. My cousin did; today he drifts, barely able to cope, overweight, diabetic."

"I heard that most hippies came from upper middle class homes."

"Maybe you have to come from security to embrace insecurity—poverty—like Francis leaving his family wealth."

"I've never known anyone growing up poor who didn't want to be rich."

"Exactly." I wondered how many ascetics came from poverty.

Cristoforo was climbing towards us. Did Father Rinaldi really find him picking pockets in Alexandria? Had he truly taken vows of poverty? He didn't appear to live as humbly as these Capuchins, in spite of his frayed robe. He certainly enjoyed the car and the cell phone.

We returned to the entrance where we bought an image of Francis painted on a wooden panel. The saint's eyes were dark and serious, his brown figure set against a blue background. I recalled he suffered from eye disease and underwent surgery in Rieti. He prayed he be given strength to withstand the pain of cauterization, and claimed he felt no pain at all. Another miracle, I thought.

We walked slowly, silently, down the hill, across the stone bridge over the river, and up to the car, the saint's image heavy in my hand.

We sped south along the N71 and turned east along the shore of Lake Trasimeno, heading toward Assisi. Straining to see through the thick mist, I recalled Francis had retreated to an island in the lake in Lent of 1211. He brought two loaves of bread and told the boatman to return on Good Friday. But I could see only a bare outline of land.

We curved through the Umbrian hills and circled Perugia. Passing through a broad valley of farms, we ascended Mount Subasio to the medieval village of Assisi.

We parked in a lot outside the town, and Jack opened my door. "Let's find a lunch place. There must be something with a good view up here. Cristoforo, would you join us?"

Jack and I exchanged glances, and the friar nodded gravely. "I show you a good place. The sister of a brother runs it."

I smiled at the wording. "The sister of a brother?"

"*Si.*"

We walked through a portal in the old town wall and followed a cobbled lane. On a promontory to our left, rose the Basilica of Saint Francis, silhouetted against the blue sky; birds soared about its bell towers. We continued uphill into the town, past shops selling ceramic plaques and painted crucifixes, postcards and writing papers. As the midday sun burned our backs, we climbed stairs to a small terrace, where *Bella Assisi* was painted in red on a white awning. Cristoforo whispered to a middle-aged woman who wiped her hands on an apron. She led us to a table.

We ordered spaghetti *con funghetti, crostini di prosciutto*, mixed salad, and a bottle of Chianti. Cristoforo ordered the soup of the day, minestrone with white beans.

Jack turned to the friar. "Cristoforo, we need to talk."

"*Si?*"

"Why are you driving us? What is the real reason?"

A fleeting look of discomfort, then one of acceptance, crossed the monk's face. "*Prego, Signori,* I will explain."

"Please do." I studied him.

With dismay, he opened his broad palms. "I am sorry, *Signora,* I did not want to frighten you, to worry you. Sister Agnes tells me—many times she reminds me—not to worry you. This is her phone—she calls me each day."

"It's okay, Cristoforo," I said, "but you *do* worry me." I paused. "Agnes really calls you every day?"

"It is because of the corporal, your cloth. . . ." He looked at my bag. "Do you have it still? Do you keep it safe? Many want such a thing."

A waiter poured our Chianti and set out silverware wrapped in paper napkins and a basket of crusty bread.

I pulled the linen square from my handbag. "Many would want this? But why? Is it holy or precious or miraculous? Other linens have consecrated wine spilled on them. This means more to me because of

Father Rinaldi and how he died."

Cristoforo's eyes grew bright. "*Sì*—Father Rinaldi was a saintly man. He was a Franciscan. He was a man of the earth, the flowers, the birds. The cloth of such a man is . . . perhaps, a shroud. Sister Agnes thinks this may be true."

Jack watched the friar intently, then poured more Chianti. "Do you think we're in some kind of danger?"

"In Italy we honor these things, and with honor, fame, and fame, profit. You are a man of business, *Signore.* You know this. Others in Rome talk about your cloth. They desire it. So I keep company with you."

I refolded the cloth carefully. "Are you saying Father Rinaldi may be a saint?"

The friar looked at me with soulful eyes. "Father Rinaldi was a man of great love. Love heals, *Signora.* Maybe he gives this cloth his power of love, of *santo.* But *allora*, do not fear; I watch over you. I have many friends—in many towns. You trust me, and maybe we spend more time together?"

Jack and I nodded.

Cristoforo looked relieved, as though a great weight had been lifted with his confession. "I am glad to tell you this."

Our lunch arrived, and the friar threw his hands in the air. "For this meal, make us full of thanks! In the name of Jesus, Amen." He swung his arms down and made the Sign of the Cross over his heart.

He ate quickly and stood, gently placing his thick hand on Jack's shoulder. "But I show you San Francesco, the basilica. My friends will show us the *seminario* and the grave. We meet at the church doors at one o'clock? And, *Signori*, thank you for the delicious lunch."

He strode across the terrace, nodded to the owner, and disappeared down the lane.

We met our friar in front of the church where Cristoforo introduced us to short dark Allesandro and tall fair Marco. Marco, the scholar, spoke little English, so Allesandro, who had studied English in his native Malta, translated. The brown-robed students guided us through the upper basilica, where Giotto's frescoes told stories of the Old Testament, the New Testament, and Saint Francis. Cristoforo remained nearby, watchful.

"Saint Francis," Allesandro translated, "created these frescoes, although he was already gone to God. He caused men to think different, to think humble, to see the birds and the trees, to see each other. Giotto and Cimabue painted frescoes this way, and many others came from Rome to decorate this basilica. More human, no? Not like the icon style of the medieval world. More like you and me, realistic."

We descended stairs to the lower basilica where every vault, every wall, was frescoed.

"It goes on and on," said Jack, rubbing his chin. "It's amazing."

The three friars led us into the crypt, where pilgrims venerated Francis's remains in a dark chapel. A simple lace-covered altar stood in front of a wrought-iron grate. We knelt with the others.

"His relics rest in an urn inside," Cristoforo whispered.

I held my linen cloth, thinking how a single man could change history. With his love for the individual, he prepared the ground for the rebirth of classical humanism. The Renaissance celebrated man, albeit as God's creation, and with the emphasis shifting from God to man, a new worldview was born. This new direction eventually led to God being seen as man's creation, a wispy, comfortable illusion.

But in the meantime, much good would result. The individual would be empowered to speak. The common man would learn to read and write, to vote his opinion on matters of state. The printing press would propel this current of change, and by the eighteenth century this humanism would spread from art to politics. The Enlightenment would trigger revolutions against the privileged and powerful in both America and France.

Did I inherit this individualism, this insistence on my rights, rights to a pain-free, happy life, to peaceful nights? But God counteracted such extremes by showing a way out of self-preoccupation, for he too became more personal. With the Reformation preachers of the sixteenth century, Christ entered our homes and workplaces and taught us how to walk with him. The average man read the widely printed Scriptures and could seek truth for himself; he no longer needed a priest to speak to God.

Allesandro and Marco led us behind the tomb. We stepped through a low door and descended stairs to the thirteenth-century chapel of the first Franciscans, a small vaulted space. Those early friars were probably young men like our student guides, I thought, fresh with faith, inspired by a spirit of love and sacrifice. We ascended to the monks' large refectory where a *Last Supper* covered the end wall, overlooking long tables set for supper.

We emerged onto an airy loggia and gazed through sunlit arches to the valley below where the heat had burned away the mist. The Basilica of Saint Mary of the Angels, built around the first chapel of Saint Francis, sat like a single rose in a meadow, her dome catching the light.

Allesandro translated Marco's words, beaming with the desire to explain. "We are simple men. We love God. We work hard. We care for the poor, the sick and the dying, like Francis wanted. But our work is much bigger today, and so, too, our churches. God planted an acorn in Francis's heart, and now it is an oak tree." He pointed to Saint Mary's on the plain. "The little chapel called the Porziuncola now has a big basilica built over it. But the little chapel is still inside. You understand?"

We nodded and followed them to gates opening on the street. As we thanked them and said our good-byes, they looped small wooden "Tau" crosses on leather laces over our heads, to rest on our hearts, the glow of the gentle saint shining in their eyes.

We watched the two young men saunter up the hill to their rooms, chatting and waving their hands.

"They're such happy fellows," Jack said as he took my hand.

"Nearly on fire with love . . ."

Cristoforo nodded and pointed up the hill. "You wish to see Santa Chiara?"

We followed him to the thirteenth-century Basilica di Santa Chiara where Clare's body lay incorrupt. Pausing on a sweeping terrace, the friar turned to us, his intense eyes softening, and began the story of Saint Clare, friend of Francis.

"Clare is rich and beautiful. She wants to be poor and humble like Francis. She is only eighteen and her family disapproves. She runs away, down the hill." He waved his hand toward the basilica in the valley. "She rides, with her sister Agnes, to meet Francis."

"It would be romantic," Jack said, "if we didn't know better."

"*Si, Signore!* It is romantic, but romantic like the old way, like adventure."

I smiled. *Romantic* had indeed lost its original meaning. It once referred to tales of knights, to heroic epics. If love was involved, it was a secondary theme. In the nineteenth century, any work of fiction was considered a romance.

"Francis cuts their hair," the friar continued. "He gives them rough clothing, flour sacking. He takes them to San Damiano. Clare begins a new order."

I recalled another story. "And when the Saracens attacked her convent, Clare held the Reserved Sacrament up to the window. The Saracens fled."

"*Si, Si!*" Cristoforo said, his eyes wide. "You know about her, *Signora*."

"A little." I had been incredulous when I first heard the tale, but in time had come to believe the Sacrament could wield such power, if God desired it.

Clare and Francis were young, attractive, and wealthy. They forsook an easy life to marry poverty, to wed Christ. Was it the Holy Spirit that pushed them out of material comfort into a world of spiritual joy? Were the two worlds so very incompatible? Perhaps one engulfed, overshadowed, the other.

Cristoforo led us inside. "This church was first called San Giorgio. Here the boy Francis learns about God. Here Francis is buried, before San Francesco is built." Cristoforo paused before a chapel off the south aisle. "This is the crucifix of San Damiano—God spoke to Francis through this crucifix."

I gazed at the colorful painted cross over the altar. The arms lay against a russet background, an amber halo circled the long brown hair, and saints gathered around. The rustic simplicity, the vivid hues, the figure of the Son of God reaching to man, saying, *Behold, here I am, doing what needs doing*—these things touched me. Christ's humanity and humility filled the chapel.

"I've seen this crucifix before," Jack said.

I nodded. "It's been replicated all over the world by Franciscan communities. But I thought the original was in San Damiano."

"It was brought here for safekeeping," the friar said. "The Poor Clares watch over it."

"And Clare?" I asked. "Is her body here?"

"I will show you."

We descended into the crypt and followed an underground ambulatory running beneath the high altar. Looking into the glass tomb, we could see Clare's body resting on a golden bed, clothed in a black robe with a white headscarf.

"They found the body," Cristoforo said, "in 1850, under the altar. She was, how to you say, still . . ."

"Intact," I said, "incorrupt, not decomposed."

"*Si*, incorrupt, but now she is darkening."

"That's remarkable." Jack raised his brows with doubt. He rubbed his chin.

The friar turned to him. "It is a sign of holiness, a sign of *santo*."

I looked at the black-robed nun who loved God so. Did God permeate her very flesh? I wanted to see where she had lived. I wished I had known her. One day I would. "Cristoforo, is San Damiano far? Do we have time to visit?"

"Not far."

We emerged from Clare's basilica onto the bright piazza and purchased a Franciscan crucifix from a stout shopkeeper across the street. I laid the neatly wrapped parcel in my bag alongside my linen cloth, and we walked down the hill, past the white basilica amidst the soaring birds. The church of San Damiano was beyond the city wall, nestled into the hillside.

The eighth-century Romanesque chapel was rustic with a tiled nave and wooden pews, a plain altar and red burning candle beneath a painted crucifix. The church smelled of earth and damp stone. I gazed at the crucifix where God spoke to man, intersecting time, commanding the rich young merchant.

We left Cristoforo kneeling in the chapel and visited the adjoining oratory and dormitory. Here the sisters slept on straw mats and here Clare died. In this humble convent, Clare nursed Francis's wounded body; here Francis wrote the *Canticle of the Creatures* as his eye disease slowly blinded him. In this space, Clare confronted the Saracens, holding high the sacred and powerful host, and finally, as she lay dying she cried, "Thank you, God, for creating me."

The bells rang two and Jack checked his watch. "Maddie, we'd better go if you want to see La Verna."

We found our friar in the chapel, his thick hands clasped together as he gazed upon the crucifix. I touched his robe.

He looked up at me, his eyes filled with joy.

We drove through green rolling hills, north to La Verna, the friar humming "All things bright and beautiful, all creatures great and small . . . ." I dozed, my mind full of Francis, Clare, and the smiling eyes of our Franciscan friends. The colorful painted crucifix rested in my palms. For the time, Mollie had receded to a phantasmal shadow.

Cristoforo's careful explanations at lunch had put my mind somewhat at rest; he seemed no longer the silent menace, but rather our guide and protector. For the first time, I trusted the friar, perhaps the greatest blessing of the day.

We followed the highway north to Sansepolcro, then deeper into the Casentino mountains toward Chiusi della Verna. The road narrowed and Cristoforo drove with a concentrated purpose, taking the twists and turns with increased skill. I closed my eyes and held my breath.

Jack, in the front passenger seat, turned to look at me, as though checking on the welfare of a child. "So what exactly happened to Francis at La Verna? What *are* stigmata exactly?"

I breathed deeply. "A Count Chiuso gave the hermitage to Francis as a place of rest. In 1224, Francis and three followers journeyed there to keep a pre-Michaelmas fast."

"Michaelmas?"

"The September feast of Saint Michael and All Angels."

Cristoforo leaned on his horn as he passed a small Citroen. I grabbed the seat back.

"Go on," Jack said.

"Francis asked Christ to let him suffer the pain of his crucifixion."

"Why?"

"Good question—why ask for pain? They say he wanted to experience the love Jesus felt for the world as he died. I suppose Francis believed that he couldn't know the love without knowing the suffering."

"Hmm . . ." Jack returned his gaze to the front window and the swiftly disappearing road ahead.

"So, on September fourteenth a seraph angel with six flaming wings appeared to him. The angel—actually an Angel of the Lord, Christ himself—pierced Francis's hands, side, and feet, and Francis knew Christ's love."

"Amazing."

"The wounds continued to bleed, and he died within two years."

"I wonder if he regretted his request."

"I doubt it."

Cristoforo maneuvered the car into a gravel parking lot. "We are here—Sanctuario della Verna, a Franciscan monastero. Many pellegrini come for retreat. *Per favore*, will you excuse me? Friends expect me." He grabbed his brown skirts and strode up the hill, whistling a familiar hymn, "Love divine, all loves excelling . . . ."

125

Joining other pilgrims walking up a wide drive through a forest of pine, fir, and beech, we passed the Chapel of the Birds, where sparrows once welcomed Francis with their chorus. We followed a cobblestone path, passed through a wrought-iron gateway, and climbed to a large terrace fronting a fifteenth-century basilica, overlooking the broad countryside. At the edge of the terrace a massive wooden cross intersected the sky, as though raising its arms in blessing. I inhaled the crisp air of the Casentinos as the sun warmed my skin, floating between heaven and earth on this rocky crag of light and air. Groups had gathered on the terrace, chatting and laughing, seeming unaware of the *Silenzio* signs.

The basilica door listed the prayer offices, and I saw that one would soon begin. We entered the white vaulted nave and sat in a pew near the south aisle. Two large blue-and-white Della Robbia sculptures framed the altar, depicting Christ's Nativity and Mary's Assumption. In a bay chapel, a glass cabinet displayed Francis's bloodstained bandages, his drinking cup, his wooden bowl, and his walking stick.

As pilgrims filled the church, friars processed into the choir behind the altar and began singing the Psalms antiphonally.

As they chanted, I knelt and thanked God for Francis Bernadone. This simple man's love of God was greater than his love of self, allowing Christ to unite with him through common wounds. Maybe in this way God drew Francis into the created world, giving him the power to talk with God's creation, to heal man and beast. I prayed that my love for God would not be muddied by self-love. I sat back and let the lyrical chants weave about me, my linen cloth in my lap.

A thurifer, swinging clouds of sweet smelling smoke, stepped from the chancel, followed by a solemn crucifer, and the friars. We followed too, processing out to the frescoed Corridor of the Stigmata. Jack nudged me and pointed to our friar, and I was relieved to see the frizzy black head and the familiar lope. We continued into the tiny Chapel of the Stigmata, built into the cliff-face, and took seats in a wooden choir. A glass-covered stone in front of the altar marked the place where Francis received the wounds of Christ. Flowers and a burning candle had been placed alongside the stone.

The monks read from Francis's writings, chanted the *Litany of the Saints*, and processed out. We followed them down a narrow stone path between high walls, into a tunnel, and back out to the Corridor, then turned down a side path to Francis's cave. There the saint's stone bed could be seen, carved out of the rock, similar to Le Celle.

Francis's wounds gave him joy, ecstasy. How could this be? A dove fluttered in my heart, piercing me with a suffering love, a difficult love.

Had I been honest about my part in Mollie's death? I knelt, grasping my linen cloth, and in my mind saw her first steps as she toddled toward me, trusting me to catch her. Her death was more than an accident, more than a tragic loss of life, for her death had been caused by betrayal, a betrayal of trust.

Another piece of my puzzle had been worked out, a bit of my anguish glimpsed, understood. Mollie had trusted me and I had failed her. Wiping my eyes, I rose to find Jack, full of the sense of having made one more step, having healed one more wound.

He was in the gift shop with Cristoforo, purchasing a ceramic Madonna and Child. The white sculpted figures were set against a blue background, framed with yellow, peach, and rose flowers, a bright contrast to earthy Francis. We walked silently back to the car and drove through the forest. As the sun set behind the mountains, I considered the mystery of Francis.

Francis's physical wounds brought him joy. Jesus, too, suffered physical wounds to save us, to heal us by his blood, to provide the one path to eternal life, to happiness on earth and in heaven. Why was this necessary? Again, the body and soul united, just as they united in the incarnation of God in the man-Christ and in the suffering of the saints. Surely, our bodies were a kind of incarnation, physical houses of the spiritual, imperfect ones to be sure. Yet somehow, the suffering of the body perfected the soul, even healed the mind.

Could grief be ameliorated, lessened, changed into something else? Could suffering offer a kind of sanctification, a growth of holiness? Could the God-in-us transform our interior wounds through his suffering on the cross? Did the love of the Creator expressed two thousand years ago have the power to heal my heart today? With every prayer, I opened more doors, only to find more questions.

And what was the role of the Church in all of this? The Church, the Bride—and Body—of Christ, the Communion of Believers throughout time, had been given a great charge. The Church was to ensure that God's incarnation continued in each of us, so that we would be ready for the Last Judgment at the End of Time. Was the Son of God incarnate in me? Could his presence destroy my night demons? My mind whirled with visions of the Eucharistic host working into my heart, purifying a path, burning the ghouls to ash. And I prayed once more, *Take not thy Holy Spirit from me.*

I glanced at Jack as we approached the exit for Florence. He dozed, his chin resting on his chest, a low rattle escaping his open mouth. As we pulled up to our hotel, he looked about and stretched.

"How about a quick swim before dinner?" he asked. "There should be just enough time."

That evening, sitting at an antique desk in our tiny room, I searched for words to describe my remarkable day, words turning my hours into sentences that made sense. Bells chimed seven as I gazed at the Florentine hills and the light notes of the pianist floated from the loggia. The russet city basked in the sun's last rays; scooters grunted up the road to Fiesole. Another day was put to rest; another evening would begin. A congregation of birds in the olive trees sang their evensong, and the cypresses climbed like church spires.

My prayer book lay on the dresser with Saint Peter and the Madonna of Saint Luke; my rosary and Father's linen lay alongside. I added the small Franciscan crucifix and the sculpted Madonna from today. These were my pilgrim's badges, the stages of my journey, and they comforted me, giving order to my hours, chapters to my days.

Tomorrow, Siena. What would I learn from Saint Catherine? Like Francis, she died young, and like Francis, she received the stigmata. Hers was another body united to God through suffering—and joy.

Chapter Ten
Siena

Thus have I looked for thee in the sanctuary,
that I might behold thy power and glory.
Psalm 63:3

Cobbled lanes meander over Siena's red-earthed hills just as they did in the eleventh century, creating an ocher maze friendly to people but hostile to cars.

When the Romans conquered the Etruscans in the first century BC, Caesar Augustus named the town Sena Julia, probably after the local *Senone* tribe. The Lombards, the Franks, and the eleventh-century prince-bishops all in turn ruled Siena until, in the twelfth century, the township won independence. The new city-state fought her neighbors, suffering sieges, filling dungeons, and avenging family blood; the Sienese lived in mini-fortresses with thick stone walls and secret passageways. In 1559, Siena became subject to Florence and in the late nineteenth century, joined the modern Italian state.

We found our hotel just outside the town wall, surrounded by orchards and vineyards. The fourteenth-century Certosa di Maggiano had been built to ensure prayers for the founder's soul. *Certosa* translates to "charterhouse." These endowed convents followed the stipulations of the will or charter.

Jack checked in and Cristoforo stacked our luggage in the bare cloister. The friar soon left for a retreat house nearby.

As we walked to our room, we passed through salons filled with antiques and Venetian portraits of Roman emperors astride their stallions. We peeked into a Victorian library paneled in alder. Pleased that the talkative porter spoke English, we learned a bit of the certosa's history.

Pausing to look out a window, he narrowed his dark eyes. "The

trees along this road between here and the walls were used for hanging."
He set our bags down and waved his arms as though revealing dark
secrets.

Jack glanced at the porter with surprise. "Really? You mean
hanging as in executions?"

"*Si.* In 1554 the Spanish Emperor laid siege to Siena. Any farmer
who tried to enter the city was . . . hung from a tree! During the siege the
monks built a barricade that was guarded by French soldiers. When the
Emperor's men forced the monks out, the French set the certosa on fire.
But four monks returned and rebuilt."

He grabbed the bags, working his way up a spiral staircase to a
landing. "In the eighteenth century. . . the Austrian emperor seized the
certosa . . . and made it a parish church." He pulled a massive iron key
from his pocket, worked it into a carved keyhole, and opened the heavy
door. "You have the largest suite, *Signori.* It goes back here and through
there, and farther on, and you can see here are cupboards and the bath
and . . ." He opened and closed doors, showing us the many rooms, a
maze of cubicles linked with doorways.

"*Grazie, grazie, grazie.*" Jack slipped several lira into his palm.

"*Grazie, Signori, buona sera!*" He nodded and backed out the door,
clanging it shut.

Our rooms faced two directions. On one side, we looked to a dry
fountain in the bare cloister and on the other side, to vineyards striping
the Tuscan hills. In the distance, olive trees clustered around russet
farmhouses.

Jack slipped his arm around my shoulders. "My, oh my, my
Madeleine, this *is* picturesque . . . and peaceful. You're getting enough
picturesque and peaceful to smother any nightmares. How did you sleep
last night? I didn't hear you cry out." He kissed me on the cheek.

I hesitated. Even so, I hoped words might help. "It was an oddly
different dream," I said, gazing at the vines, "but still terrible. Mollie was
coughing and choking, turning blue. I carried her down a hall, crying for
help, the same panic welling up. . . ."

I turned to Jack, his face so full of concern. "I don't know. I'm not
sure this trip is making any difference. My days are better, but the nights
are still hard, maybe even worse. I'd rather not talk about it."

The weight behind my eyes was constant now, pushing and
pressing, never letting up, often ballooning to a headache. I had found
the best antidote was to ignore it, to think of something—anything—else.

"Then let's unpack. It's early. We'll lunch in Siena, return for a swim in the garden pool, have a nap, then a nice dinner downstairs. What shall you wear tonight? The dining room looked intriguing, candlelight and mystery, very medieval. We'll have a perfect dry martini in that bar with the emperors on the horses. We can imagine intrigue and danger." Jack lifted my garment bag onto the bed.

I tried to pull myself together. "Sure," I said.

I had no trouble imagining intrigue. Pale-face haunted me, an unsolved mystery. Forcing a smile, I unzipped my bag and hung up slacks and dresses. I struggled to open a warped drawer with a minute key and reached for a sweater.

I found my linen and gently ran my fingers over it. My lower lip quivered, warning me. Trembling, I moved toward Jack and laid my head on his chest. Tears were near.

He held me and stroked my hair. "That's good," he said. "Let it all out."

I cried into his shoulder in rhythmic waves, choking gasps escaping my lungs.

A little shaken, yet feeling some relief, I held a cold compress to my puffy eyes, then followed Jack and Cristoforo to the Piazza del Campo for lunch.

Each summer, crowds gathered in the piazza to watch the Palio delle Contrade horse race, in which districts competed for the glorious banner, the *palio*. But today the piazza was quiet, a broad rectangle of amber stone.

Jack looked up from his guidebook as we circled the arena. "Did you know that the horse and rider go to their parish church on the morning of the *palio* for mass and a blessing? The horse goes too! That I would like to see."

I smiled, comforted by his good humor. These Italians *were* full of life. "It *is* difficult to imagine."

We chose Il Mangia for lunch and sat at a linen-covered table on the edge of the piazza—Cristoforo took a seat near the entrance. We lunched on *linguini con formaggio,* minestrone, and *insalata verde* and sipped a local Chianti.

I gazed into the piazza, imagining the sixteen horsemen riding proudly around the perimeter, waving their flags, the crowds screaming.

But today tourists meandered; musicians played accordions and fiddles. On the far side of the square, the old town hall and campanile rose between houses of amber stone.

"This is nice," Jack said. "It's pleasant, taking the afternoon slow, sipping wine, enjoying the flavor of the town. How about going back to the *certosa* for a little siesta?" He caressed my cheek with his fingertip.

I smiled. "Sure, but first . . ."

"First what, Maddie?"

"Could we see Catherine's home first?"

"Catherine?"

"Catherine of Siena, one of the great saints. She's patron saint of Rome, Italy, and Europe. And she lived right here in town—it can't be far."

"I've heard of her." Jack sounded resigned. "So tell me her story. You're going to, sooner or later."

I ignored the sarcasm. "Let me find my notes."

I pulled the sheet from my bag and checked on my linen cloth, still there. I scanned the biography for unusual details, ones that might be interesting to Jack. "Catherine was the twenty-fourth, some say twenty-fifth, child of a wool-dyer."

Jack looked up. "Twenty-fourth?"

"Right, and she was a twin."

"Perhaps her mother should be sainted, or her father."

"Good point. Her family was large even by the standards of the times. She was born in 1347, one year before the Black Plague hit Europe, when Tuscany lost a third of its population."

"That's portentous."

"It is." I skimmed on. "From a very young age, she dedicated her life to God. At sixteen she became a lay Dominican, taking vows of chastity, poverty, and obedience, but remaining in the world."

"She remained in the world? With those vows, you've got to be kidding."

"She followed the severe Anchorite rule, living at home, praying and meditating, eating little, sleeping little. After three years, she began to care for the sick and poor. Others joined her."

"So she wasn't a real nun? She didn't live in a convent?"

"She was a tertiary, a third order—monastics who take vows of poverty and obedience. Many tertiaries marry, have families, and work in secular jobs."

132

"Wasn't she supposed to be rather attractive? I recall seeing a picture somewhere."

"She was considered quite beautiful." I sipped my coffee.

"Was she martyred? Is that why she was canonized?"

"Not martyred, but she died young. In one of her visions, Christ commanded her to work in the world, so she wrote to cardinals, popes, and princes, imploring peace and advising on affairs of state. She was actually illiterate, so she dictated her letters. She intervened in many local conflicts. She traveled on diplomatic missions and urged the pope to return to Rome from Avignon during the Great Schism."

"Wow, a political saint! And a woman, in those times. And illiterate."

"Precisely. Then, in the church of Santa Cristina in Pisa, while praying before a painted crucifix, she received the stigmata, which remained invisible until her death at thirty-three. Today her body lies in Rome, in the church of Santa Maria sopra Minerva, where she spent her last years."

We followed Brother Cristoforo to Sanctuario Cateriniano, Catherine's birthplace and family home, today four chapels: the Upper Oratory (the kitchen), the Lower Oratory (her father's dye shop), the Oratory of the Camera (her bedroom), the Church of the Crucifix (the family garden). We saw the kitchen hearth where the child Catherine fell into the fire and emerged unharmed.

While Jack took pictures, moving from chapel to chapel, the friar and I knelt in the first pew of the Chapel of the Crucifix. The Christ on the cross was a colorful painted figure like the Christ of San Damiano, only larger, embracing, the eyes thoughtfully compelling. The crucifix was mounted on a red panel in an apse of creamy marble and gold inlay; vases of wildflowers sat on the lace-covered altar. It was before this crucifix that Catherine prayed when she received the stigmata.

Cristoforo's thick fingers worked his wooden beads as his lips moved silently.

Sitting back, I opened a brochure describing Catherine's experience. Her confessor, Raimondo di Capoue, was present and recorded what he saw.

After having celebrated mass and given her communion, she remained insensible for quite some time. And as I was waiting for her to return to her senses, in order to receive, as often happened, some spiritual consolation from her, in an instant her tiny body, which had been prostrate little by little, was raised up and, as she was on her knees, she stretched out her arms and hands, remaining rigidly for some time in that position with her eyes closed; finally, as if she had been mortally wounded, she suddenly collapsed and shortly after, regained consciousness. Then she called for me and said, "You must know, Father, that by the mercy of our Lord Jesus, I already bear in my body his stigmata. . . . I saw the Crucified Lord coming down towards me enveloped in a blinding light; and by the force of my desire to meet my Creator, my body was made to elevate itself. Then from the scars of his most sacred wounds I saw descending upon me five blood-stained rays, which touched my hands, my feet, and my heart. . . . And I immediately felt such pains in all these parts of my body, especially in my side, that if the Lord had not performed another miracle I don't think that I could have survived such a trial."

Catherine did survive and returned to her rounds of work, prayer, and fasting. In some mysterious way, her frugal and penitential life—her wounds of body and soul—gave her joy. And finally, as a walking-wounded, she became a political activist. I wanted to understand this bizarre equation. Her power could not have been her own, and she was not mentally unstable. She was the voice of reason, guidance, and love. Was God working through her? *Lord, can you use my wounds too? Can you turn them into joy?*

I joined Jack, waiting in the courtyard, and soon, with our friar, we followed a cobblestone path through a long colonnade to the nearby thirteenth-century Basilica di San Domenico, Catherine's church. Here she prayed for the world; here she experienced visions of Christ. We left Cristoforo speaking with a Dominican friar and found Catherine's chapel bay where her life frescoed the walls.

Moving toward the high altar, Jack stopped abruptly and pointed to another chapel lit by flickering votives. "You're right about her body being in Rome. But her head is here."

I stared, stunned. Catherine's skull was encased behind a grilled window in a massive golden house, surrounded by more frescoes and carved stone. The skull appeared only partially decomposed, and I could see the high cheekbones of her face. Indeed, she *had* been beautiful.

What was the power of these bones? Through the years, the bodies of saints had been divided and placed beneath altars, sanctifying the holy tables. Ever since the first Christians worshiped over the graves of the martyrs, the faithful have believed that something holy, something miraculous, something spiritual, still resided in the material remains, or in some way God used those remains as a channel. Posthumous miracles would occur at both of Catherine's altars, in Rome and Siena. What connected the soul to the body? What was left when a saint died? Did the saint in heaven work through her bodily remains on earth? Was the body a channel for God?

We found Cristoforo in the bright square. As my thoughts wound around Catherine's body and soul, and my questions circled her mysteries, a little boy with large dark eyes handed me a white daisy and a folded paper, then ran off to a tour group. Clutching the flower and paper, I followed Jack to a nearby gift shop. Cristoforo followed the boy.

We purchased a ceramic plaque. The sculpted image showed Catherine with her head wrapped in a pale scarf, her body draped in black. She held a long lily branch and gazed down, her eyes half-closed. What had she found that I had lost?

I unfolded the paper the boy had given me, titled *The Eucharistic Miracle of Siena: the Basilica of San Francesco.*

"*Now* we can go back to the hotel." Jack placed his hand on the small of my back.

"Please, not yet—just one more stop. It won't take long. Look at this, Jack!"

Jack sighed, his eyes glazed with frustration. I saw he was burning out and maybe I was too. Still, this church seemed nearby, and if the description was true, the history was similar to mine.

My head was beginning to pound, a steady throb. "We need to walk off the pasta and wine." I tried to sound upbeat and patted his tummy, usually trim, but showing signs of two weeks in Italy.

Jack handed me my plaque, wrapped in brown paper. "Madeleine, you really should see a therapist. You're not yourself and these churches are making things worse."

"No, Jack . . ." I looked around for Cristoforo as a slow panic rose from somewhere deep. The church couldn't be that far.

"You've got to let go of it," Jack was saying. "I want my old Maddie back, the one who slept deeply and loved life. You're drifting away . . . into yourself. I feel so helpless, standing by, not able to protect you, to help you . . . . Heck, you can't even look at me when I talk to you!" His voice was high, pleading, edged with panic.

I turned to him, my rising fury clouding my judgment even as I worked to keep my tone under control. "You want me to see a therapist? I have to let go of it? I don't think so. This is a spiritual problem, one of heart and soul and body, and I *am* progressing. Maybe I have to hit bottom first. And you do help," I added, my hand on his arm, "just being here." I tried to calm the anger in his eyes before it escalated further, but it was too late.

"Well, I've had enough of your churches for one day—*and* your saints. Let's go back to the hotel." Jack had moved into his commanding role, a gear he shifted into without thinking, a habit of years of getting things done.

"Please, I do want to see San Francesco—a miracle happened there, like mine. Won't you come with me? *Please?*" I knew I was pushing and I hated my whine, but I couldn't stop.

"No thanks—you go ahead. You just don't know when to quit, do you? Enough is enough!"

Jack hailed a taxi, got in, and slammed the door. The car headed toward the city walls. My heart beat hard, my stomach suddenly queasy. The headache was pulsing strong. Was the Eucharistic Miracle of Siena worth Jack's anger?

Cristoforo approached as I rubbed my temple with my forefinger.

"The boy was from America," he said. "He told you about San Francesco?"

I nodded.

"Where is Signore Seymour?" The friar's thick brows pulled together.

"We had a little disagreement, Cristoforo. He's gone back to the hotel."

"I stay with you, for you have the cloth. Signore will take care of himself, he will be careful?"

"We won't be long. Tell me about San Francesco—the Eucharistic Miracle—while we walk to the basilica. I hope you know the way. Jack took the map."

I walked quickly to match Cristoforo's long pace as we headed across the square.

"In 1730 thieves steal the ciborium," Cristoforo explained, "the holder for reserved hosts. The ciborium has great value. It is silver. They want the silver, not the hosts. Three days later the hosts are found in the alms box of a different church. They have the basilica's stamp, its sign of ownership. The hosts are returned to San Francesco in a great procession." The friar waved his hands in the air, then looked down at me, pausing. "The hosts are important, for Christ is in them."

"Yes. I believe that too."

We followed the medieval lanes, watching for cars and scooters.

"Many years go by," Cristoforo continued, "and the hosts are the same, there is no change. They are examined often and still no change. Scientists test them. They are fresh. The Holy Father says, 'This is a miracle' and 'God is here.' "

Suddenly the basilica appeared on the far side of a broad piazza, its red brick façade tall and wide with a small rose window over the lintel.

We stepped into a dark nave and walked toward a glimmering high altar; green Prato stone striped the apse. I looked up to the high dome, painted a vivid celestial blue and scattered with stars. Cristoforo led me to a southern transept chapel where several faithful knelt before an altar. Wax dripped from burning votives onto an iron stand, and leaflets like the one the boy gave me lay on a table.

Cristoforo waited nearby. I placed Catherine's image on the wooden pew and set the poppy, wilted by the warmth of my hand, with the leaflet alongside. Taking out my own bloodstained cloth, I studied the tabernacle. Housed in a delicate silver temple on an ornate pedestal and stacked neatly behind glass were the hosts of the Miracle of San Francesco. I knelt, finding the hosts' incorruption difficult to believe, but knowing it to be true.

As my headache receded in the cool calm of the chapel bay, I prayed once more for healing, for the end of nightmares. I prayed too for Jack, for his understanding, his patience. I knew other consecrated hosts held the Presence of Christ, but God had preserved these through the centuries as a particular sign of hope. Catherine, Francis, Dominic, Prassede, Pudenziana, and Agnes, living layers of history, journeyed before me. Through the years, these people of God traveled on, asking me to join them in a pilgrimage of the Church to heaven, our true home. Do we feed upon these earlier saints and martyrs, enriching our souls with their blood and tears? Our world holds such different assumptions, yet their past has created our present, influencing our perceptions, our apperceptions.

Is this how the Church evolved in time, to union with God? Did my journey today add to the sum of future Christian experience? As my eyes rested on the silver tabernacle shining in the dark basilica, I could see in my mind Peter of Prague celebrating the Eucharist in Bolsena, the hosts bleeding, dripping onto the corporal. These were real people, real events, real flesh and blood, all reaching over the centuries to me, to my here-and-now. Would someone gaze at Father's altar linen one day? Would this be another layer of experience that would move God's people farther along?

A bell rang five. I stood and stretched my cramping legs, then looked about. Was that Cristoforo in the side aisle speaking to his friends? I recalled my husband's anger. Again sick at heart, I wrapped the plaque and slipped my linen into my bag. My headache resurging, I hurried to join the friar. I needed to find Jack.

I pushed open the heavy door to our suite only to meet an empty silence.

"Jack . . . Jack?"

I checked the closet. His clothes hung neatly. I sat on the couch, wondering what to do. Why did I push him so? Was I fanatical about these churches? I stared at the door, a tight lump forming in my chest.

I reached for his carry-on in the corner, pulled out his passport, and flipped it open to his picture. His serious mug shot held all that I loved about him—his life of challenges overcome with hard work, his practical acumen, his deep sense of right and wrong, the humor behind his eyes. *What had I done?*

A card fell out and I picked it up. It smelled of lavender water.

Susan Beck, Ph.D.
Beck, Hargate, and Powell
Liberty Building, San Francisco
415-663-9220

On the back, Jack had written a phone number and the words *Zurich Institute*, then under that, two other numbers, both in Italy. I looked through the travel documents—hotel confirmations, itinerary, restaurant reviews—and found the bill from Villa San Michele in Fiesole.

138

There were several calls to Zurich, to the same number that was on the back of the card. Suddenly I had a flash of the blond in Venice, the one who was speaking to Jack outside San Zaccaria. And there was the woman in Bologna too. Could that have been this Susan? The daughter of Lynn Beck? What was going on?

I waited for a time, watching the door. Then as the sun dropped behind the hills, I walked to the window. Fuchsia wisps of reflected light, low over the horizon, were fading quickly and a few lights appeared in the farmhouse below. I would ask Jack about this Susan when he returned. There was no point in worrying without all the facts.

I took two aspirin and curled up in the lumpy overstuffed sofa. In the weak light of a floor lamp, I tried to read the small print of my history of Saint Antimo, our next stop, as I listened for footsteps on the stairs and wrestled with the riddle of Susan Beck and my husband.

In 781, according to legend, the Emperor Charlemagne camped near Monte Amiata, south of Siena, with his army, his men sick and dying. As he prayed for help, an angel answered, "Gather this herb, dry it out over the fire, reduce it to a powder, give it to the afflicted with some wine so that they drink it; all infection will be cured, and your army will remain unharmed."

When his army recovered, Charlemagne built Sant' Antimo in thanksgiving, naming it for the letter A, to be the first of twenty-five monasteries he would build. A fourth-century martyr, Antimo was imprisoned, drowned, and decapitated by Emperor Diocletian. Pope Hadrian gave the saint's relics to Charlemagne who placed them under the high altar of his new abbey. With imperial protection, Sant' Antimo Abbey grew, so that by 1050, nine monasteries, forty-six churches, and thirty-two other properties were under its oversight or allied with it.

Where was Jack? It was getting dark.

But Siena grew powerful and claimed abbey lands, reducing Sant' Antimo to one-fifth its former size. No longer protected by the emperor, the abbey declined, until the pope established an order of Benedictines in 1291. Over the next century, the community saw wave after wave of reform and decline.

In the summer of 1377, Catherine of Siena journeyed to Sant' Antimo, urging the monks to greater discipline and preaching to the crowds. Raimondo di Capoue wrote:

> I often times saw more than a thousand people, men and women, as if called by invisible trumpets, arriving together from the mountains and other places of the province of Siena, in order to see Catherine and to hear her voice. Then everyone, having heard and seen her, led by remorse, wept without end over their sins. Many of the guilty, charged with great sins which they never had confessed, having never worthily received the Sacrament of Penitence, ran to the confessors, among which I was one, and confessed with such sorrow, that no one could doubt that a rain of thanks had come from the sky into their hearts.

By the end of the fifteenth century, the abbey had joined the local diocese. The church was preserved, but the conventual buildings were abandoned and quarried. In 1870, Siena began restorations; a century later the diocese sent a priest to celebrate daily mass and settled a French order of canons. Today these men chant the daily offices and masses, filling the old vaults with Gregorian plainsong, welcoming the faithful and the curious . . .

A key jangled in the lock and the door creaked open. I sat up with a start and stared at a man's silhouette against the wall.

It was Jack, holding a giant sunflower. "I'm sorry, Madeleine . . . I'm so sorry. I walked off all my irritation."

"I was worried. It's all my fault." I recalled Susan Beck with a sharp pain as I took the flower and wrapped my arms about him. "I thought I had driven you away. How do you put up with me?"

He held me close and stroked my hair. "Somehow, Maddie, I manage, but you're worth it. After all, you've put up with me all these years. I do like to control things too much."

"Have you had dinner?"

"I got a bite in town. How about you?"

"No—I fell asleep on the couch. What time is it?"

"Seven-thirty. Let's go down to the bar and get sandwiches."

"Give me five minutes."

I washed my hands and face, and slipped into a long skirt; I combed my hair into an enamel clasp Jack bought me in Venice and added a little rouge and lipstick. I rummaged for some earrings and a necklace, then dabbed some cologne on my wrists.

Jack sighed with appreciation. "You look nice . . . and smell good too. What's that fragrance?"

"Thanks. Guerlain something. You gave it to me for Christmas."

I had been a bit extreme, a fanatic. Even a neurotic, some would say.

Mollie haunted me again that night, but her image was blurring. I chased her down cobbled alleys, around sudden corners. The floodwaters receded as Venice moved further into my past, and a brilliant light beckoned me, absorbing my phantom baby in its aura.

Jack's voice was distant, then closer, and I woke crying, struggling to choose between them, Mollie then and Jack now.

Thursday morning was crystal clear, a Tuscan May morning, with temperatures in the mid seventies and promising to rise. I settled into the back seat of the car, holding my secrets, filing Susan Beck into future conversations. I feared confronting Jack; what would he say? It was better for now to keep the peace.

We headed out early, south to the Abbazia di Sant' Antimo on Father Rinaldi's list, adding two more sites to make a round-trip. We planned to take the S73 southwest to the Chiesa di San Galgano, cut east across the mountains to Abbazia di Monte Oliveto, and south to San Antimo. Jack packed extra film, and I packed water, sunscreen, and of course, my linen cloth.

We sped through rippling green hills divided into square plots of early vegetables; we glimpsed medieval villages on limestone cliffs. Cristoforo raced up the two-lane road, passing slower cars, swerving here and breaking there, finally coming to a halt atop Monte Siepe near a red brick chapel, San Galgano.

When the worldly Galgano Guidotti had a vision of the Archangel Michael, he gave up his violent ways and retreated to Monte Siepe, where he buried his sword in a stone, transforming it into a cross. After his death, Cistercians built a chapel over his grave and the miraculous sword-in-the-stone, and founded an abbey in the valley below.

We stepped through an arched doorway into a small sanctuary of red-and-white tiles. In the center of the domed nave the sword-in-the-stone was encased in glass, much like the stigmata stone of Saint Francis at La Verna.

Galgano, Francis, and Catherine all had supernatural visions. Were the accounts of angels visiting our world today so difficult to believe—accounts of healings, comfort, and guidance? I had read firsthand reports of angels who appeared as UFOs. Some angels took the form of men or women. Skeptics claim such visions are merely extensions of one's psyche, imagined or wished for. Yet history records angels visiting our world, guarding and warning us since our exile from Eden.

In the silent chapel I thought of the three children who had appeared from nowhere, directing me. Could they have been angels?

We drove down the hill to the abbey ruins. The giant walls and massive piers echoed such a world of angels, the white stone rising from the green meadow. We stepped through the high grass of the abandoned nave lined with soaring columns, open to the skies. At least the peace of the monastery remained.

Jack aimed his camera toward a window in the apse. "This reminds me of Tintern Abbey in Wales."

"It's a lot like Tintern," I whispered into the quiet air. Was it all an illusion, this aerie presence, induced by sun and introspection? "I can see why the Romantic poets and painters—Wordsworth, Shelley, Keats, Turner—loved these places. You feel in touch with the spiritual without any commitment, obedience, or requirement. It's kind of like dessert without the main course, if you know what I mean."

"Not exactly." Jack focused on doves cooing on a ledge. "You lost me in the Romantic poet part." He was clicking everywhere, a romantic madman with a Nikon. "Stand over there."

"You know what I mean—touchy-feely, feel-good religion with nothing concrete." I could imagine the last photo—my mouth open, my hands gesticulating wildly.

"You're returning to your red-light-on-the-altar Reserved Sacrament speech." He had finished the roll, and as the film rewound took a fresh thirty-six out of his pocket.

"But why not go for the real thing instead of the imitation? Even if it requires a leap, a commitment, a rule, at least it's real."

"You may be right." He put his arm around me and steered me to the car where Cristoforo waited, intently studying the map.

"*Signori,* you go to Monte Oliveto Maggiore next, *sì?* I think I have found the best way from here. We follow this road. . . ."

We took off, our friar hunched over the wheel, whistling the hymn "Praise to the Lord the Almighty, the King of Creation . . . ." Speeding down the two-lane highway, we entered a forest, then continued through the hills. We flew like the angels, low and close to the earth.

Jack was scanning the entry for Monte Oliveto. "This place sounds like another Galgano chapel."

"Maybe it started out that way." I glanced at him, a bit carsick, and refocused on the swiftly moving road.

"It says Bernard Tolomei of Siena founded it in 1313. Like Galgano, he was a wealthy Sienese searching for a simpler life. He had a vision of white-robed monks climbing a ladder to heaven so he formed a Benedictine order. Sounds like Jacob with a monastery."

We parked in a large paved lot and followed a well-kept path through tall pines, over a drawbridge, and under an arched portal. Walking down a wide drive, we came to a cluster of red brick buildings. A door opened to a cloister where thirty-six frescoes illustrated the life of Saint Benedict. Students and tour groups crowded before the pastel walls, half-listening to chatty guides.

The commotion pulled me abruptly into the modern world, and for some reason brought Susan Beck to mind. I would speak to Jack later.

We followed Cristoforo out of the packed cloister and into the quiet of the empty abbey.

"The noon office starts soon," the friar whispered. "I will meet you at the car in an hour?"

We nodded and he disappeared through a chancel door.

A white vaulted ceiling loomed over a dark wood choir that filled the nave, intricately carved with birds, tabernacles, landscapes, and musical instruments. We took seats in folding chairs between the choir and the altar, so that we faced the high altar, with our backs to the monks' choir.

We turned to see ten white-robed Benedictines file in. They began to sing, their voices soaring through the vaults; tourists in shorts and tee shirts ambled through the side door and paused to stare. Some joined us and others moved from painting to sculpture, consulting their guidebooks. I focused on the altar and the music, trying to ignore the tourists, trying to ignore Susan Beck.

The artist-monks, having expressed the inexpressible, filed out, and the tourists moved closer to the choir stalls, examining their fine marquetry.

Cristoforo met us at the door. "You would like lunch?"

Jack looked interested. "How about Montalcino? Is it far?"

"Not far."

Maybe I would speak to him then. Since Venice, our mutual dishonesty over this strange woman was raising a thick wall between us, and I longed to tear it down. But at what price? Did I want to know who she was and what she meant to my husband? The thought of losing Jack terrified me.

The road wound through vineyards and up a hill to the medieval village of Montalcino, its fortress and bell towers dominating the valleys of three rivers: the Orcia, Arbia, and Ombrone.

"Montalcino," Jack said as we drove through a narrow gate in the town wall, "is home to some of the best wines in Tuscany."

"We have some at home, don't we? In your cellar?"

Jack smiled. "Sure do, but I'd like to add a few more bottles."

"So this is the great Montalcino."

Cristoforo dropped us off in the center of town, and we found a trattoria bordering the dusty piazza that served sandwiches and wine by the glass. The friar returned from parking the car, ordered a double espresso, and took a nearby table where he could watch the guests.

I dabbed my eyes, watering from the dust. "You'd think we could at least see the vineyards. But then, these towns were built for military defense, not for tourists." *Now*, I thought. Now I'll ask about the Beck woman.

"Still, it *is* Montalcino," Jack said, like a pilgrim in a shrine. "I want to do a little wine browsing after lunch. They've got to have a few wine bars here—*enotecas*—for tasting."

I couldn't ruin the moment. I watched tourists pause in the shade of an awning on the opposite side, waiting for a shop to open. Others sat on the cathedral steps, waiting too. The sun had retreated behind a spreading haze, and the grays and browns of the stone façades shimmered in the pressing heat of the early afternoon.

"Jack, I need to ask you something."

Jack was thumbing his guidebook. "Did you know they have a yearly thrush-hunting festival? They have an archery competition, costumes, parades, neighborhood banners, dancing."

"Sounds colorful. But Jack . . . while you were gone yesterday . . ."

"Where are our sandwiches?" He looked around for the waiter, then, frowning, turned to me. "You wanted to ask me something?"

I sipped my wine, holding onto the rosy depths as though they offered safety. "I . . . noticed something yesterday while you were gone."

"You noticed something? I'm sorry, Maddie, I came back, didn't I? Let's forget about it."

"But I wanted to ask you–"

"Let's move on, okay? I said I was sorry. Let's just forget about it."

The sandwiches arrived, layers of meat and cheese in rolls. I had lost my courage. The question could wait, but I was sure he was hiding something. We had never hidden things before from each other, at least nothing like this.

I took a bite of a thick *panini* and scanned the piazza. "They say the locals here sheltered resistance fighters during the Nazi occupation." I shivered—had this square seen executions?

A lone man caught my eye. He waited in front of a bookstore, his back to us, intently reading titles through the glass. He was bald; he clasped a straw hat in one hand and wiped his forehead with the other. His bearing was familiar. He turned slightly and glanced at us. I breathed deeply, keeping my thoughts to myself, telling myself it was all in my head.

Jack signed the check and as we walked toward a wine shop, the man sauntered in the opposite direction. Inside, the room was dark, the barman friendly; bottles lay in bins and on racks, angled for viewing. Cristoforo scanned the room and waited at the door.

Jack tasted several recent vintages, holding the glass up to the light for color and legs, inhaling the bouquet, swirling the ruby liquid in his mouth and spitting into a basin.

The barman kissed his finger tips. "*Molto bene*," he said, "*molto bene.*"

"Young with promise," Jack replied, leaning on the polished bar and looking him in the eye. "But it's nice—do you have ordering information? Do you ship?"

We left, the deal done, free shipping thrown in. The barman pumped our freckled hands with his tan one, grinning as though he had pulled one over on some naive Americans, and walked us to the door. He handed us his card and several brochures on the vineyards and the making of a great Brunello.

"That's three cases, all total, I've sent home," Jack said with satisfaction as we made our way down the hill to the car. "You can't even find this stuff in the States."

We followed Cristoforo to the car, the friar folding his hands thoughtfully. "Now we go to Sant' Antimo? It is a holy place. Many came in the early days. It was on the road to Rome."

Jack glanced at him doubtfully. "The road to Rome? How so? We're out in the middle of nowhere."

The friar pulled the car keys from his robe. "The Via Francigena."

"One of the pilgrims' routes," I said as I pictured the many who traveled to Rome, on foot, on horseback, in wagons, in rags. They carried scallop shells around their necks for water and food; some sought healing, some adventure. *Much like me*, I thought. Pilgrimages could be adventurous indeed.

Cristoforo nodded and lowered his large frame behind the wheel.

I gazed out the car window as we followed the curving road. A breeze had cleared some of the haze, and sunlight shimmered on the high grass. We drove south through the hills and suddenly, around a bend, a

Romanesque abbey appeared, amber stone in a green meadow of vines, olive trees, and orange poppies. We turned down a quiet lane lined with cypresses leading to the abbey with its long nave, softly rounded chevet, and stalwart bell tower.

"It's like a jewel in God's palm." I sighed.

Bells echoed, calling us to afternoon prayers. We parked near a tour bus and followed other pilgrims to the abbey. Stepping through the ancient doorway, we paused in the back. The nave was nearly full.

Six white-robed monks processed in and took their places in a wooden choir between the shallow nave and the stone altar. Alabaster columns rose to a balustrade and clerestory windows; a large wooden crucifix hung in the air over the altar. Its thirteenth-century Christ was simply carved with short hair, trim beard, and eyes closed as if in prayer—or pain. His lips were thin, determined. A silvery light flowed through the high, unadorned window beyond, filling the apse with a golden glow.

We found seats halfway up the nave. As I prayed my thanksgivings for this abbey, I recognized the chanting. "It's a mass," I whispered to Jack.

Cristoforo nodded. It was Thursday, May 15, still Ascensiontide. Sunday would be the Feast of Pentecost. I did not know the feast day—there were many daily festivals on the Roman calendar—but I was grateful. The Gregorian chant wove among us, circled the altar and the giant crucifix, and mingled with the thurifer's smoke drifting to the windows. The incense-infused light opened a door in my soul.

We followed the liturgy in green missals and loose prayer sheets. I gazed at the sacrificial Christ on the cross, my cloth spread on my palms in offering, in confusion, in supplication, and gave myself up to something greater, something permeating the linen, something swirling about me, something on the altar, something in my heart. This was not a moment of verbal prayer or even contemplation. This was a moment of ecstasy. *Washed in the blood of the lamb*, the evangelicals would say—that is how I felt—washed, washed by love, God's suffering love, Christ's cleansing blood. Peace filled my soul, and, I thought, *I am healed.*

The mass ended and the monks processed out. I remained for a few minutes longer, absorbing the last moments of Christ's sacramental presence, like a sunbather catching the late afternoon rays.

I followed Jack toward the doors, leaving Cristoforo kneeling, and we stepped outside to meet the bright world of earth and sky. Jack snapped pictures, aiming for the trees, the façade, the scripted sign listing service times. He turned to the bell tower, the conventual buildings, the cloister, the vegetable garden. He zoomed in on an orange poppy.

"Did you sense it, feel it?" I asked, eager to share.

Jack smiled at me, then returned to focusing. "Did I feel it? I think I know what you mean. There was nothing to analyze or decide, nothing to know or question. All you do is go, simply be present, and let God do the rest. Is that what you mean?" He clicked.

"Exactly," I said, relieved he understood. "Sant' Antimo is so different from, say, the elaborately decorated cathedrals. Of course, the mass is the same everywhere, always making Christ real for us. But in places like Siena I think of Catherine, or in Assisi, of Francis, or in Bologna, of Dominic. In Sant' Antimo there were no looming historical figures commanding my attention. So I didn't think, I simply experienced. I give up control."

"It's like other Cistercian abbeys." Jack refocused, his long fingers turning the lens. He tried squatting to get a better angle. "Like Senanque in Provence. The abbey was under restoration at the time, and we couldn't attend a service, but even with the drilling and the dust, there was that simplicity." He aimed at the chevet, framed by cypresses. "Nice."

"And it's as if the stone has absorbed the prayers over time." I picked an orange poppy and studied it, twisting it between my fingers. "Jack . . ."

"Yes?" *Click. Click.* He stood and turned toward the distant hills folding so gently. *Click.*

"Who is Susan Beck?" I watched his eyes. He blinked hard.

"Susan Beck? Now why do you ask that?" He turned away. *Click. Click.*

"I just wondered . . ."

Then he faced me, looking wary but resigned. "Dr. Susan Beck is the daughter of Dr. Lynn Beck of San Francisco. You recall I wanted you to see Lynn. I mentioned her daughter to you. Why do you ask? Are you suddenly interested in seeing one of them?"

"I . . . er . . . I found her card in your passport."

"You were going through my things?" He scowled.

Jack knew the best defense was a good offense, but I ignored the attack.

"When you didn't show up, I was worried. I looked for your passport, and her card fell out."

148

He shook his head and lowered himself onto a large boulder. "I guess you found me out. I hate to lie to you, Maddie."

I squeezed next to him and scrutinized his face. He seemed relieved. He seemed sincere.

"So you lied?" Part of me still didn't want to know.

"We had drinks. She was in town for a few days."

"Was she the blonde in Venice?" I was both angry and frightened. What would come next?

He nodded.

"You said she was an art student."

"I had to, Maddie, the way you've been acting lately. She's been helpful on the phone. I needed someone to talk to about your condition."

"*My condition?*"

"You've been behaving a bit strange lately, almost paranoid."

"And in Bologna when we checked in—was that her too?" *She's been following me.*

"We've been in touch. Now don't go all squirrelly on me. I really think she could help you."

"Oh you do?"

"She specializes in supernatural—paranormal—phenomena."

"Phenomena?" I fought to control my anger, my hurt. *Dear Jesus, what is going on here?*

"Just see her, Maddie, please? She's with a top-notch institute in Switzerland."

He's going to commit me.

I stared at the glowing abbey, my lip quivering. "There's nothing she can do. And besides, Sant' Antimo changed me. I'm much better." I watched him, but he looked unconvinced. "I *am*."

"Time will tell, won't it?" He fixed his gaze on the distant hills.

I sensed his love, the frustration beneath the sarcasm, and reached for his hand. "I'll see her. Will she be in Rome this weekend? You're not going to send me away, are you?"

"Don't be silly. But I did invite her to dinner tonight." The film rewound, the familiar whir filling the quiet. Jack reached for another roll.

I swallowed hard. "That's nice. When were you going to tell me?"

"I've been meaning to, but haven't had the nerve and thought I might call and cancel. Her mother told me she was her own person, had her own style—didn't always do things conventionally, by the books. Lynn may be right. What do you think? Should I cancel?"

"No, don't cancel. I'd like to meet her." She would be another ghost faced. And who knew, she might be helpful.

Cristoforo was approaching from the abbey. I placed the poppy inside my service leaflet, then followed Jack and the friar to the car.

As we headed north, I gazed unseeing at the countryside, my mind returning to the safety of the amber abbey in the green meadow, the alabaster columns, the swirling incense, and most of all, the mystical presence of Christ.

Cristoforo seemed unusually calm, driving with deliberation, taking the turns slowly, meditatively. I sensed the mass had affected him too.

He hummed another hymn: "Rock of ages, cleft for me, let me hide myself in thee; Let the water and the blood, From thy side, a healing flood, Be of sin the double cure, Cleanse me from its guilt and power..."

150

Chapter Eleven
Il Gesu

They shall be satisfied with the plenteousness of thy house;
and thou shalt give them drink of thy pleasures, as out of the river.
Psalm 36:8

S usan Beck was early, waiting in the bar. She clasped a martini, her long red nails tapping the bowl of the glass. Slim bare legs dangled from the stool and a short skirt inched higher as she swiveled toward us. She couldn't have been over thirty.

She smiled a broad white smile. "It's so very good to meet you." She slipped off the stool and shook my hand firmly.

"A pleasure." I lied politely and focused on her green eyes.

A black lace camisole clung to her breasts and an open red leather jacket narrowed to her waist. Her hair hung straight, two thick strands of pale gold framing an oval face and falling toward deep cleavage. She reached for a cigarillo burning in the ashtray. Watching Jack for her next move, she tapped the tray with the tip.

"Let's go to the table," Jack said with obvious discomfort.

Let him squirm was my first thought. *Can she really be a psychiatrist?* was my second. Unconventional, her mother said.

The dinner was awkward, but I was glad to meet her, one more ghost given flesh and bones, one more unknown faced. She clearly had designs on my husband, but Jack ignored the signals. She spoke of transference and wishful thinking, and how I shouldn't be ashamed. She explained with some condescension that many people deluded themselves with spiritual fantasies, that we could work them through in a few sessions, and that she would be available in Rome over the weekend. I felt like working *her* through a few sessions.

Jack looked at me, waiting.

"Thank you, Dr. Beck," I began.

"Please call me Susan," she purred.

I waved away a puff of smoke as we waited for our main courses. "Susan, I really appreciate your time."

"No problem. I was in Bologna for a book signing and drove down as a favor to Jack . . . er . . . Mr. Seymour. Do you have a copy?"

"I'm afraid I don't."

"*Divine Sex: How the Church has Brainwashed Millions*. You might find it revealing." She winked at Jack. "Let me give you a copy. It's been on the best-seller lists for weeks and climbing steadily." She pulled a slim volume from her briefcase and began signing the title page.

"You're so gracious." I paused, watching Jack, his face beet red. "But as for a meeting in Rome, I regret that our schedule is rather full. I'm sure Jack will be happy if I see your mother in San Francisco next week—if things don't improve."

Jack nodded. "That sounds reasonable."

Susan Beck looked disappointed and pulled out a second pack of cigarillos. She waited for Jack to offer a light.

"Do you mind not smoking?" I asked.

"Of course I don't mind! I'm so sorry." She flashed a tentative smile of apology to Jack and put the pack away. "Now, do tell me about your travels."

"We loved Lake Como." Jack was clearly relieved at the change of subject. "Have you been there?"

"I haven't had the pleasure," she cooed, "but I'd love to go someday."

"There's a wonderful place for lunch in the center of the lake . . . what's the name, Maddie?"

I tried not to growl. "Bellagio."

"Right, Bellagio. You take the ferry up the lake. . . ."

Cristoforo was waiting as we said good-bye to Dr. Beck in the foyer. His usually impassive face was distraught. "I must go to Rome tonight, *Signori*."

"What is it, Cristoforo?" I touched his arm, feeling the rough cloth.

"Can't it wait until morning?" Jack asked.

"It cannot wait. Agnes is . . . is dying. I must be with her. She is, you see, like . . . my mother."

"Sister Agnes!" I saw her in my mind, so strong and so sure, so alive and so full of something I wanted for myself. "What happened?"

"She is old and weak and it may be her time. She has pneumonia. The doctor says she is not doing well." Cristoforo rubbed his hands, concentrating. "I take the train. It is okay. I will be there soon." His words were edged with panic.

"Then let me get you a taxi to the station." Jack turned toward the porter's desk.

"*Grazie. Allora,* I see you in Rome."

"Tomorrow." I kissed him on each cheek. "And Cristoforo?"

"*Sì?*" He pulled out his rosary.

"It will be okay."

"*Sì, Signora.* It will be okay." He looked at me with grateful eyes and turned toward the door.

"I'm so sorry, Maddie." Jack was propped up against his pillows, his closed book on his lap. It was nearly midnight.

"I'm the one who should be sorry." I zipped my garment bag and set it next to Jack's luggage; we would be ready to leave first thing in the morning. We had packed in silence, my anger choking my words. Indeed, words swirled in my head, unable to find one another, fragments stillborn.

I turned out the light and laid my head against his chest, listening to the beat of his heart.

He sighed, letting out tension-filled air. "I shouldn't have invited Dr. Beck. She's . . . very persuasive. She seemed to have all the answers."

"And you *wanted* answers. I know I've been worrying you, acting a bit neurotic by today's standards. You did what you thought right."

He turned toward me and kissed me softly on my lips, my forehead, my eyes. "I'm beat—we'd better get some sleep."

His apology diffused my anger to the point of quiet acceptance. I turned out the light and gazed into the dark, thankful for my patient husband, thankful for his steady presence. Soon his regular breathing had become a deep snore.

A thin shaft of moonlight lit the antique nightstand. My prayer book and palms lay next to my rosary and silver-edged Mary, my blue-and-white Madonna, and my Saint Catherine with her lily. The dried poppy sat at the foot of the Saint Francis crucifix. The Venetian maple angel smiled from my linen cloth, the clay figure of Saint Peter next to it.

Sleep would not come. I rose and moved into the sitting room, opened my laptop and connected to the Internet. As I suspected, today was the feast day of several saints. The chief festival for May 15 was John Baptist de la Salle, the founder of the Christian Brothers. Thinking of all the schools his fraternity had established, I was thankful for his life.

It appeared that May 15 was also the feast day of Isidore of Chios, a third-century martyr. A Roman soldier who converted to Christianity, Isadore refused to offer sacrifice to the emperor. His tongue was cut out, he was beheaded, and his body was thrown into a well. Saint Myrope recovered his body and buried him, and for this, she was flogged to death. I recalled Pudenziana and Prassede, the caring sisters. The story was familiar, one of belief in Someone worth dying for, a story of a faith that spread like wildfire through the Mediterranean and into the northern countries. Again and again, the lives of these early Christians inspired me to seek the truth, to never give up the search, to not be afraid of what I might find.

I closed my laptop and returned to bed. Jack had rolled onto his side and was breathing quietly. The moon had retreated behind a cloud, and as a warm breeze blew through the open window, I prayed for Agnes and Cristoforo. Somehow, I knew that if God willed it, he would reach her bedside in time. I prayed, too, for Susan, who seemed to be trying too hard to be someone she was not meant to be. Jack's confusion over the woman was encouraging, and I sensed he had gotten more than he had bargained for.

Something had happened in Sant' Antimo. I traveled avenues of incarnation, of Christ's healing presence in the world and in my body. How I wanted to understand, how I wanted to own the answers, pack them neatly into my heart, mind, and soul. And in some ways, I glimpsed the truth, gave up control, and experienced love anew. Was that it? Was there—could there be—more? Would Mollie come to me again tonight? Could I finally close my eyes in peace?

I carried my altar linen like a miraculous medal. Did I imagine its comfort, its strength, its power? In this journey, it covered and protected my soul. I hoped the Coronati Convent could manage without it. After all, it *was* my decision—I could keep it if I chose. I could exercise my free will.

154

My lids grew heavy and, finally, I slept. Mollie did appear, but this time she lay quietly in my arms, not shrinking, not accusing, simply dozing, as she used to do after the 2 a.m. feeding in the early months. We waited, rocking in the same old chair from long ago, Mollie and me, the wall nightlight casting a pale glow in the dim room.

Friday morning we drove to Rome and Brother Cristoforo met us for lunch in our hotel's rooftop restaurant. The maitre d' looked askance at the friar's threadbare robe and half-day beard, rubbed his chin, and shook his head. He grabbed three menus and motioned for us to follow.

Cristoforo appeared sad, his eyes rimmed with dark hollows. I guessed that Sister Agnes had passed away during the night.

"She has gone home . . . to God." The friar looked out the window to the distant dome of San Pietro. "I sat with her. I was there when she left us. She grew weak when Father Rinaldi died, yet she needed to finish her prayers for him."

"I'm sorry, Cristoforo." I felt her loss too—she had been a powerful presence at Quattro Coronati.

Jack had not opened the wine list, and our menus remained closed. "We're sorry, but glad you could be with her." He had grown fond of the friar over the last few weeks.

Cristoforo leaned toward us. "She said to me, 'Brother, you must smile more.' " His lips curved slightly. "Then she looked far away. She saw something—someone. She cried, 'Love . . . Love . . . Love . . .' " He dropped his voice to a whisper and gazed into my eyes. "I think . . . she saw Jesus."

I smiled, filled with the certainty of the golden abbey. "I'm sure she did."

The friar's eyes were moist, the whites lined with red. "She was all joy, *Signori*. When she went to her cell, a cloud covered the sun. I am not all joy, not like her. I am more, how do you say, somber? The convent will not be the same. I will not be the same."

We paused in silence, each of us working through his own thoughts; then Jack motioned to the waiter. He ordered two glasses of the house wine and we opened our menus.

Cristoforo breathed deeply, looked over Rome, and folded his hands on the table. "She said something else, *Signora*."

"Something else?" I set my menu down.

"She said, 'Do not take the cloth until she is ready. She must give in love.' "

Jack looked relieved.

As the waiter served our wine, I felt only confusion. "Of course, when I'm ready."

Jack raised his glass. "To the life—and love—of Sister Agnes."

I sipped my Chianti and gazed out the window to the ocher domes. *When would I ever be ready?*

Cristoforo drove us across town, past the Coliseum, and up the hill to the convent. We found young Elena in the cloister, wearing the same flowered dress, her hair tied in a band, with the golden retriever Michelangelo beside her wheelchair. Cristoforo excused himself to check on the children.

"It is a sad and happy reunion, my friends." Elena's voice was hoarse. "I understand she is in heaven, and I know I will see her again, but the parting is hard. She was a mother to me."

"I know." I rested my hand on her shoulder. Agnes had been a mother to many.

"Will another sister take over?" Jack asked.

Elena nodded, looking more confident as she stroked Michelangelo. "Sister Cecilia will probably be elected. I too have a plan, God willing."

"Oh?" I knelt to scratch the dog behind the ears. His liquid eyes blinked with pleasure and he nuzzled my other hand, looking for treats.

"There is a new surgery for my back. I am to be admitted Monday." Elena's voice rose high and thin, like a tight thread about to break. "My chances are fifty-fifty—and possibly more damage. I prayed with Sister Agnes and she said I should do it. But she is gone and now I am not sure."

I touched my bag nervously. "I'm certain Agnes would want you to go through with it."

Jack nodded, gazing thoughtfully at the young girl. "If there's a chance, you have to do all you can. It's the best choice."

I heard a door open and close.

156

Elena looked beyond me and smiled. "Here is my new friend. I must say good-bye for now."

A short stocky man with dark glasses and a Forty-Niners cap approached and took the handles of Elena's chair. He wore a stethoscope over his polo shirt. "You must rest, my dear," he whispered, his head close to hers. He spoke English with an American accent. He glanced at us and unlocked the break on Elena's chair, preparing to wheel her away.

"Jack," I said, "that's . . . that's . . . that's him!"

The man paused. He took off his glasses, carefully replaced them with wire rims, and removed his hat.

Elena stared at us, clearly puzzled.

His cheeks reddened. "I suppose explanations are in order." He looked to be in his midthirties and indeed, balding. He had small green eyes the color of jade, set in a round face.

"I should say so!" Jack cried. "Maddie, this is your phantom pursuer? Just who are you, may I ask?"

"I'm Elena's doctor."

"Her doctor?" I frowned at Elena as though she had betrayed me, then scowled at the doctor.

"I'm her doctor," he repeated, his blush deepening.

Elena shook her head, as though she were responsible for the seemingly awkward moment. "I'm sorry. Please allow me to introduce you properly. Mr. and Mrs. Seymour, this is Dr. Garvey McGinty. He is American, on sabbatical, helping us at the clinic."

Jack looked at me. "McGinty? Isn't that the fellow the bishop said was after our cloth?"

The doctor fixed his gaze on the flagstone floor. "I fear it's confession time. That's my uncle. He's a good man, but a bit pushy. He told me about you and the altar corporal. He thinks it's a relic and might have miraculous powers."

"You wanted it for the clinic?" I was beginning to understand. "But why didn't you ask?"

"What uncle?" Elena turned toward the doctor.

"I wanted it for Elena." Dr. McGinty gazed affectionately at the young girl.

"Would someone please tell me what is going on?" Elena looked from face to face, traces of anger creeping into her voice.

"My dear," Garvey McGinty said to Elena, "you wondered where I've been? I suppose I fancied myself some kind of James Bond or chivalric knight. I only wanted to borrow the cloth in time for your surgery. If I'd had their itinerary, it would have been easier."

"You frightened my wife!" Jack glared. "The itinerary—you mentioned our itinerary—you took my papers in Milan?"

"I tried to, but lost courage when I saw you in the lobby. So I returned them before I had a chance to copy them. I did remember some of the places, though." He clutched his cap nervously, working the fabric between pudgy fingers. "I do apologize. It was very wrong of me."

I turned to Jack, then the doctor. "Dr. McGinty, you've given us a bit of a scare. But we're glad it was only you. Even Cristoforo wasn't sure."

"I only met the good friar this morning. Elena, I am so very sorry."

"I understand, Garvey, but it was wrong of you. That *is* stealing, even if you call it borrowing."

"I do see that now. Will you forgive me?"

"Of course." Elena grinned at all the attention. "But why didn't you simply ask if you could borrow the cloth?"

"Sister Agnes said no, that Mrs. Seymour needed it. And I didn't know when they would return." The doctor turned to us and bowed. "Please, I'm truly sorry to have frightened you." He put on his hat and took the chair handles. "And now, my dear, you'd better rest."

We exchanged farewells, and I promised Elena we would see her before we left Rome. The doctor wheeled her toward the clinic, and I watched the short pale man, my last ghost, disappear through the doorway.

Cristoforo returned, a notebook clasped in his thick hand.

Jack smiled. "Why, I think he's in love with the girl."

"You may be right," I said. "Isn't that sweet . . . "

Cristoforo turned to us. "*Signori*, when do you go home?"

"Monday." Jack was still grinning and scratching his chin.

"Sunday is a great celebration," the friar said eagerly. "Will you come? Twelve young ladies take vows at Santa Sabina to be novices. They marry Christ."

"What about Agnes?" I asked. It seemed a time to mourn, not celebrate.

Cristoforo looked at me seriously. "Her funeral is later this week. But this service would give Agnes great joy and is a blessing for us—it will lift our spirits high. It is like life and death, death and life. They often go together. For we know we will see our little mother again. For us, she is not truly gone."

158

Jack nodded, turning to me. "It's like when my sister had a baby a week after our grandfather died. It was a gift. A real gift at a sad time." He smiled at Cristoforo. "We wouldn't miss it for the world. It will be a perfect last day in Roma."

Agnes's strength and Elena's hope lingered with me. "A perfect last day. Will Elena be there?" I thought of my cloth, my precious linen, tucked safely away.

"*Si*, Elena will be there."

That night I dreamed of Elena. She sat in her wheelchair, holding Mollie, a big four-year-old Mollie, and the chair rolled downhill, out of control. I woke up sweating and focused on the clock: *2:49*. Walking to the window, I peeked through the heavy draperies out to the city of saints and sinners, as the muted sounds of horns and motors invaded the night.

I thought of Sister Agnes and Father Rinaldi, their love for others and their sacrificial lives. I searched for the missing piece to my healing, for it continued to elude me. Still, the piece was near, and there was time. We had one more church to visit, Il Gesu. I picked up my rosary and climbed into bed, beginning an *Our Father*, moving slowly through the five *Joyful Mysteries*. Towards the beginning of the *Sorrowful Mysteries*, I faded into sleep.

Saturday morning we squinted in the bright sun as we climbed the steps of the elaborately Baroque Chiesa del Gesu, the Church of Jesus. Entering the gilded nave, we walked on tiles of silver and bronze, between walls of marble and gold. Massive muscular sculptures told faith-stories as chants echoed in a northern chapel bay. Good battled evil, as marble figures flew through the heavens or screamed from hell.

The Gesu Church, the main Jesuit church in Rome, was founded as a preaching church two decades after Luther posted his reforming theses on the chapel door in Wittenberg castle. The Church responded to this

Protestant Reformation with sanctuaries like Il Gesu, built with an open nave, effective for teaching the faithful. Over time, Chiesa del Gesu became layered with gold as the papacy peaked in wealth and power.

A crippled Spaniard began the order that would rebirth Roman Catholicism. Ignatius of Loyola, born in 1491 to a noble family, was wounded in the siege of Pamplona. As his leg healed, he read the lives of the saints and was inspired to become a knight for Christ. But how could he know what God called him to do? He developed the *Spiritual Exercises* where the student seeks God's will through confession, contemplation, and prayer.

Ignatius studied in Paris and soon disciples joined him in a basement chapel on Montmartre. The pope approved the rule and named the new order the Society of Jesus, the Jesuits. In contrast to other orders, the Jesuits abolished the choral mass to allow more time for work; they did not wear habits; they emphasized missions, education, and care of the sick. They traveled the world to counter the Protestant reformers, founding schools and missions in Germany, Japan, India, and the Americas. They built a tightly knit organization, militaristic in structure and tone.

We walked through Il Gesu's glittering nave and turned up the north transept to the Chapel of Saint Ignatius. Marble statues towered on each side of the ornate altar and a sculpture of Loyola rose over an urn housing his remains.

Jack returned to the center aisle to take pictures of the *trompe d'oeil* ceiling where figures appeared to leap from the vaults.

I sat in a pew and studied the dramatic white statues. According to the guidebook, one was *Religion Vanquishing Heresy*. A strong, poised woman in flowing robes represented Religion. Her right hand held the Lamp of Truth, and her left hand held a cross. She leaned down, and her bare foot shoved the leg of a muscular half-robed man who grappled with a serpent. The man was Heresy, and he gripped the tail of Satan, the Father of Lies. In the corner under Religion, a cherub read from the Bible. Religion was kicking out Heresy with Truth, the cross, and the Scriptures.

"What is truth?" Pontius Pilate asked.

Jesus claimed, "I am the Way, the Truth and the Life. . . . He who has ears to hear, let him hear."

The words thundered in my ears. How was I to know objective truth, the way things really were, how the universe was set up, why I was here, where I was going? Was I no more than an ape's descendant? Did I take the word of the saints, of the Church, of this Galilean preacher? Why shouldn't I believe Freud or Nietzsche or Camus—or Susan Beck— and assign this religious fantasy to the rubbish pile, dissect my dreams, stroke my perceptions because they are mine, my personal expression in a world where no objective truth exists? Why shouldn't I overdose on alcohol and pills, or shoot moving targets in an office or school? Surely, the only deterrent was the threat of lethal injection, strapped in a death chair, viewed by the curious, the outraged, and a few mourners. Society could provide no moral ought, no Ten Commandments, for the only reality lay in my head.

Once again, I rejected this existential, narcissistic view. Since most of us believed in scientific truth, why was it difficult to believe in objective truth about God? Nothing disproved his existence, and so much supported it. I again felt the overwhelming evidence of history, of the thousands of testimonies to God-truth, to Christ-truth, affirming, again and again, the reality of who we are, where we are going, and what—who—we are meant to be. I sensed the wind of the Holy Spirit, that *Spirito Sancto*, blowing through the years, forming and reforming, creating and recreating.

Here, in the midst of Il Gesu's grandeur, I tried to piece together the puzzle of perception. It seemed we view the past through filters of time and prejudice as we examine written and oral testimonies to the events of our world. Not only is this history colored by the character and passions of these witnesses, but also by our own tinted lenses. How can we know? Did God really send his Son to reveal himself? We must slog through the mud of distortion, assemble the evidence, watch for patterns in human conduct, and conclude. Centuries of testimony argued forcibly that God did, indeed, reveal himself by sending his Son to us.

Heresy clutched the serpent. I thought of my battle with self-deception, of my ongoing flagellation for a negligence long ago forgiven, of my quicksand of remorse and grief. Perhaps I, too, wrestled with Satan. Did I welcome him or push him away?

In Sant' Antimo I had experienced a simple solution to the load I carried. Washed by Christ, I gave up control, I let go. Perhaps this trip was indeed a search for truth, for a way to accept the truth of redemption. Did I do this, accept this, in that bright stone nave with the dusty light? Was there more?

As I gazed at the woman who brandished the cross like an Amazon warrior, her foot kicking this man of muscle, I prayed that I too could hold onto the truth, believe what Christ said and not lapse into doubt and anguish. I prayed I could believe that in spite of what I did, Christ wiped the slate clean, washed the sin away, that I could believe I was loved and could love others, and that I could act upon my belief, kick out the lies in my life. I fought the tears of grief and self-pity that gripped me. *No more of that.*

I knew what to do. It was so clear. I took the cloth out of my bag, my baby blanket of comfort. Then I looked for Jack. I ran into the bright square, waving my linen like a flag of peace, or surrender, or . . . victory.

Jack sat in the sun, soaking up the rays as he liked to say, reading his restaurant guide. "You're radiant!" he said as he clapped the book shut.

"And you are red." I steered him and his fair face into the shade. "I have so much to tell you. Let's have lunch. Where shall we go this time, oh noble knight?" I thought the joy would kill me.

"So Ignatius showed you the truth?" Jack studied his scampi thoughtfully.

We sat under a giant umbrella and attacked shellfish with fingers and mini-forks, tearing crusty bread and dipping it in olive oil. A movie crew was filming on the steps of the Pantheon, a chaotic grouping of deflectors and reflectors, aides and technicians, tripods and cameras, hovering around two actors, working to turn reality into an illusion that would in some sense be more real.

"I believe he did," I said, "or at least his church did, his legacy did."

"He fought the Protestants, right?"

"He and his followers were missionaries, founding schools and missions, emphasizing the Eucharist. They taught what they saw was the truth."

"So what truth did Ignatius show you?"

"I've made a decision. Prayer is not enough. Mystical churches are not enough. It's time for me to act, to offer. My nightmares reek of self— self-pity and self-obsession. The lady kicking out that fellow with the snake opened my eyes. I'm giving my linen cloth to the convent." But even as I said the words, I wanted to take them back.

"Are you sure?"

I swallowed hard, determined not to allow mere feelings to order my life. "I'm sure. And Elena needs it. Let's ask for the check. There's so much to do. I've been such a slouch."

Jack gazed at me as if I had been transformed into a Congressional candidate. "With pleasure, *Signora* . . . So we return to Quattro Coronati?" He signaled the waiter for the check.

"*Si*, back to Quattro Coronati."

The taxi wound up the Coelian hill.

I carried the linen in my handbag, Father's blood-soaked cloth, the cloth of his love, of his death, of his Lord's sacrifice, a cloth growing heavier with each minute. Could I part with such a dear memory, such a close reality? Then I recalled Elena's tears, Sant' Antimo's light, and Il Gesu's marble woman kicking out lies, lies of self-pity. *Yes, I will open myself to love, so that I, too, may love. I must give up this cloth.*

We stepped into the silent chapel. Today no organ played, but the red candle burned steadily.

I fell to my knees in the front pew, my mind and heart and soul swirling in a tornado of will. I stared at the crucifix, calming myself to receive Christ's love. Slowly, he drew me into him, into peace. I remembered something Father Rinaldi said years ago, about the one thing he always confessed—*I haven't loved enough.* This time, instead of asking for healing, I asked for love. *Teach me to love, Lord. I do not know how.*

Calmer, I looked at my husband, kneeling beside me. I prayed my thanksgivings for Jack and asked that Elena be given courage and healing. I prayed for the convent, for the orphanage, for the children. I prayed like Ignatius—*show me thy will.*

We found Brother Cristoforo walking in the cloister, reading his prayer book. I put my hand on his arm. "Could we see Elena, Cristoforo? I have something to give her."

Hope flashed across his face. "*Si*, I will find her."

We waited on a stone bench and watched the fountain bubble as light and shade played on the columns. Soon the friar returned, pushing Elena in her chair.

"You returned! I'm so glad," she said. Her wooden rosary was wrapped around her fingers.

I opened my bag. "I have something for you." I laid the cloth, faded with blood-wine stains, travel dirt, and tears, over her paralyzed legs. "You keep this for now."

Elena rested her hands on the cloth. "*Signora*, thank you; you are very good. I am still so frightened. Mother Agnes is gone—will you come again?" Her moist eyes pleaded with me.

I nodded. "I will."

"We fly home Monday," Jack reminded me.

"But," I said, "we will be at Santa Sabina tomorrow. Will you be there, Elena?"

Elena nodded, her gaze holding mine.

"Good. Now, could I ask a favor? Would it be possible to see the nursery?"

Jack looked at me with surprise.

Elena smiled. "It would be a pleasure."

Cristoforo took hold of Elena's chair, and we followed. "We have two more babies, making seven. Carlina had twins on Feast of Ascension! *Gratia Deo*! She makes her vows tomorrow with the others. She will work in orphanage and raise her children. *Allora, ecco,* we are here."

Carlina looked up with a broad, proud smile. Discretely covered by a large cape, she held a baby to each breast.

"*Signora*," she said, "could you help *un momento*? Take Antonia? She needs to be, how you say?—burped. Agnes, she still hungry." The young mother thrust the infant into my arms.

Jack shot me an alarmed glance and watched me closely. I held Antonia, feeling nothing but love for this perfect daughter of God. Her face had lost much of her newborn redness, and dark hair waved over her scalp. Ten days old, she squinted and sucked in her lips, her tiny hands making fists. I lifted her over my shoulder and gently rubbed her back as we walked to the window. She fussed, squirming against my heart, trying to escape her digestive bubble of pain.

I thought of my Mollie as I looked out to the silty waters of the Tiber. I knew she forgave me, and I knew I would see her again. I remembered the song I sang to her and tried it out on Antonia: "Hush little baby, don't you cry. . . ." My grief burned, an open wound, but it didn't matter. This tiny life mattered. The other children in the room mattered. These nuns mattered. Antonia burped a tiny *aagh* and relaxed, quiet now.

I felt Jack's gaze as I heard him chat with the others. He was ready to save me at any minute.

I turned and grinned. "She's beautiful," I whispered to Carlina. "You must be very proud."

Jack smiled, relieved.

"*Si, si*," she said, "but they are all beautiful, no?" She waved to the other beds with their sleeping forms.

Antonia slumped into a dense, warm bundle beneath my shoulder. "I think she's asleep," I whispered.

I laid her carefully in one of the baskets along the wall and pulled up a thin, faded, pink blanket. Carlina nodded her approval. I thought of all the childless women that waited to adopt. This would be my work.

Sunday, the Feast of Pentecost, was breezy but warm. A few clouds scuttled across the sky as we stepped through the lobby doors.

Jack nodded to a porter for a taxi. "This wind will blow the haze out of the city."

I did not recall dreaming during the night, but had woken with a groggy sense of having come home from far away.

As the taxi took us to Santa Sabina in the Aventino, an ancient suburb of imperial Rome, Jack scanned his notes from the Internet.

"We've been here before, Maddie. You'll recognize the orange garden and the views of the city and the river. There are monasteries that used to be house-churches. Remember that keyhole with the view of San Pietro? That's up here too."

"I do, Professor Seymour, I do. What else did you discover?"

Jack chuckled at his new title. "The Aventino was a wealthy neighborhood. They believe this church began in a mansion."

"Santa Sabina was once a mansion?"

"They think so. Excavations revealed the house of Marcella, a Roman matron, a follower of Saint Jerome." He peered over his glasses. "Who was Jerome?"

"One of the Church fathers—a desert hermit. He translated the Scriptures into Latin." A popular subject of art as well, I thought.

"Evidently this Marcella gathered a group of ladies in her house for worship—a certain Peter of Illyria was their priest. When the Goths invaded, the house was destroyed, but Peter built a new basilica. I guess a good deal of Rome was rebuilt after 410."

"But who was Sabina?"

Jack consulted his notes, pencil scratchings on a hotel pad. "Historians think she was a second-century martyr in Umbria, most likely converted by her servant. After the Goths, Sabina's relics were brought here and placed under the altar of Peter's new church."

"Can we visit the excavations? Is the crypt open?"

"They didn't say."

"Probably not. Who takes care of the church now? Is there an order in residence?" I gazed out the window as we wound up a hill into a neighborhood of tall shade trees and large villas.

"Dominicans—the pope gave the church to Saint Dominic to found a monastery. Thomas Aquinas lived and worked there too. Aquinas is pretty famous."

"Both Dominic and Aquinas were there—wow!" Saint Thomas Aquinas was receiving a renewed interest in our modern world, being the "saint of reason," the founder of Scholasticism. It has been said that eras embrace their opposite. Today, a time of individualism and freedom, looks to Aquinas for rational boundaries. The Victorian age, a time of empire and discipline, cast its Romantic eye on Francis, God's wandering troubadour.

We arrived early and strolled through the neighboring park. Fragrant orange trees blossomed, their branches swaying in the breeze. A swing set tilted in a corner. From a viewing terrace we could see across the Tiber to the Trastevere district, once a marshy wharf bustling with trade.

"So these novitiates are marrying Christ?" Jack said.

"In a way. They give up other roles to devote their lives to him. But this is a third order and less strict. They don't always wear habits, and they may enter the world and hold secular jobs, marry, have families."

"I suppose a good deal of this is a matter of metaphor, a way of explaining, much like great art." Jack gazed thoughtfully at the thick bell tower of Santa Sabina.

"Some is metaphor. Some is reality." I smiled and reached to straighten his tie.

He turned, cupped my face in his hands, and kissed me tenderly on the lips. "I for one, am glad *you* married *me*. How are the nightmares, by the way, since you met the lady wrestler in Il Gesu?"

"Quiet, even receding. I don't remember any from last night. I've been too busy planning. I woke up this morning thinking of babies, healthy babies."

"Do you still want to set up a foundation for the orphanage?"

"With all my heart. But it will take a good deal of fund-raising, Jack"

"It'll be a challenge." He gazed over the city. "I think I'll approach old McGinty first. For that matter, his nephew might not be a bad prospect." He smiled with anticipation. I could see him tallying names in his head.

The bells in the tower rang as we walked through the orange garden and into Santa Sabina.

Tall Corinthian columns lined the bright and airy basilica, towering over the congregation assembled in the long nave. Elena and Cristoforo knelt in the front with others from the convent. We found seats in the back as ten white-robed Dominicans entered from the north aisle and circled the altar.

Parts of the church dated to the fourth century. Like Roman ghosts, the old stones carried into the present that other terrible time, a violent time, a time of torture and execution by crazed emperors, a time of slaughter and pillage by savage tribes.

Today, before the novitiates took their vows, the Eucharist would be offered just as it had been then; the infinite would enter the finite, as God gave us himself in the humble bread and wine. Banning the pagan ghosts of the past, this transformation ensured a new way, a way of redemption. Chants echoed from an upper balcony as today's light streamed through clerestory windows onto yesterday's fluted columns. The church danced to the counterpoint of time.

The young women in white blouses and black skirts, their faces partially veiled, sat in the front row, their friends and family behind them. Each girl approached the altar, spoke her vows before the bishop, kissed his ring in obedience and respect, and returned to her seat, glowing. Carlina, tears of joy streaking her face, smiled to us as she rose. Jack took my hand, squeezed it, reached for his handkerchief, and dabbed his eyes. The girls sang a lilting melody, and their song floated high through the upper windows and over Rome. Surely, the angels sang too.

I reached for Jack's hanky.

We found a quiet corner of the garden in the midst of the chattering reception.

"*Signora*, are you sure?" Cristoforo studied me with brown eyes. "You have no doubts?"

Elena watched me closely, one hand stroking Michelangelo and the other on the arm of her chair.

"No doubts. Let Elena keep it for as long as she needs—such a cloth must be used. It belongs to the convent." I knew that God's power was not limited to that cloth or to the icons of my journey. I knew he could work through anything, anytime, anyplace. I knew now that he could work through me.

"Thank you, *Signora*," Elena said, her eyes large. "I have placed it in a glass case on our altar until my surgery."

Cristoforo clapped his hands together. "We will make a special house for it, a reliquary, *si*? Many pilgrims will come. Father Rinaldi was well loved, for he loved well. The Holy Father cannot make him *santo* for he left the Roman Church. *Allora*, we know better, and many others too. Miracles may happen with this cloth, Signora."

"A miracle happened for me, Cristoforo," I said. "You will let us know how the surgery turns out?"

"*Si.*"

Cristoforo kissed us on our cheeks and traced the Sign of the Cross over our heads. He grinned, revealing several missing teeth and two gold ones. "Go in peace, my children. May God be with you."

We said farewell to the middle-aged friar and the young girl on the verge of womanhood, and Cristoforo wheeled Elena toward Dr. McGinty on the far side of the garden. I was sure he was humming "I sing a song of the saints of God, patient and brave and true . . . ," another of Father Rinaldi's favorites.

Hand-in-hand, Jack and I walked to the terrace overlooking the river.

"Let's stretch our legs," Jack said, "and enjoy this beautiful day."

"Maybe stroll by the river?"

We descended a cobblestone path and headed toward Isola Tiberina, an island in the Tiber. We passed Santa Maria in Cosmedin, a Greek Orthodox church with the Bocca della Verita carved into the façade, the Mouth of Truth. Legend claimed that the mouth would close on a liar's hand; I would seek truth elsewhere.

Silently, we made our way through the buzzing intersection of three ancient imperial districts—the Aventino, the Palatino, and the Capitolino. Approaching the ruins of the Teatro di Marcello, we turned left onto the old stone Ponte Fabricio and crossed the river. We left behind the horns and scooters and traffic, and found ourselves in a leafy oasis surrounded by rushing water. The wind had swept the skies clear, and the sun warmed our backs.

We continued along the main street of Isola Tiberina and came upon the church of San Bartolomeo.

Jack looked at me. "A church! And it's Sunday and the bells are ringing like crazy. Now what can that possibly mean?"

I smiled. I knew this medieval sanctuary held the relics of Bartholomew, considered by scholars to be the apostle Nathaniel. I glanced at Jack. "Just a quick peek?"

We crossed the broad courtyard and entered. The priest was beginning the consecration, standing behind an altar slab resting on Bartholomew's boat-shaped sarcophagus. The church was full; in the front pews a group of young people sang fervently. We stood in the back and watched, making the Sign of the Cross as the celebrant raised the bread and wine; soon the faithful stepped forward to receive. The priest gave his final blessing, and they meandered out, chattering in their melodic Italian.

We walked the aisles, stunned by frescoed vaults and airy side chapels, such a contrast to the weighty altar over Bartholomew's bones. The church was a glittering epilogue of my pilgrimage, a last gift.

We stepped outside to a broad terrace behind the basilica, where a tall obelisk stood against the sky like a ship's prow. I stared out to the swiftly moving waters on either side as the wind lessened and the sun burned my cheeks. We sat on a stone bench.

"I'll miss Elena and Cristoforo," I said wistfully.

Jack put his arm around me. "She's a sweet girl and I liked the friar, after all. I wasn't too sure about him at first. We'll keep in touch."

"You've made some big promises, Jack."

"You mean fund-raising? I needed a challenge. We'll kick it off with a small donation of our own and maybe host a few dinners with some of our San Francisco friends. It'll be fun."

"And we'll have a reason to visit Rome, and see Elena and Cristoforo."

He nodded. "You'll be a trustee once we get it going."

"Really? A trustee of what, exactly?"

"The Coronati Foundation."

It sounded important. "And what exactly do we trustees do?"

"You make sure things are running properly, which means visiting often."

"Good."

Jack scrutinized my face. "Your dark circles are gone."

"Slowly fading, maybe? I've been sleeping. Giving Father Rinaldi's cloth to the convent was the final release. I've been so selfish, thinking only of my own pain and not the pain of others. I came close, you know, to keeping it for myself, my own selfish self. Now it can help others find God, giving them something physical to hold onto. Maybe it will heal bodies as well as souls."

"What did it, do you think? What banished the ghosts? Belief? Faith? Learning about the saints? Dragging me around Italy? Pasta and *pomodoro* sauce? The cloth relic? The list could go on. . . ."

"Please!" I cried, laughing. Then I paused, listening to the silence broken only by the cry of a gull and the rush of the river below us. "Christ—it was Christ." I stared at the current, then turned to my husband. "He became so real, Jack. As we moved from place to place, shrine to shrine, each time I asked God—begging, complaining, whining—I had some kind of answer. Sometimes it was words in my head. Sometimes it was a great sense of being loved, being held, being stroked like a child on my father's lap. And the more I prayed for healing, the more I sensed Christ's presence in the Eucharist."

"It was as if you got to know him better?"

I nodded. "I not only felt closer, but learned more about him, his ways, his nature. I learned *how* he loves, not just *that* he loves."

"And how does he love?"

"He loves through real things, through his created world, through bread and wine, through other people, those who love you and those you love. He loves through sharing and through suffering. He loves, I think you could say, sacramentally."

"And the sisters who buried the dead in Rome?"

"They shamed me. They showed me my anger toward my sister-in-law, my self-preoccupation, and my self-destroying envy."

"And the great heresy fighters? Ambrose and Augustine and Dominic?"

"They made me think about truth and what it is, exactly, that it

170

does indeed exist apart from my opinion, my feelings."

"I never understood," Jack said, "the point of Zaccaria in Venice. What did the father of John the Baptist have to do with Mollie's death?"

"I think that was belief, the first step of simple faith. Remember Zaccaria didn't believe the angel? I didn't believe the priest who absolved me years ago in the confessional. I didn't accept God's love. I didn't believe it was real."

Jack nodded. "Love is a tricky business—so delicate, so strong, and so opinionated really. Everyone has their own way of loving, even God, I guess."

"And if you accept God's love you can love yourself, to use modern lingo." I turned to him as a sudden thought hit me. "And Dominic was Father Rinaldi's idea, but we stumbled upon the Madonna of Saint Luke on our own. That icon gave me such hope! Dominic taught me to trust revealed truth. Mary was my friend, one who understood. She comforted me."

"Heart and mind," Jack said. "We need both." He kissed me on the forehead.

"And in Saint Francis," I said, smiling, "mind and heart united with body and soul. His body became a reflection of his soul. First, his body became inconsequential to him because of his love for others. Second, his body received the wounds of Christ, physical pain reflecting his love for Christ. Catherine experienced that too."

"I think the importance of Francis was suffering."

"Yes—Francis showed me that suffering is okay. Suffering does not always mean guilt. Redeemed suffering, suffering that continues though its cause has been forgiven, means we can love. Francis's wounds didn't heal, but became the actual source of joy. That was when I began praying for God to use my wounds too."

"And Sant' Antimo? Something happened there. You were more at peace after that."

"I think I let go."

"What were you holding on to?"

"Guilt for Mollie's death, guilt for being so selfish, anguish at not having more children, as though I was being punished, punished forever, and some kind of selfish pleasure in dwelling on it. That's where the nightmares came in. I'm starting to sound like Freud."

"What made you let go?" Jack's voice was barely audible as he looked into the distance toward Saint Peter's dome, a rosy half circle against the blue sky.

"Again, it was Christ. At Sant' Antimo, as the priest consecrated the bread and wine, the light filtering through the incense clouds, I felt Christ sprinkled over me, around, and through me. I knew he was there. And I knew he would help. I stopped thinking, emptied my heart, and let him fill it. I gave up my will—my control. I felt safe, like I felt when I married you. I trusted Christ to love me, really love me." I looked up at him and traced my finger along his cheek. "Body and soul, wounds and all."

Jack held my shoulders, then kissed me tenderly. "Body and soul, kid, wounds and all. In fact, I probably love you *more* because of your wounds."

"That's it—wounds transformed! I realized that, as I stared at the statue of *Truth Vanquishing Heresy*. The truth I learned, and I believe it's objective, revealed truth, is that suffering can be transformed by love—by God—into action, into active love. In fact, that may be what love really is, transformed suffering, wounds put to use."

Jack stood and offered me his hand. "Very deep, but I like the result—you're happy again. And I have a new project, and it's in Rome. My golf game was getting old. Come—let's have Sunday brunch at the rooftop restaurant."

"Yes." I was still lost in thought, my worlds and words tumbling together.

We crossed the bridge, leaving the pretty, sunlit island awash in the waters of the Tiber.

That evening, as we packed for our flight home, I checked my e-mail for last minute messages. "Jack, look."

He peered down at the slanted screen.

Dear Mom,

Hope your travels are going well.

I'm rather in a predicament at the moment. Lisa Jane proposed—that sure caught me off guard!—don't know if I'm ready but I don't want to lose her. Don't worry, I haven't said no. She said life is too short to coast along. I'm thinking it over—it's a big commitment. You like being married, though, don't you? But it seems like such a leap right now.

Love, Justin

I looked at Jack. He laughed. "She sounds like you. *You* proposed to *me*. Are you going to reply? Give a little expert advice?"

I paused. "No—it's his choice, after all, and one he must live with. I can't control everything."

"It's more fun to let go a little." Jack was kissing the back of my neck, slowly, tenderly, and I turned to face him. "More of an adventure," he added. "I'm not too good at it, but that's what they say."

"I'm beginning to understand that."

Chapter Twelve
Coming Home

O Lord, thou has searched me out,
and known me.
Psalm 139:1

I t was good to be home.

On Trinity Sunday, Jack and I knelt in our usual pew at Saint Thomas's and prayed our thanksgivings. I thanked God for Justin and Lisa Jane, who I trusted to work things out themselves, for Sister Agnes and Brother Cristoforo, possibly saints, for Elena and her successful surgery. I thanked him for all the miracles in my life, all the pilgrims before me and to come, and I thanked him for Jack.

Peach roses sat at one end of the linen-covered altar. The missal lay open at the opposite end, angled for the celebrant's view. Robed in Trinity green, the young priest, intoning with a deep voice, raised the silver chalice, and the bells trilled their high-toned chorus, announcing that God the Son had mystically entered the wine, changing it into his blood. He then raised the bread, and we worshiped Christ who had come among us in this mysterious way. We lined up with the faithful and received Our Lord in the timeless sacrament of new creation.

Once again, the unnameable, unfaceable Yahweh of old who banished Adam and Eve from the Garden of Eden, who flooded the earth and vanquished Israel's enemies, today bridged the great divide of man's Fall. His Son, through suffering, could now enter our hearts, minds, and bodies. Only through this kind of love could he truly know us, enter our experience, our world. And today, as Christ entered our world in the bread and the wine, we partook of his. We knew a bit of eternity, a foretaste of heaven. We caught a glimpse of the mansions he promised.

Like a mother offering her pain in giving life to her child, the

174

sacrifice of God the Son rebirthed us. The infinite entered the finite. His sacrifice was re-enacted, re-membered, made corporeally real on this altar.

Today, however, I understood the importance of another offering, the offering of my life and all that I was and was meant to be. No longer could I skim over that part of the liturgy. The gift of life offered in the mass had a requirement, a catch. I must take the first step toward God in the offering of myself to him. Only then could God's return offering be fully effected and my soul infused with his grace. The Jesus Church taught me that, and I began to understand Christ's ambiguous statement: *For whosoever shall save his life shall lose it.*

"*And here we offer and present unto thee, O Lord,*" the priest prayed, "*ourselves, our souls and bodies, to be a reasonable, holy, and living sacrifice unto thee . . .*"

Saint Thomas's was small compared to the basilicas and abbeys of Italy, but in essence it was the same, connecting man to God, earth to heaven. I received the heavenly creatures of bread and wine and returned to my pew full of Christ, reborn, touching, tasting, the holy. I pondered the union of our bodies—Christ's and mine.

My body had turned a bend in time, gone around a corner into middle age. I was grappling with my past and counting the days of my future. My flesh would continue the journey to ashes—there was no stopping it no matter how many hosts I received. Some days I sensed my body crumbling to dust before me, encouraging my soul in its preparation for heaven. Even in aging, God reversed Satan's victory—Eden's curse of death. For he had turned my dying body into God's triumph, a tool in his grand plan, an earthly container, yes, a reliquary.

For now, we were one, this great God and little me—another mystery. I glanced at Jack who was sitting back in the pew, thumbing his hymnal. For now, at this moment, we were all one, one with those in the past and one with those in the future. Perhaps this union would carry me on the last leg of my earthly journey, to Mollie, to home.

Maybe God used this union to perfect us—as he used suffering, I now knew, to perfect us. When we suffered we shared his wounds, and we became open to receive him into our souls. Somehow, our pain opened that door. The Kingdom of Heaven was within us, obscured by self, but, like the mustard seed, fed by every sacrament and prayer, every offering. Perhaps the healing of my nightmares—that mystery of body and soul—was effected through the nightmares themselves, for in suffering, Christ could work his grace in me. I would not have sought him as I did, had I not suffered. Suffering opened the door.

Jack touched my arm and whispered in my ear, "We've got a new priest."

"He's young."

"There's a reception after mass."

"Good."

The organ boomed the first chords of "Joyful, joyful, we adore thee, God of glory, God of love . . . ," and I stood with Jack, singing with all my heart and soul.

Chapter Notes

Chapter Two, Roma

Relics: The word relic comes from the Latin *reliquiae* for remains, that left behind. Christian relics included bodily remains as well as clothing and objects associated with the saint. The division of saints' bodies to provide relics was discouraged up through the sixth century in the West, and into the fourth century in the East. By the mid-seventh century, relics were given to churches to sanctify them and bring them close to Rome, the "mother" church. In 787, the Second Council of Nicaea decreed that for a church to be consecrated, it must have relics.

Paul's stay in Rome: II Timothy 4:21 (written from Rome): "Do thy diligence to come before winter. Eubulus greeteth thee, and Pudens, and Linus, and Claudia, and all the brethren."

Emerentiana: Emerentiana and Agnes had the same wet nurse as babies. In the Roman world, this made them "milk" sisters.

The fish: The fish, a symbol of Christ, of the newly baptized, and of the Eucharist, has been used since the second century.

Agnes as the sacrificial lamb: When Adam and Eve disobeyed God, a perfect, innocent sacrifice would be needed to atone for man's sin. The People of Israel sacrificed lambs for this purpose, and the rite was conducted on the temple altar, the lambs or less costly sacrifices sold nearby. Christ is referred to as the "Lamb of God," the *Agneus Dei,* for with his death and resurrection, he replaces the old sacrifice, creating a new rite for the People of God, one without animal sacrifice.

Chapter Three: San Pietro

Nero's fire and subsequent persecutions: In 64 AD a fire broke out in the Circus Maximus and burned for nine days, destroying two thirds of the city. Rumors spread that Nero set the fire so that he could build a new palace. Searching for scapegoats for the fire, he executed Christians. The Roman historian Tacitus

(55-120 AD) wrote: "(they were) called Chrestiani . . . derived from Chrestus, who in the reign of Tiberius, suffered under Pontius Pilate, Procurator of Judea . . . Nero . . . found a set of profligate and abandoned wretches who were induced to confess themselves guilty; and on the evidence of such men a number of Christians were convicted. . . . They were put to death with exquisite cruelty, and to their sufferings Nero added mockery and derision. Some were covered with skins of wild beasts, and left to be devoured by dogs; others were nailed to crosses; numbers of them were burned alive; many, covered with inflammable matter, were set on fire to serve as torches during the night. . . ." Quoted by Will Durant in *Caesar and Christ*, 281.

The rights of women in Republican Rome: In Republican Rome (509-27 B.C.), women had few legal rights, and a man could kill his wife for unfaithfulness. In Imperial Rome (27 B.C. through the fourth century), women gained some influence and social rights, probably encouraged by the rise of Christianity. Likewise, in the Jewish community, the wife had few rights and her husband many, including the right of divorce. Roman women could not teach or testify in law. Jesus preached respect and equality for women, and this increased status became one of the reasons for Christianity's great success in its first five centuries, particularly evidenced in the early Roman house-churches run by Roman matrons, by the many female saints and martyrs, and by the numerous communities of female religious that thrived throughout the Mediterranean.

Saint Peter: "Blessed art thou, Simon Bar-Jona, for flesh and blood hath not revealed it unto thee, but my Father which is in heaven . . . and I say . . . that thou art Peter, and upon this rock I will build my church; and the gates of hell shall not prevail against it. And I will give unto thee the keys of the kingdom of heaven: and whatsoever thou shalt bind on earth shall be bound in heaven: and whatsoever thou shalt loose on earth shall be loosed in heaven." Matthew 16:17-19, called "The Great Commission," and interpreted variously. Roman Catholics cite this promise as reason for the papacy, Peter being the first apostle, and the beginning of a long line of "first apostles," the popes. Anglicans cite this as granting authority to priests through apostolic succession, the continuous line of ordinations since Peter, to forgive sins sacramentally, to "bind" and to "loose."

Peter walking on the water: Matthew 14:24-32.

Peter with Christ on the shore: John 21:9-11, 15-17. In verse 18, Christ predicts Peter's death: ". . . when thou shalt be old, thou shalt stretch forth thy hands, and another shall gird thee, and carry thee whither thou wouldest not."

Chapter Four: Milano

The Feast of Corpus Christi: This festival of the Body and Blood of Christ in the Eucharist is observed by the Western Church on the Thursday after Trinity Sunday. The Blessed Juliana of Liège, France (d. 1258) had a vision of such a feast around 1230. It wasn't until the Miracle of Bolsena that Pope Urban IV decreed its observance in the bull *Transiturus*. Juliana had known the pope when he was James Pantaléon, Archdeacon of Liège.

Hippo Regius: Hippo Regius is now called Bone/Annaba and is located on the Mediterranean coast of Algeria (then Numidia). Augustine's title derives from his time as Bishop of Hippo, distinguishing him from other saints of that name, such as Augustine of Canterbury of the sixth century. Born in Algeria in the town of Thagaste (now Souk Ahras) in 354 to a devoutly Christian mother (Saint Monica) and a pagan father, Augustine was schooled in Carthage. He returned years later to Algeria, where he was elected Bishop of Hippo and where he died as the Vandals swept into North Africa. He saw his people and his villages destroyed as Roman rule collapsed in the wake of pillage, rape, torture, and fire.

The Five Ambrosian basilicas:
San Nazaro Maggiore, originally the *Basilica Apostolorum*, was built on the old Via Romana, one of the major spokes radiating from the circular wall. Imperial delegations from Rome processed along this ceremonial entrance to Milan, passing under a triumphal arch and through a six-hundred-meter colonnade to the city gates. In 395, Ambrose found the relics of the first-century martyr Saint Nazarus nearby and moved them to the basilica. Only the outside walls and the saint's relics remain from that time.

The *Basilica Virginum* outside the northern wall was once *San Simpliciano*, and shows Ambrose's influence, if not his founding. *Basilica Salvatoris*, near the present day *San Babila*, outside the northeastern wall, and *San Lorenzo* to the southwest have been thought to be two other Ambrosian martyria, based on more circumstantial evidence.

The Roman wheel of fate: The Roman belief in fate—that the gods controlled man's world and man's life on earth—was countered by the Christian belief in destiny, that man could choose, could exercise free will during his life (insofar as allowed by others), and could choose God as his destiny, his final end. Saint Paul introduced the concept of Predestination, that certain people were chosen by God to be saved, making them the "Elect." Saint Augustine clarified this by saying that it is God's all-knowledge of the future that creates this "advance" choice, and that man retains his free will, sometimes a difficult concept for many of us to grasp.

Chapter Six: Venezia

The horses of Saint Mark's Basilica: The bronze horses have had an interesting travel history. Considered second-century and Roman, they found their way to Constantinople. They were stolen from the Hippodrome in 1204, installed on San Marco's façade in the mid-thirteenth century, removed by Napoleon in 1797 to be placed on the Triumphal Arch of the Carrousel in Paris, given back to the façade of San Marco by the Austrians in 1815, protected in Rome during the World Wars I and II, restored in 1979, and finally placed in the Museo Marciano in Venice. The replicas one sees today on the façade of the church are forged from copper, silver, and gold.

The Apocalypse and the symbols of the four evangelists: The four living creatures of the Apocalypse—the end of the world and the Second Coming of Christ—were described by John in the Book of Revelation. Considered to be the four evangelists (Matthew, Mark, Luke, and John), the creatures became symbols for the gospel writers as early as the time of Saint Augustine (late fourth century). John writes of the vision he has on the island of Patmos: "And before the throne there was a sea of glass like unto crystal: and in the midst of the throne, and round about the throne, were four beasts full of eyes before and behind. And the first beast was like a lion, and the second beast like a calf, and the third beast had a face as a man, and the fourth beast was like a flying eagle. And the four beasts had each of them six wings about him; and they were full of eyes within: and they rest not day and night, saying, Holy, holy, holy, Lord God Almighty, which was, and is, and is to come." Revelation 4:6-8.

Venice's trade: In 1075, a law decreed that each returning ship from the East must furnish San Marco with some precious object.

"Only believe, and . . . be made well." Luke 8:50.

"And the light shines in the darkness . . . he was not the light, but came that he might bear witness of the light." John 1:5, 8.

"I am the voice of one crying in the wilderness, 'Make straight the way of the Lord.' " John 1:23.

Chapter Seven: Bologna

Saint Dominic: Before his birth, his mother dreamed "that she bore a dog in her womb and that it broke away from her with a burning torch in its mouth wherewith it set the world aflame." *Butler's Lives of the Saints.* It is thought that

Saint Francis met Saint Dominic in Rome in 1216.

The Albigensians were a medieval people of southern France who came to be known as Cathars, or purists, and were deemed heretical by several twelfth-century councils. Their theology was dualist, believing good and evil were equal combatants, that flesh and material creation were evil, that salvation meant that man would liberate his soul from his evil body, that Christ was an angel in disguise and not human (hence did not suffer or rise from the dead). They condemned marriage and were vegetarian.

The rosary: The term rosary comes from *rosarium* or rose garden, the rose being a symbol of Mary. A rosary is a string of beads used to keep track of prayers as well as the prayers themselves. Prayer beads existed before Christ, but the first known Christian use was by third-century Eastern monks. In the ninth century the laity used prayer beads to follow the monastic offices. The 150 Psalms prayed in these daily offices were replaced with 150 *Paternosters* (the *Our Father* or *Lord's Prayer*), divided into sets of fifty. *Paternostriers,* bead-making guilds, appeared in France in the thirteenth century. Around this time, the rosary was developed, promoted by Saint Dominic, in which the Ave—the first half of the Hail Mary, Angel Gabriel's announcement to Mary—was recited using beads. Eventually the two methods were combined.

The "Inquisitions": There were different "inquiries" into heresy at different times, usually using methods common to the age and not involving nearly the bloodshed modern myths portray and supported by a majority of the population.

Chapter Eight: Firenze

Savonarola: The great Renaissance artists Michelangelo and Botticelli admired the Prior of San Marco and the former referred regularly to his sermons.

"And the peace of God, which passeth all understanding, shall keep your hearts and minds through Christ Jesus." Paul's letter to the Philippians 4:7.

Stigmatics: There are at least 321 historically recorded stigmatics who have suffered one or more of the wounds of Christ's passion (hands, feet, side). The existence of the wounds is not argued by science, but their cause is. The wounds do not heal normally and usually result in death; except for one case they have no foul odor, and in many cases have a sweet aroma. The stigmatics (some have been canonized, some beatified, and some neither) ask to share Christ's wounds, usually in ecstatic prayer, in a desire to experience his sufferings. Some, such as Catherine of Siena, have prayed that the stigmata be unseen, but that the suffering continue. There appear to be more women stigmatics than men. Saint Francis is the first recorded case of stigmata. The most recent is Blessed Padre Pio, a twentieth-century priest currently being considered for canonization.

"Christ is not entered into the holy places made with hands, which are the figures of the true; but into heaven itself, now to appear in the presence of God for us." *The Book of Common Prayer*, 22 (Hebrews 9:24).

Chapter Ten: Siena

Raimondo di Capoue: Quoted from Mons. Lodovico Ferretti, o.p., *Saint Catherine of Siena* (Siena: Edizioni Cantagalli, 1996), 47-8.

Catherine's image: This ceramic image is based on the considered-to-be faithful portrait of Catherine by Andrea Vanni (1322-1414) which hangs above the altar in the basilica.

The angel's words to Charlemagne: "Gather this herb, dry it out over the fire, reduce it to a powder, give it to the afflicted with some wine so that they drink it; all infection will be cured, and your army will remain unharmed." Abbey of Sant' Antimo, *A Stone that Sings, the Abbey of Sant' Antimo* (Castelnuovo dell'Abate: Edizioni Sant' Antimo, 1995), 10.

The partisans in Italy in World War II: For a remarkable firsthand account of this terrible time see Iris Origo's *War in Val d'Orcia*, a diary written by an Anglo-American married to an Italian landowner (owner of the estate La Foce between Siena and Lake Trasimeno) who was responsible, in the feudal tradition, for over a hundred farmsteads on his land. The estate today is open in the summer for dinner concerts.

Chapter Eleven: Il Gesu

"What is truth?" John 18:38.

"I am the Way, the Truth and the Life." John 14:6.

"He who has ears to hear, let him hear." Matthew 11:15.

Chapter Twelve: Coming Home

"For whosoever shall save his life shall lose it." Mark 8:35.

"And here we offer and present unto thee, O Lord, our selves, our souls and bodies, to be a reasonable, holy, and living sacrifice unto thee." *The Book of Common Prayer*, 81.

Selected Bibliography

Abbey of Sant' Antimo, *A Stone that Sings, the Abbey of Sant' Antimo* (Castelnuovo dell'Abate: Edizioni Sant' Antimo, 1995).

Blackhouse, Robert, *Christian Martyrs* (London: Hodder & Stoughton, 1996).

Brown, Peter, *The Cult of the Saints, Its Rise and Function in Latin Christianity* (Chicago: The University of Chicago Press, 1981, 1982).

Brown, Peter, *Augustine of Hippo* (Berkeley: University of California Press, 1967).

Butler's Lives of the Saints, Eds. Herbert J. Thurston, S.J. and Donald Attwater (Allen, Texas: Thomas More Publishing, 1956, 1996).

Cahill, Thomas, *How the Irish Saved Civilization* (New York: Doubleday, 1995).

Cahill, Thomas, *The Gifts of the Jews* (New York: Doubleday, 1998).

Cronin, Vincent, *The Florentine Renaissance* (London: The Folio Society, 2001).

Durant, Will, *Caesar and Christ* (New York: MJF Books, 1971).

Ferretti, Mons. Lodovico, O.P., *Saint Catherine of Siena* (Siena: Edizioni Cantagalli, 1996).

Hager, June, *Pilgrimage, a Chronicle of Christianity through the Churches of Rome* (London: Weidenfeld & Nicolson, 1999).

Hibbert, Christopher, *Rome, the Biography of a City* (London: The Folio Society, 1997).

Hibbert, Christopher, *Venice, Biography of a City* (London: Folio Society, 1997).

Hibbert, Christopher, *Florence, the Biography of a City* (London: The Folio

Society, 1997).

Johnson, Paul, *A History of Christianity* (New York: Atheneum, 1976).

Martin, John, *Roses, Fountains, and Gold* (San Francisco: Ignatius Press, 1998).

McLynn, Neil B., *Ambrose of Milan, Church and Court in a Christian Capital* (Berkeley: University of California Press, 1994).

Origo, Iris, *War in Val d'Orcia,* 1943-1944 (Jaffrey, New Hampshire: David R. Godine, Publisher, Inc., 1947, 1998).

Oxford Dictionary of the Christian Church, Eds. F.L. Cross and E.A. Livingstone (New York: Oxford University Press, 1997).

Ricci, Teobaldo, *Historical Background and Spirituality of "Le Celle" of Cortona.* Translated by Leonard Gilliland, taken from Legend of Perugia, n.80, Omnibus of Sources, 1056 (Cortona: 1994).

Underhill, Evelyn, *Mystics of the Church* (Harrisburg, PA: Morehouse Publishing, 1975).

Underhill, Evelyn, *Shrines and Cities of France and Italy* (London: Longmans, Green and Co. Ltd, 1949), Ed. Lucy Menzies.

Visser, Margaret, *The Geometry of Love* (New York: North Point Press, Farrar, Straus and Giroux, 2000).

Woods, Thomas E. Jr., *How the Catholic Church Built Western Civilization* (Washington, DC: Regnery Publishing, Inc., 2005).

About the Author

CHRISTINE SUNDERLAND has been interested in matters of belief since she was sixteen and her father, a Protestant minister, lost his faith. Today she is Church Schools Director for the Anglican Province of Christ the King and Vice-President of the American Church Union (*Anglicanpck.org*). She has edited *The American Church Union Church School Series*, *The Anglican Confirmation Manual*, and *Summer Lessons*. She has authored *Teaching the Church's Children* and seven children's novellas, the Jeanette series, published by the American Church Union.

"In order to write *Pilgrimage*," Christine says, "I traveled extensively in Italy to Christian historical sites. It was a fascinating quest."

Christine holds a B.A. in English Literature and is an alumnus of the Squaw Valley Writers Workshop and the Maui Writers Retreat. *Pilgrimage* is the first of a trilogy.

For more information on Christine Sunderland:
www.ChristineSunderland.com
www.capstonefiction.com

Printed in the United States
81757LV00003B/10-15